喚醒你的英文語感！

Get a Feel for English !

喚醒你的英文語感！

Get a Feel for English !

愈忙愈要學
社交英文

作者／Quentin Brand

C O N T E N T S

第二部分 **擴展人脈**

第三部分 **聊天的主題**

結　語

附　錄

前　言

The Leximodel

引言與學習目標

有人說，在高爾夫球場上敲定的生意比在會議室裡還多。的確，雖然想法或提案是在會議室裡討論與評估，但做成決定的場合往往是後來的酒吧或餐廳，因為生意和人有關，也和信任與交情有關。

這表示在全球化的時代裡，以非母語來交際以及跟來自其他文化的人建立商業網絡的能力是一項重要的商業技巧。無論是和重要的舊夥伴維持良好的關係，還是和新夥伴建立互信，這種技巧都不可或缺。有企圖心的生意人會想辦法改善寫英文電子郵件或是做英文簡報的技巧，但不要忽略了，改善洽談與交際的技巧也很重要。不過，由於洽談牽涉到跨文化的溝通；交際則牽涉到談論生意以外的話題。所以這往往表示你要對別人敞開心胸、談論你的看法，並分享一些個人的觀點與人生經驗。有很多人不敢這麼做，但有很多人則是生性害羞。

本書旨在說明一些洽談的技巧，並提供一些適用於各個交際場合的實用用語，協助各位不再畏懼以英語和外國人交際。希望本書能幫助各位更輕鬆地找到生意夥伴，並成為一個更懂得交際的人。

現在請各位花點時間看看下列的問題，並寫下你的答案。先做這個 Task，做完後再往下看。

Task 前言 1

想想下列的問題，並寫下你的答案。

1. 你為什麼購買本書？
2. 你想從書中學到什麼？
3. 你在用英語交際時遇到哪些困難？

看看以下這些針對上述問題所提出的可能答案，勾選和你的想法最接近的答案。

1. 你為什麼購買本書？

❏ 我買這本書是因為我想學習對工作有幫助的英語。

❏ 我真的忙得不得了。我不想浪費時間去學工作上用不到的東西，或是練習在職場中派不上用場的語言。

❏ 我在封面上看到「社交英文」這幾個字。有時候我必須出國談生意，或是接待外國來的客戶或買主。我正在找一些書，可以幫助我和生意夥伴往來交際、協助我結交新的生意夥伴，並讓我更有自信。

❏ 我想要一本透過練習來引導的書，同時還要有簡單的參考要點。這本書可以讓我隨身攜帶與查閱，就像一本專為交際所寫的英文字典。

❏ 我想要一本了解我想要什麼的書！

2. 你想從書中學到什麼？

❏ 我想學到最常會用到的字彙和文法，以增進我的英語交際技巧。

❏ 我想要學到正確的洽談方式、適合談論的話題類型，以及要怎麼避免枯燥或冒犯他人。

❏ 我希望這本書告訴我錯在哪裡，並加以改正。我希望這本書就像是我的私人語言家教。

❏ 我想要學到國際性的英語。我的買主有些是英國人，有些是美國人，我在歐洲、印度和東南亞也都有買主。我希望這本書能改善我的聽力。

❏ 我希望這本書能改善我的發音，讓我說得更流利。

❏ 我英文念得不太好，而且很討厭文法。我覺得文法很無聊，而且比去參加全都是老外的聚會還可怕！可是我也知道，文法非懂不可。所以我希望可以不必學一大堆文法，就可改善我的英文。

❏ 我想找到可以靠自學來改善英文的方法。我在說英語的環境中工作，但我知道自己沒有善用這個優勢來培養專業的英文能力。我希望這本書能告訴我怎麼做到這點。

3. 你在用英語交際時遇到哪些困難？

❏ 我根本不知道該說些什麼！找話題真的很難，因為我和生意夥伴之間有很大的文化差異，我實在不想找個乏味或不恰當的話題。

❏ 我不知道要怎麼打開話匣子，或是要怎麼延續話題。我真羨慕那些一開口就可以聊上好幾個小時的人。

❏ 當我聽不懂別人的口音時，我不知道該怎麼辦。我總不能一直說：「對不起，請

你再講一遍！」
❏ 當很多外國人在一起交際時，我老是覺得插不上話，因為我根本不曉得他們在講什麼。
❏ 我不知道要怎麼引人發笑或是講笑話。
❏ 我是一個生性非常害羞的人，所以交際對我是一大折磨。可是它對我的工作很重要，我非交際不可。
❏ 我需要更多的自信。

你可能同意以上這幾點的部分或全部，你也可能有其他我沒有想到的答案。不過先容我自我介紹。

我是 Quentin Brand，我教了十五年的英文，對象包括來自世界各地的商界專業人士，就像各位這樣，而且有好幾年的時間都待在台灣。我的客戶包括企業各個階層的人，從大型跨國企業的國外分公司經理，到擁有海外市場的小型本地公司所雇用的基層實習生不等。我教過初學者，也教過英文程度高的人，他們都曾經表達過上述的心聲。他們所想的事和各位一樣，那就是要找一種簡單又實用的方法來學英文。

各位，你們已經找到了！這些年來，我開發了一套教授和學習英文的方法，它是專門用來幫像各位這樣忙碌的生意人解決問題。這套辦法的核心概念稱作 Leximodel，是以一嶄新角度看語文的英文教學法。目前 Leximodel 已經獲得全世界一些最大與最成功的公司採用，協助其主管充分發揮他們的英語潛能，而本書就是以 Leximodel 為基礎。假如你讀過與研究過本系列的前幾本書：《愈忙愈要學英文 Email》、《愈忙愈要學英文簡報》，那你一定已經知道 Leximodel 在學習與使用上有多實用與多簡單。

本章的目的在於介紹 Leximodel，並告訴各位要怎麼運用。我也會解釋要怎麼使用本書，以及要如何讓它發揮最大的效用。看完本章，各位應達成的「學習目標」如下：

❏ 清楚了解 Leximodel，以及它對各位有什麼好處。
❏ 了解 chunks、set-phrases 和 word partnerships 的差別。
❏ 在任何文章中能自行找出 chunks、set-phrases 和 word partnerships。
❏ 清楚了解學習 set-phrases 的困難之處，以及要如何克服。

❑ 清楚了解本書中的不同要素，以及要如何運用。

　　但在往下看之前，我要先談談 Task 在本書中的重要性。各位在前面可以看到，我會請各位停下來先做個 Task ，也就是做練習。我希望各位都能按照我的指示，先做完 Task 再往下看。

　　每一章都有許多 Task ，它們都經過嚴謹的設計，可以協助各位在不知不覺中吸收新的語言。做 Task 的思維過程比答對與否重要得多，所以各位務必要按照既定的順序去練習，而且在完成練習前先不要看答案。

　　書中有很多 Task 須要配合 CD 。這些 Task 的後面會有 CD 的內容文字和翻譯來讓各位對照。但為了訓練聽力，請務必先確實聽完 CD ，然後再閱讀文字。第一次聽的時候可能會聽不太懂，但可以多聽幾次。你每聽一次，就會多聽懂一點，而這也是訓練聽力的必經過程。

　　當然，為了節省時間，你大可不停下來做 Task 而一鼓作氣地把整本書看完。不過，這樣反而是在浪費時間，因為你要是沒有做好必要的思維工作，本書就無法發揮最大的效果。請相信我的話，按部就班做 Task 準沒錯。

The Leximodel

可預測度

在本節中，我要向各位介紹 Leximodel。 Leximodel 是看待語言的新方法，它是以一個很簡單的概念為基礎：

Language consists of words which appear with other words.
語言是由字串構成。

這種說法簡單易懂。 Leximodel 的基礎概念就是從字串的層面來看語言，而非以文法和單字。為了讓各位明白我的意思，我們來做一個 Task 吧，做完練習前先不要往下看。

Task 前言 2

想一想，平常下列單字後面都會搭配什麼字？請寫在空格中。

listen   _____
depend   _____
English   _____
financial   _____

你很可能在第一個字旁邊填上 **to**，在第二個字旁邊填上 **on**。我猜得沒錯吧？因為只要用一套叫做 corpus linguistics 的軟體程式和運算技術，就可以在統計上發現 listen 後面接 to 的機率非常高（大約是 98.9%），而 depend 後面接 on 的機率也差不多。這表示 listen 和 depend 後面接的字幾乎是千篇一律，不會改變（listen 接 to； depend 接 on）。由於機率非常高，所以我們可以把這兩個片語（listen to、 depend on）視為固定（fixed）字串。由於它們是固定的，所以假如你的答案不是 to 和 on，就可以說是寫錯了。

不過，**接下來兩個字**（English、 financial）**後面會接什麼字就難預測得多**。但我可以在某個範圍內猜測，你在 English 後面寫的可能是 class、 book、 teacher、 email、 grammar 等，而在 financial 後面寫的是 department、 news、 planning、 product 、 problems 或 stability 等。但我猜對的把握就比前面兩個字低了許多。爲什麼會這樣？因爲能正確預測 English 和 financial 後面接什麼單字的統計機率低了許多，很多字都有可能，而且每個字的機率相當。因此，我們可以說 English 和 financial 的字串是不固定的，而是流動的（fluid）。所以，與其把語言想成文法和字彙，各位不妨把它想成是一個龐大的字串語料庫。裡面有些字串是固定的，有些字串則是流動的。

總而言之，根據可預測度，我們可以看出字串的固定性和流動性，如圖示：

The Spectrum of Predictability 可預測度

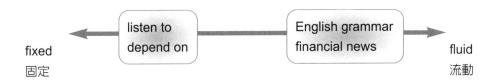

字串的可預測度是 Leximodel 的基礎，因此 Leximodel 的定義可以追加一句話：

Language consists of words which appear with other words. These combinations of words can be placed along a spectrum of predictability, with fixed combinations at one end, and fluid combinations at the other.

語言是由字串構成。字串可根據可預測度的程度區分，可預測度愈高的一端是固定字串，可預測度愈低的一端視流動字串。

Chunks 、 Set-phrases 和 Word Partnerships

你可能在心裏兀自納悶：我曉得 Leximodel 是什麼了，可是這對學英文有什麼幫助？我怎麼知道哪些字串是固定的、哪些是流動的，就算知道了，學英文會比較簡單嗎？別急，輕鬆點，從現在起英文會愈學愈上手。

我們可以把所有的字串（稱之爲 MWIs = multi word items）分爲三類：chunks 、 set-phrases 和 word partnerships 。這些字沒有對等的中譯，所以請各位把這幾個英文字記起來。我們仔細來看這三類字串，各位很快就會發現它們眞的很容易了解與使用。

我們先來看第一類 MWIs ： chunks 。 Chunks 字串有固定也有流動的元素。listen to 就是個好例子： listen 的後面總是跟著 to（這是固定的），但有時候 listen 可以是 are listening 、 listened 或 have not been listening carefully enough（這是流動的）。另一個好例子是 give sth. to sb.。其中的 give 總是先接某物（sth.），然後再接 to ，最後再接某人（sb.）。就這點來說，它是固定的。不過在這個 chunk 中， sth. 和 sb. 這兩個部分可以選擇的字很多，這是流動的，像是 give a raise to your staff「給員工加薪」和 give a presentation to your boss「向老闆做簡報」。看看下面的圖你就懂了。

They | listened / are listening / have not been listening carefully enough | to | the presentation.

We need to | give | a proposal / a present / some thought | to | the client / Mandy / the new plan | .

　　部分為 fluid　　　　部分為 fixed

相信你能夠舉一反三，想出更多例子。當然，我們還可以把它寫成 give sb. sth. ，但這是另外一個 chunk 。它同樣兼具固定和流動的元素，希望各位能看出這點。

Chunks 通常很短，由 meaning words（意義字，如 listen 、 depend）加上 function words（功能字，如 to 、 on）所組成。相信你已經知道的 chunks 很多，只是自己還不自知呢！我們來做另一個 Task ，看看各位是不是懂了。做完這個 Task 前，先不要看答案哦！

Task 前言 3

閱讀下列短文，找出所有的 chunks 並畫底線。

Everyone is familiar with the experience of knowing what a word means, but not knowing how to use it accurately in a sentence. This is because words are nearly always used as part of an MWI. There are three kinds of MWIs. The first is called a chunk. A chunk is a combination of words which is more or less fixed. Every time a word in the chunk is used, it must be used with its partner(s). Chunks combine fixed and fluid elements of language. When you learn a new word, you should learn the chunk. There are thousands of chunks in English. One way you can help yourself to improve your English is by noticing and keeping a database of the chunks you find as you read. You should also try to memorize as many chunks as possible.

中　譯

　　每個人都有這樣的經驗：知道一個字的意思，卻不知道如何正確地用在句子中。這是因為每個字都必須當作 MWI 的一部分。MWI 有三類，第一類叫做 chunk。Chunk 幾乎是固定的字串，每當用到 chunk 的其中一字，該字的詞夥也得一併用上。Chunks 包含了語言中的固定元素和流動元素。在學習新字時，應該連帶學會它的 chunk。英文中有成千上萬的 chunks。閱讀時留意並記下所有的 chunks，將之彙整成語庫，最好還要盡量背起來，不失為加強英文的好法子。

答　案

現在把你的答案與下列語庫比較。假如你沒有找到那麼多 chunks，就再看一次短文，看看是否能找到語庫中所有的 chunks。

社交必備語庫　前言 1

• ... be familiar with n.p. ...	• ... every time + n. clause
• ... experience of Ving ...	• ... be used with n.p. ...
• ... how to V ...	• ... combine sth. and sth. ...
• ... be used as n.p. ...	• ... elements of n.p. ...
• ... part of n.p. ...	• ... thousands of n.p. ...
• ... there are ...	• ... in English ...
• ... kinds of n.p. ...	• ... help yourself to V ...
• ... the first ...	• ... keep a database of n.p. ...
• ... be called n.p. ...	• ... try to V ...
• ... a combination of n.p. ...	• ... as many as ...
• ... more or less ...	• ... as many as possible ...

★ 📁 語庫小叮嚀

◆ 注意，上面語庫中的 chunks ， be 動詞以原形 be 表示，而非 is 、 was 、 are 或 were 。

◆ 記下 chunks 時，前後都加上 ...（刪節號）。

◆ 注意，有些 chunks 後面接的是 V（go 、 write 等原形動詞）或 Ving（going 、 writing 等），有的則接 n.p.（noun phrase ，名詞片語）或 n. clause（名詞子句）。我於「本書使用說明」中會對此詳細說明。

好，接下來我們來看第二類 MWI ： set-phrases 。 Set-phrases 比 chunks 固定，通常比較長，其中可能有好幾個 chunks 。 Set-phrases 通常有個開頭或結尾，或是兩者都有，這表示完整的句子有時候也可以是 set-phrase 。 Chunks 通常是沒頭沒尾的片斷文字組合。 Set-phrases 在社交談話中很常見。請看下列的語庫並做 Task 。

Task 前言 4

下列語庫為社交談話常用的 set-phrases ，請把你認得的勾選出來。

社交必備語庫　前言 2

* I agree completely.
* I agree.
* I don't see it quite like that.
* I personally think + clause ...
* Yes, but don't forget that + clause ...
* The ... n.p. ... is very good here.
* I'll have the n.p. ...
* Can I have the n.p. ...?
* Have you tried this?
* Where did you get your n.p.?

★ 📁 語庫小叮嚀

◆ 由於 set-phrases 是三類字串中最固定的，所以各位在學習時，要很仔細地留意 set-phrases 的每個細節。稍後對此會有更詳細的說明。

◆ 注意，有些 set-phrases 是以 n.p. 結尾，有些則是以 n. clause 結尾。稍後會有更詳細的說明。

　　學會 set-phrases 的好處在於，使用的時候不必考慮文法。只要把它們當作固定的語言單位背起來，原原本本照用即可。本書的 Task 大部分和 set-phrases 有關，我會在下一節對此有更詳細的說明。但現在我們先來看第三類 MWI： word partnerships。

　　這三類字串中，word partnerships 的流動性最高，其中包含了二個以上的意義字（不同於 chunks 含意義字與功能字），而且通常是「動詞 + 形容詞 + 名詞」或是「名詞 + 名詞」的組合。Word partnerships 會隨著行業或談論的話題而改變，但所有產業的 chunks 和 set-phrases 都一樣。舉個例子，假如你是在製藥業服務，那你用到的 word partnerships 就會跟在資訊業服務的人不同。同樣地，假如你要聊聊最近所看的電影和你最喜歡的運動，二者所需的 word partnerships 也會不一樣。現在來做下面的 Task，你就會更了解我的意思。

Task 前言 5

看看下列的各組 word partnerships，然後將其所適用的行業寫下來。請見範例。

1.

- government regulations
- patient response
- key opinion leader
- drug trial
- hospital budget
- patent law

產業名稱：　　　　*醫藥界*

2.

- risk assessment
- credit rating
- low inflation
- non-performing loan
- share price index
- bond portfolio

產業名稱：＿＿＿＿＿＿＿＿＿＿

3.

- bill of lading
- shipment details

- customs delay
- letter of credit

- shipping date
- customer service

產業名稱：＿＿＿＿＿＿＿＿＿＿

4.

- latest technology
- system problem
- input data

- user interface
- repetitive strain injury
- installation wizard

產業名稱：＿＿＿＿＿＿＿＿＿＿

答案
2. 銀行與金融業
3. 外銷／進出口業
4. 資訊科技業

　　假如你在上述產業服務，你一定認得其中一些 word partnerships。在本書的「語感甦活區」，我會介紹許多不同社交話題的 word partnerships，並告訴各位要怎麼依照個人的興趣蒐集、記錄 word partnerships。

　　現在我們對 Leximodel 的定義應要修正了：

Language consists of words which appear with other words. These combinations can be categorized as chunks, set-phrases and word partnerships and placed along a spectrum of predictability, with fixed combinations at one end, and fluid combinations at the other.

　　語言由字串構成，這些字串可以分成三大類—— chunks、 set-phrases 和 word partnerships，並且可依其可預測的程度區分，可預測度愈高的一端是固定字串，可預測度愈低的一端是流動字串。

新的 Leximodel 圖示如下：

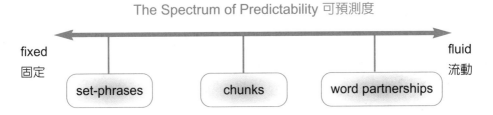

學英文致力學好 chunks，文法就會進步，因為大部分的文法錯誤其實都是源自於 chunks 寫錯。學英文時專攻 set-phrases，英語功能就會進步，因為 set-phrases 都是功能性字串。學英文時在 word partnerships 下功夫，字彙會增加。因此，最後的 Leximodel 圖示如下：

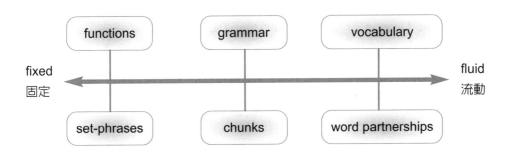

Leximdodel 的優點以及其對於學習英文的妙用，就在於無論說、寫英文時，均無須再為文法規則傷透腦筋。學習英文時，首要之務是建立 chunks、set-phrases 和 word partnerships 的語料庫，多學多益。而不是學習文法規則，或者苦苦思索如何在文法中套用單字。這三類 MWI 用來輕而易舉，而且更符合人腦記憶和使用語言的習慣。本節結束前，我們來做最後一個 Task，確定各位對於 Leximodel 已經完全了解。如此一來，各位就會看出這個方法有多簡單好用。在完成 Task 前，先不要看語庫。

 Task 前言 6　　　　　　　　　　　　　　　　CD 1-02

請聽 Track 前言 1 中的對話，找出 chunks 、 set-phrases 與 word partnerships ，並分別用三種不同的顏色畫底線，最後完成下表。請見範例。

A: Have you seen the new James Bond movie?

B: Oh, yes. You?

A: Yes. What did you think of it?

B: I thought it was better than the others — I really liked it. What did you think of it?

A: Yes, I liked it, too. It was exciting, but not over the top. Do you know what I mean?

B: Mmm. That's what I thought too. I really liked the car chase, and the opening credit sequence was very exciting. And I always enjoy watching Pierce Brosnan.

A: Oh, yes. He's brilliant. Did you like the title song?

B: Not as much as last time, actually. What's the name of the American actor who was in the supporting role?

A: Uhm, Edward Norton, or something like that. Did you like him?

B: Yes. He was excellent. They worked well together, don't you think?

A: I don't know. I think the woman was better. She provided a good love interest. Lucky James Bond!

B: Yes!

● 中　譯

A：你看了新的○○七電影嗎？

B：看了。你呢？

A：看了。你覺得怎麼樣？

B：我覺得它比其他幾部好看，我滿喜歡的。你覺得怎麼樣？

A：是啊，我也很喜歡。它雖然稱不上精彩絕倫，但卻不失刺激，你明白我的意思吧？

Ｗ ｏ ｒ ｄ　Ｌ ｉ ｓ ｔ

chase [tʃes] *n.* 追逐　　　　　　　　sequence [ˋsikwəns] *n.* 連續鏡頭

B：嗯，我也這麼覺得。我滿喜歡它的飛車追逐，而且開頭的演員陣容表也很棒。我一直很欣賞皮爾斯·布洛斯南。

A：對呀，他很厲害。你喜歡它的主題曲嗎？

B：其實我比較喜歡上一部片的主題曲。那個演男配角的美國演員叫什麼名字？

A：呣，好像是愛德華·諾頓之類的。你喜歡他嗎？

B：是啊，他演得很好。你不覺得他們搭配得天衣無縫嗎？

A：我不知道，可是我覺得那個女的比較好，她帶來了不少愛情趣味。詹姆斯·龐德真走運！

B：沒錯！

Set-phrases	Chunks	Word Partnerships
Have you seen ...	*... be better than ...*	*James Bond movie*

答　案

請以下列語庫核對答案。

社交必備語庫　前言 3

Set-phrases	Chunks	Word Partnerships
• Have you seen...	• ... be better than ...	• James Bond movie
• What did you think of it?	• ... like sth. ...	• American actor
• Do you know what I mean?	• ... be exciting ...	• car chase
• That's what I thought too.	• ... enjoy Ving ...	• opening credit sequence
• ... or something like that.	• ... the name of ...	• title song
• Don't you think?	• ... be excellent ...	• love interest
• I don't know.	• ... work well together ...	• supporting role
	• ... over the top ...	
	• ... as much as ...	

★ 📁 語庫小叮嚀

◆ 注意，set-phrases 通常是以大寫字母開頭，或以句點結尾。而刪節號（ ... ）則代表句子的流動部分。

◆ 注意， chunks 的開頭和結尾都有刪節號，表示 chunks 大部分為句子的中間部分。

◆ 注意所有的 word partnerships 都至少包含兩個意義字。

　　假如你的答案沒有這麼完整，不必擔心。只要多練習，就能找出文中所有的固定元素。不過你可以確定一件事：等到你能找出這麼多的 MWI ，那就表示你的英文已經達到登峰造極的境界了！很快你便能擁有這樣的能力。於本書末尾，我會請各位再做一次這個 Task ，以判斷自己的學習成果。現在有時間的話，各位不妨找一篇英文文章，像是以英語為母語的人所寫的電子郵件，或者雜誌或網路上的文章，然後用它來做同樣的練習。熟能生巧哦！

本書使用說明

到目前為止，我猜各位大概會覺得 Leximodel 似乎是個不錯的概念，但八成還是有些疑問。對於各位可能會有的問題，我來看看能否幫各位解答。

我該如何實際運用 Leximodel 學英文？為什麼 Leximodel 和我以前碰到的英文教學法截然不同？

簡而言之，我的答案是：只要知道字串的組合和這些組合的固定程度，就能簡化英語學習的過程，同時大幅減少犯錯的機率。

以前的教學法教你學好文法，然後套用句子，邊寫邊造句。用這方法寫作不僅有如牛步，而且稍不小心便錯誤百出，想必你早就有切身的體驗。現在只要用 Leximodel 建立 chunks、set-phrases 和 word partnerships 語庫，接著只需背起來就能學會英文寫作了。

本書如何使用 Leximodel 教學？

本書介紹很多在非正式會話中經常使用的 set-phrases，並說明要怎麼學習與運用。文中也會針對一系列常見的話題，介紹其中常用的 word partnerships。並教各位要怎麼留意每天都可以看到的語言，藉此說明如何增進各位談論這些話題的能力。

為什麼要留意字串中所有的字，很重要嗎？

不知道何故，大多數人對眼前的英文視而不見，明明擺在面前卻仍然視若無睹。他們緊盯著字串的意思，卻忽略了傳達字串意思的方法。每天瀏覽的固定 MWI 多不勝數，只不過你沒有發覺這些 MWI 是固定、反覆出現的字串罷了。任何語言都有這種現象。這樣吧，我們來做個實驗，你就知道我說的是真是假。請做下面的 Task。

Task 前言 7

看看下列的 set-phrases，把正確的選出來。

- ❏ Regarding the report you sent me ...
- ❏ Regarding to the report you sent me ...
- ❏ Regards to the report you sent me ...
- ❏ With regards the report you sent ...
- ❏ To regard the report you sent me ...
- ❏ Regard to the report yous ent me ...

不管你選的是哪個，我敢說你一定覺得這題很難。你可能每天都看到這個 set-phrase，但卻從來沒有仔細留意過其中的語言細節。（**其實第一個 set-phrase 才對，其他的都是錯的！**）這就證明了我在教 set-phrases 時提到的第一個告誡沒錯。無論如何，一定要加強注意所接觸到的文字。

雖然各位應該要加強注意所接觸到的語言，但仿效的對象必須以母語人士為限，其他人則不夠可靠。所謂「英文為母語的人士」，我指的是有受過教育的美國人、英國人、澳洲人、紐西蘭人、加拿大人或南非人，但不一定是白人。如果英文非母語，就算是老闆也不可完全信任。公司中若有人在十年前到美國念過博士，英文能力公認好得沒話說，也信不過。要特別注意：有部分英文為母語的人士的英文很不可靠，就如同有些國人的中文很不可靠一樣。所以你起碼要選擇受過高等教育的母語人士，或已經建立品牌的英文出版物。

如果多留意每天接觸到的固定字串，久而久之一定會記起來，轉化成自己英文基礎的一部分，這可是諸多文獻可考的事實。刻意注意閱讀時遇到的 MWI，亦可增加學習效率。 Leximodel 正能幫你達到這一點。

需要小心哪些問題？

本書中許多 Task 的目的，即在於幫你克服學 set-phrases 時遇到的問題。**學 set-phrases 的要領在於：務必留意 set-phrases 中所有的字。**

從 Task 前言 7 中，你已發現其實自己不如想像中那麼細心注意 set-phrases 中所有的字。接下來我要更確切地告訴你學 set-phrases 時的注意事項，這非常重要，請仔細閱讀。學習和使用 set-phrases 時，需要注意的細節有三大類：

1. **短字**（如 a 、 the 、 to 、 in 、 at 、 on 和 but）。這些字很難記，但是瞭解了這點，即可以說是跨出一大步了。 Set-phrases 極為固定，用錯一個短字，整個 set-phrase 都會改變，等於是寫錯了。
2. **字尾**（有些字的字尾是 -ed ，有些是 -ing ，有些是 -ment ，有些是 -s ，或者沒有 -s）。字尾改變了，字的意思也會隨之改變。 Set-phrase 極為固定，寫錯其中一字的字尾，整個 set-phrase 都會改變，等於是寫錯了。
3. **Set-phrase 的結尾**（有的 set-phrase 以 n. clause 結尾，有的以 n.p. 結尾，有的以 V 結尾，有的以 Ving 結尾），我們稱之為 code 。許多人犯錯，問題即出在句子中

set-phrase 與其他部分的銜接之處。學習 set-phrase 時，必須將 code 當作 set-phrase 的一部分一併背起來。 Set-phrase 極為固定， code 寫錯，整個 set-phrase 都會改變，等於是寫錯了

教學到此，請再做一個 Task ，確定你能夠掌握 code 的用法。

Task 前言 8

請看以下 code 的定義，然後按下頁的表格將字串分門別類。第一個字串已先替你找到它的位置了。

n. clause = noun clause（名詞子句）。 n. clause 一定包含主詞和動詞。例如： I need your help.、 She is on leave.、 We are closing the department.、 What is your estimate? 等。

n.p. = noun phrase（名詞片語），這其實就是 word partnerships ，只是不含動詞或主詞。例如： financial news、 cost reduction、 media review data、 joint stock company 等。

V = verb（動詞）。

Ving = verb ending in -ing（以 -ing 結尾的動詞）。以前你的老師可能稱之為動名詞。

- glass of wine
- decide
- do
- go
- having
- help
- I'm having a party.
- knowing
- good game of tennis
- see
- talking
- nice holiday
- golf handicap
- did you remember
- doing
- great actress
- he is not
- helping
- John wants to see you.
- look after
- my new mobile phone
- sending
- I'd like some more tea.
- I don't remember.

29

n. clause	n.p.	V	Ving
	glass of wine		

答案

請以下列語庫核對答案。

社交必備語庫 前言 4

n. clause	n.p.	V	Ving
• I don't remember.	• golf handicap	• help	• helping
• I'd like some more tea.	• great actress	• do	• knowing
• did you remember	• good game of tennis	• see	• doing
• John wants to see you.	• my new mobile phone	• look after	• having
• I'm having a party.	• nice holiday	• decide	• sending
• he is not		• go	• talking

★ 語庫小叮嚀

◆ 注意 n. clause 的 verb 前面一定要有主詞。
◆ 注意 noun phrase 基本上即為 word partnership。

所以總而言之，在學習 set-phrases 時，容易出錯的部分有：

1. 短字
2. 字尾
3. Set-phrases 的結尾

不會太困難，對吧？

如果沒有文法規則可循，我怎麼知道自己的 set-phrases 用法正確無誤？

關於這點，讀或寫在這方面要比說來得容易。說話時要仰賴記憶，所以會有點困難。不過，本書採用了兩種工具來幫各位簡化這個過程。

1. **學習目標記錄表**。本書的附錄有一份「學習目標記錄表」。各位在開始拿本書來練習前，應該先多印幾份學習目標記錄表。由於要學的 set-phrases 和 word partnerships 有很多，可以選擇幾個來作重點學習。利用記錄表，把你在各章的語庫中想要學習的用語記下來。我建議每週 10 個。

2. **CD**。由於在交際時，清楚的發音是留給對方好印象的其中一個關鍵，所以本書很強調發音。各位會一直需要用到 CD，這不僅對發音有幫助，也有助於加強聽力，並且會讓學習更有趣、更有效。利用 CD 來練習你挑出並寫在記錄表上的 set-phrases，每天花 10 分鐘來聆聽與複誦，會比禮拜天晚上花 2 個小時還有效。

　　與其擔心出錯，以及該用或違反哪些文法規則，不如參照本書語庫裡的用語以及 CD 裡的內容，熟能生巧。現在請做下面的 Task，不要先看答案。

Task 前言 9　　　　　　　　　　　　　　　　　　　CD 1-03

請聽「Track 前言 2」，然後在題號後寫下你聽到的內容。

1. _____

2. _____

3. _____

4. _____

5. _____

答案

1. Have you seen the new season of Sex and the City began on Friday?

2. What did you think it?

3. Do you know what I meant?

4. That what I thought too.

5. Don't you thinks?

Task 前言 10

檢查上題的答案。你會發現每句話都有錯誤，請研究這些錯誤，並寫出正確的句子和錯誤原因的編號（1. 短字； 2. 字尾； 3. set-phrases 的結尾）。見範例。

1. Have you seen the new season of Sex and the City began on Friday?

   Have you seen the new season of Sex and the City that began on Friday? (3)

2. What did you think it?

   _____

3. Do you know what I meant?

   _____

4. That what I thought too.

   _____

5. Don't you thinks?

   _____

答　案

2. What did you think of it?　　　　(1)

3. Do you know what I mean?　　　　(2)

4. That's what I thought too.　　　　(1)

5. Don't you think?　　　　(1)

　　如果你的答案和上列的南轅北轍，請回頭再把本節詳讀一次，要特別注意 Task 前言 8 以及以 set-phrases 細節的三個問題為主旨的段落。你也可以再練習一次 Task 前言 6，以了解其中的 set-phrases 是如何運用。

　　本書有許多 Task 會幫各位將注意力集中在 set-phrases 的細節上，你只須作答和核對答案，無須擔心背後原因。

本書的架構為何？

　　本書共有三個部分。「第一部分」會教各位學習「怎麼」開口。各位會學到西方人與亞洲人在談話風格上的差異、要怎麼更有效地與人互動、要怎麼開啓話題並表現出興趣，以及各種談話風格的差異。

　　「第二部分」是以擴展人脈的技巧為重點，尤其是要如何在用餐時逗客戶開心，以及要怎麼在聚會上盡量爭取擴展人脈的機會。

　　「第三部分」會教各位在社交場合中要聊些「什麼」，有哪些話題聊起來既有趣又得體。各位會學到許多跟這些話題有關的字彙，並學到一些技巧，以針對本身感興趣的話題來建立與更新個人的專屬字庫。

　　「第一部分」和「第三部分」各有一個「社交必備本領」，它的目的在於整理各位所要學習的觀念，並提供各位一些有趣的思考方向。在整本書中，各位還會看到一些與西方人的文化和行為層面有關的「文化小叮嚀」。如果把它應用在會話中，各位將會覺得既有趣又實用。

　　各位可以依序讀完這三部分，也可以直接跳到最感興趣的部分。

　　現在請花點時間看看目錄，以熟悉即將展開的學習旅程。

　　本書所介紹的用語大部分都是以 set-phrases 和 word partnerships 的形式出現。這些用語會出現在各章的「社交必備語庫」，各位可以拿 CD 來當作範本練習。經常地使用 CD 對於各位的學習是很重要的。書末的「附錄一」集結了各章的語庫，方便各位學習使用。

我如何充分利用本書？

　　在此有些自習的建議，協助各位獲致最大的學習效果。

1. 為了提供更多記憶 set-phrases 的機會，本書會反覆提到一些語言和概念，因此倘若一開始有不解之處，請耐心看下去，多半念到本書後面的章節時自然就會恍然大悟。
2. 假如你在閱讀本書時有機會和外國人交際，不妨試著運用一些你學到的用語。要有信心，並抓住每個練習的機會。
3. 每個 Task 都要做。這些 Task 有助於記憶本書中的字串，亦可加強你對這些字串的理解，不可忽視。
4. 建議你用鉛筆做 Task。如此寫錯了還可以擦掉再試一次。
5. 做分類 Task 時（請見第三章 Task 3.3），在每個 set-phrase 旁做記號或寫下英文字母即可。但是建議有空時，還是將 set-phrases 抄在正確的一欄中。還記得當初是怎麼學中文的嗎？抄寫能夠加深印象！
6. 利用書末附錄的「學習目標記錄表」追蹤自己的進步，並挑選自己洽談時要用

的用語。選擇的時候，不妨記住以下重點：

- 選擇困難、奇怪、或新的用語。
- 如果可以的話，避免使用你已經相當熟悉、或覺得自在的用語。
- 特意運用這些新的用語。

7. 如果你已下定決心要進步，建議你和同事組成 K 書會，一同閱讀本書和做
   Task 。

在研讀本書之前，還有哪些須知？

Yes. You can do it!

翻開第一章前，請回到「學習目標」，勾出自認為達成的項目。希望全部都能夠
打勾，如果沒有，請重新閱讀相關段落。

祝學習有成！

聊天的風格
與技巧

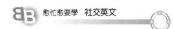

社交必備本領 1
五個如何「有效交際」的必備本領

金言語錄

To listen closely and reply well is the highest perfection we are able to attain in the art of conversation.
　　　　　　　　　　　　　　　　　　　　　　　　　　　　— La Rochefoucauld
仔細聆聽、適當地回答是談話藝術的最高境界。
　　　　　　　　　　　　　　　　　　　　　　　　　　—— 拉・羅什富科

人物檔案

拉・羅什富科是 17 世紀的法國哲學家，路易十四國王的宮廷學者。在當時的宮廷中，如果你想要成爲有權力、有影響力的人，就必須具備交際與擴展人脈的本領。他認爲聆聽很重要。對於必須用英語交際的生意人來說，這點就十分受用。

詳讀下列這五個必備本領，並在研讀本書的第一部分時想想它們的意思。

五個如何「有效交際」的必備本領

如何：

1. 讓對方多說一些
2. 問有趣的問題
3. 設法了解對方
4. 假裝很有興趣
5. 假裝聽懂他所說的話

---

1 讓對方多說一些

🗝 大部分的人都喜歡有機會談論自己，或是表達自己的意見；大部分的人也都喜歡有個好的聆聽者，能對自己所說的每件事點頭稱許。

🗝 假如你能讓對方多說一點，這就表示你可以少說一點！如此一來，你就不必太過擔心自己的說話技巧。

🗝 假如你能讓對方多說一點，並當個好聽眾，你就會贏得談話高手的美名；如此一來，你的人際關係自然會好！

2 問有趣的問題

🗝 如果要鼓勵對方多說一些並當個好聽眾，你就必須問些有趣的問題。各位會在第二章學到如何做到這點。

🗝 西方人喜歡談論自己的興趣和意見，而不喜歡談論自己的家庭生活；但東方人往往相反。所以在問問題時，要盡量問對方的興趣，而不要問他的私人生活。

🗝 盡量避免問可以預料答案的問題。我有一位外國朋友在台灣住了好幾年，她在名片上印了下列資料：

1. 我沒有結婚。
2. 我沒有生小孩。
3. 我會說中文。

這些年來，不斷回答同樣的問題已經使她不勝其擾，於是她就把答案印在名片上，好讓自己不必再回答！

3. 設法了解對方

🗝 有很多人擔心，不知道該和陌生人或者必須交際的人談些「什麼」。假如你把焦點擺在對方而不是自己身上，不要去管必須和他交談讓你有多煩惱，那你就不會覺得那麼緊張了。

🗝 設法找出一些雙方共有的興趣或經驗，然後談論這些問題。

🔑 你可能會發現，對方跟你去過同一個國家渡假，此時你們就可以針對這個經驗交換意見。

🔑 你可能會發現，你們對電影的喜惡相同，此時你們就可以談論電影。

🔑 你可能會發現，自己的小孩和對方的小孩年齡相仿。此時你們就可以談談為人父母的煩惱、壓力及樂趣。

🔑 不用擔心該談些「什麼」，只要設法去認識對方就好。盡量在最短的時間內成為他的朋友。

4 假裝很有興趣

🔑 當對方在說話時，你要保持笑容、表示興趣、大力點頭，然後說：That's really interesting! What do you mean?「真是有趣極了！你的意思是？」假如你無法全部聽懂，但對方似乎對這個話題很有興趣，那你也要表現出興致高昂的樣子。

🔑 相信我，假如對方從頭講到尾，而且覺得你對他說的話很感興趣，他就「不會注意」你談自己談得不多。第三章對於這點會有更詳細的說明。

🔑 在社交談話中，重要的不是說了「什麼」，而是友善的互動所形成的「感覺」。對對方所說的話表示興趣有助於形成這種良好的感覺。

5 假裝聽懂他人所說的話

🔑 不要一直想著下列的問題：要是我聽不懂他的話怎麼辦？要是他的腔調很重，或者我的聽力不好怎麼辦？

🔑 讓對方放鬆並樂於談論自己，這樣他可能甚至不會注意到你大概只聽懂一半他所說的話。

🔑 假如你不確定對方在說什麼，那就假裝聽懂，然後多問一些問題，像是：What do you mean by that?「你這麼說的意思是？」，直到自己聽懂為止。

談話的本質

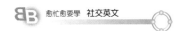

引言與學習目標

本章要來探討一些東西方的文化差異，它們在擴展人際關係和交際談話中扮演了重要的角色。這些文化差異很小，所以很多人沒有注意到，但假如你想更有效地擴展人脈並成為交際談話的高手，了解它們就很重要。即使你的交際對象不是西方人，你還是會發現這章很有用。

好幾年前，當我第一次來台灣學中文時，我想要交新朋友，於是在咖啡廳、公車上或酒吧裡跟人聊天。當時我並不曉得亞洲人和西方人在談話風格上的文化差異，所以我當然是用西方人的談話方式。雖然跟我交談的台灣人都很友善，我也的確交到了一些好朋友，但我卻開始對自己的交際能力感到不滿意。我想著：「我到底是怎麼了？」在英國的時候，我是個善於交際的人，而且很容易就能跟別人聊開來。可是到了台灣，就算我朋友的英文好得不得了，我卻老是覺得交際是件難事。後來有一天，有一個台灣朋友告訴我，我是個話很多的人，而且老愛問一大堆問題。但我之所以會問這麼多問題，是因為我想讓談話延續下去。於是我便開始思考亞洲人和西方人在談話風格上的差異。當我在亞洲各地旅行時，我開始聆聽周遭的人的談話方式，以下是我的心得。

1. **亞洲人比西方人習慣談話中的沈默**。西方人對於談話中的沈默會覺得不自在，所以他們會用很多技巧來讓談話進行下去。
2. **西方人比較常問問題**。這不是因為他們話多，而是因為如果要讓別人開口，問問題是再平常不過的方法。而且在西方人的談話中，談話高手就是指懂得怎麼讓對方開口的人。第二章對此會有更詳細的說明。
3. **西方人喜歡對各式各樣自己不一定很懂的話題表示意見**。比方說，西方人覺得自己不必是政治專家，但也會對政治情勢發表看法。又比方說，他們覺得自己不一定是音樂專家，但也會對自己為什麼喜不喜歡哪種音樂發表看法。但另一方面，亞洲人則被教導應該要謙虛，不要對自己不太懂的東西發表意見。

當然，這是非常概括的推論，所以各位也許並不認同上面所提到的一些看法。但是透過觀察，尤其是聆聽周遭的談話，我發現這個方式真的很有用。你在和外國人交談時，可以把這些心得歸納成三個非常有用的原則：

1. **讓談話進行下去，盡量避免令人不自在的沈默。**
2. **不要害怕問對方問題，尤其是關於看法的問題。**
3. **不要害怕表達自己的意見。**如果對方表達了他對某件事的看法，你也該表達自己的意見，就算意見相左也無所謂。

　　本章會詳細探討這些重點。研讀完本章，你應達成的「學習目標」如下：

　　❏ 了解西方人和亞洲人在談話風格上的差異。
　　❏ 懂得什麼是談話的 turn 。
　　❏ 了解何為 long-turn「長輪流」與 short-turn「短輪流」的交談。
　　❏ 了解何為 initiators「發話」與 responses「回應」。
　　❏ 完成聽力的 Task 。

社交談話的目的

　　這個章節有許多說明，所以我先給各位一些 Task ，設法提振各位的精神。要做好交際，好的聽力十分重要。此外，我還希望各位在理解本章的概念時，不僅要用眼睛閱讀，還要用耳朵聆聽。找個安靜的房間，然後泡杯咖啡，並一路戴著耳機來閱讀與聆聽。要盡量投入你所學習的內容中。

Task 1.1

「社交談話的目的是什麼？」花點時間想想這個問題，並寫下你的想法。

● 答　案

> 根據談話的主題、談話的情境、對話者的關係以及各自的目標，它顯然有很多不同的目的。

　　不過，各位可能想要看看下面這樣的答案。

談話的目的

互動 ←————————————→ 資訊

　　在圖的左端，談話的目的只是在於 interaction「互動」。談話的「主題」並不如談話的「動作」重要，它的目的只是在於互動與表示友善。雙方都知道「主題」不重要，談話所建立的「善意」才是它的目的。

　　在圖另一端的談話則是不同的類型，談話的目的是在於 information「資訊」的交流。此時談話的「主題」變得比較重要，而且可能比關係的建立還重要。例如：告訴對方要怎麼去飯店；或是針對雙方的合作案提供一些基本的背景資料；或是把自己的趣事告訴對方。

　　任何的社交談話都會落在「互動」與「資訊」這二端之間。此外，隨著談話的進行，談話也會在兩端之間移動。通常是在 interaction 的一端出發，然後漸漸往 information 的一端移動，因為兩個說話者愈來愈了解彼此，並開始信任或喜歡對方，所以也更願意敞開心胸。

Task 1.2

回想最近跟某人的談話，你會把這段對話擺在圖上的什麼地方？它在圖上的位置又是如何隨著談話的進行而移動？

● 答　案

關於這個問題的答案，顯然只有自己才知道。但不管是什麼樣的談話，我希望各位明白，它會出現在圖上的某個地方。

Short-Turn 與 Long-Turn 的談話

　　談話在圖上的位置決定了談話的風格，尤其是談話中 turns 的長度。現在我們仔細看看什麼是 turns。先做以下的聽力 Task，再看 CD 中的文字內容。

Task 1.3　　　　　　　　　　　　　　 CD 1-04

請聽 Track 1.1 的三段 short-turn 對話。它們有什麼共同點？

答　案

它們都是由交替的 turns 所構成。也就是，男生先說，女生再說，接著男生說，再由女生說，以此類推。這概念很簡單，也許簡單到你根本沒去注意，但所有的談話都是由這些 turns 所形成。各位可以再聽一次這些對話，並想想它們是如何運作。接著看看下列 CD 的文字內容。

Track 1.1

Conversation 1

He:　Did you have a good weekend?

She: Yes, thanks. Did you?

He:　Not bad. What did you do?

She: I went to Tamshui. You?

He:　I wasn't feeling too well, so I stayed at home.

Conversation 2

She: Did you see *Ally MacBeal* last night?

He:　Yes, I did. Did you?

She: Yes, wasn't it funny?

He:　Oh yes, I loved it. Wasn't the scene with the judge great?

She: Ha, yes, brilliant!

Conversation 3

He:　Did you hear what happened to Mike last night?

She: No, what?

He:　Well, apparently he had too much to drink and got into some kind of trouble. Typical, isn't it?

She: Oh, no. What kind of trouble?

He:　Well, I don't know the details, but ...

● 中　譯

對話 1

男：週末過得愉快嗎？

女：愉快，謝謝。你呢？

男：還可以。妳做了什麼事？

女：我去了淡水。你呢？

男：我覺得不太舒服，所以待在家裡。

對話 2

女：你昨晚有看《艾莉的異想世界》嗎？

男：有，我看了。妳呢？

女：看了，很好笑吧？

男：是啊，我愛死了。跟法官的那場戲是不是棒呆了？

女生：哈哈，沒錯，妙極了！

對話 3

男：妳聽說 Mike 昨晚發生的事了嗎？

女：沒有，怎麼了？

男：哦，他顯然是喝了太多酒而惹上麻煩。應該算是老毛病了吧？

女：噢，不會吧，是什麼樣的麻煩？

男：嗯，細節我不太清楚，不過……

Turns 可長可短。「互動」談話的 turns 通常很短，我們稱之為 Short-turn Talk。另一方面，「資訊」談話的 turns 則比較長，我們則稱之為 Long-turn Talk。請看下表，各位就會明白我的意思。

談話的目的

重要的是，各位要了解這點，並能分辨 Short-turn 和 Long-turn Talk 的不同，因為兩者之間有明顯的語言差異。接下來幾章會教各位 Short-turn 和 Long-turn Talk 的語言，但在本章我想要確定各位明白 turns，以及 turns 有哪幾種。現在來做一個聽力 Task，訓練各位的耳朵習慣這幾種對話。記住，請先聽幾次對話，再看下面的 CD 內容。

Task 1.4　　　　　　　　　　　　　　　　　　　　　　◉))) CD 1-05

請聽 Track 1.2 的談話，並在下表正確的格子中打勾。

	Short-turn Talk	Long-turn Talk
Conversation 1		
Conversation 2		

答 案

希望各位能聽出，Conversation 1 是 short-turn，Conversation 2 是 long-turn。對話一的互動比較多，而且主題以日常瑣事為主。對話二則是資訊比較多，內容是女生告訴男生一樁發生在她身上的驚奇事件。假如你沒有聽清楚這部分，請再聽一遍，特別注意女生的部分，設法判斷她的說話時間跟男生比起來占了多少比例。在第一段對話裡，男女的說話比重差不多；但在第二段對話裡，女生的說話時間就長得多。再聽幾次 CD，直到可以聽出其中的差異為止。接著請看下面的 CD 文字內容。

Conversation 1

She: Have you seen the new Hannibal Lecter movie?

He:　Oh, yes. You?

She: Yes. What did you think of it?

He:　I thought it was better than the others — I really liked it. What did you think of it?

She: I liked it, too. It was scary, but not disgusting. Do you know what I mean?

He:　Mmm. That's what I thought, too. And I always enjoy watching Anthony Hopkins.

She: Oh, yes. He's brilliant. What's the name of the young actor?

He:　Uhm, Edward Norton, or something like that. Did you like him?

She: Yes. He was excellent. They worked well together, don't you think?

He:　I don't know, I think the woman was better ...

Conversation 2

She: A funny thing happened to me the other day.

He:　Oh, yes?

She: I was just thinking about someone I went to school with, this boy I was quite friendly with in third grade. We used to hang out together — he lived next door — but then my parents moved and I changed schools and never saw him again.

He:　Mmm.

She: Well, I was walking down Nan Jing Dong Lu（Nan-jing E. Rd.）during my lunch break thinking about this boy. I have no idea why I was thinking about him.

He:　Really?

She: Yes, and suddenly I heard someone call my name. I turned around and there was this man looking at me. I didn't recognize him at all, but he obviously knew who I was.

He: Oh yeah, that's embarrassing when that happens.

She: You got it. Well, he walked up to me and said my name again and then I realized it was the boy I had been thinking about, the one from third grade!

He: Wow, that's weird!

 中　譯

對話 1

女：你看過人魔的新片了嗎？

男：哦，看過了。妳呢？

女：看過了，你覺得這部片怎麼樣？

男：我覺得它比其他幾部好看，我很喜歡。妳覺得它怎麼樣？

女：我也很喜歡。它雖然恐怖，但不噁心，你知道的我意思吧？

男：嗯，我也這麼認為。我一向很喜歡看安東尼‧霍普金斯演戲。

女：沒錯，他很出色。那位年輕的男演員叫什麼名字？

男：嗯，叫艾德華‧諾頓之類的吧。妳喜歡他啊？

女：是啊，他演得很棒。你不認為他們搭配得天衣無縫嗎？

男：我不知道，我覺得裡面的女生比較棒……

對話 2

女：前幾天我碰到了一件好玩的事。

男：哦，是嗎？

女：我想起一個以前跟我一起上學的人，那個男生在三年級的時候跟我很要好。他就住在隔壁，我們經常玩在一起。可是後來我父母搬了家，我也轉學了，從此再也沒跟他見過面。

男：嗯。

女：我在午休時間走在南京東路上，心裡想到這個男孩。我不知道為什麼會想起他……

男：是喔？

女：對呀，然後我突然聽到有人叫我的名字。我回過頭去，看到有個男人在看我。我完全認不出他來，他卻一副認識我的樣子。

男：喔，當時可真尷尬。

女：你說對了。好啦，他朝著我走過來，又叫了一次我的名字。然後我認出來了，他就是我心裡想的那個三年級的男孩！

男：哇，真不可思議！

　　現在仔細地來看看每次的 turn。

Task 1.5　　　　　　　　　　　　　　　CD 1-06

請聽 Track 1.3，並計算你聽到多少個 turn。

答　案

┃ 你應該會聽到五個。

　　每個 turn（除了第一個和最後一個以外）都是由兩個部分組成：一個 response「回應」和一個 initiator「發話」。男生的第一個 turn 只包含一個 initiator： Did you have a good weekend?，而談話也就此展開。然後女生回答說： Yes, thanks.。接著她在同一個 turn 裡用了一個 initiator： Did you?，男生則回答： Not bad.，接著是他的第二個 initiator： What did you do?。談話就這樣延續下去，每個 turn 都是由一個 response 接一個 initiator 所組成。請看看下面的 CD 內容，我把 initiator 畫上了底線，並把 response 改成斜體字。把它看過一遍，並確定自己了解我的意思。

Track 1.3

He: <u>Did you have a good weekend</u>?

She: *Yes, thanks.* <u>Did you</u>?

He: *Not bad.* <u>What did you do</u>?

She: *I went to Danshui.* <u>You</u>?

He: *I wasn't feeling too well, so I stayed at home.*

發話與回應

在了解了何為 turn 之後，再來詳細談談 initiator「發話」與 response「回應」，請先做下一個 Task 。

Task 1.6

詳讀下列文字，將 initiators 和 responses 分別以不同符號標示出來。

1. She: Did you see *Ally MacBeal* last night?
   He: Yes, I did. Did you?
   She: Yes, wasn't it funny?
   He: Oh, yes, I loved it. Wasn't the scene with the judge great?
   She: Ha, yes, brilliant!

2. He: Did you hear what happened to Mike last night?
   She: No, what?
   He: Well, apparently he had too much to drink and got into some kind of trouble. Typical, isn't it?
   She: Oh, no. What kind of trouble?
   He: Well, I don't know the details, but ...

答 案

CD 1-07

請核對下列的答案，畫底線的部分為 initiators ，斜體的部分為 responses 。核對過答案後，各位可以多聽幾次對話（Track1.4），直到可以聽出每個 turn 中的這些轉折。

1. She: <u>Did you see *Ally MacBeal* last night?</u>
   He: *Yes, I did.* <u>Did you?</u>
   She: *Yes,* <u>wasn't it funny?</u>
   He: *Oh yes, I loved it.* <u>Wasn't the scene with the judge great?</u>
   She: *Ha, yes, brilliant!*

2. He: <u>Did you hear what happened to Mike last night?</u>

She: *No, <u>What?</u>*

He: *Well, apparently he had too much to drink and got into some kind of trouble. <u>Typical isn't it?</u>*

She: *Oh, no, <u>what kind of trouble?</u>*

He: *Well, I don't know the details, but ...*

既然各位知道了 initiators 和 responses 是什麼，我們就來看看自己能不能從 Short-turn 和 Long-turn Talk 中聽出它們。它們在 Long-turn Talk 裡的用法有點不一樣。

Task 1.7　CD 1-05

請再回頭聽聽 Track 1.2，注意 initiators 和 responses 的用法在 Short-turn 和 Long-turn Talk 裡有什麼不同？

答　案

希望各位能聽出，在 Long-turn Talk 中，initiators 屬於女生，responses 屬於男生；而在 Short-turn Talk 中，initiators 和 responses 則平均分配在兩個說話者之間。

Initiators 是在「主導」對話時使用，responses 則是在「跟隨」對方的主導時使用。在 Short-turn Talk 中，主導對話的角色會一直在兩人之間轉換，就像在打桌球或打網球一樣，只是沒有優勝者而已。而在 Long-turn Talk 中，則有一方在主導，也就是說故事的那個人；另一個人則扮演比較被動的角色，包括聽故事與回應。在第二到第四章裡，各位會更了解這點。

等一下，剛才我聽到有人說，這種方法對我太複雜了！我想要一邊喝著一杯好咖啡一邊跟別人聊天。當我跟別人聊天時，我不可能去想這些事！我會瘋掉！當然，你說得對。好消息是，我並不希望各位在聊天時去想這些事，但我希望各位在學習本書的「必備語庫」以及做 Task 的時候想想看。

當然，在現實生活中，談話會比這來得雜亂，因為有人會忘記自己在說什麼、突然改變話題、雞同鴨講，或是自己講了好幾個小時、對方卻不發一語。不過，即使在

現實中模式會改變， initiate/respond/initiate 的模式還是西方人談話的基本架構。

在西方文化中，這是自然的談話結構，而亞洲人在這種 turn 的變換以及談話的應對方式上則有明顯的差異。假如各位會運用這種模式，你的社交談話技巧就會令人驚豔！假如你覺得它很難，那也不必擔心，只要去做就對了，因為一切都會漸入佳境！

為了讓各位更了解我的意思，請做下一個 Task。在完成之前，先不要看 CD 的文字內容與翻譯。

Task 1.8 CD 1-08

請聽 Track 1.5 的兩段對話。你會怎麼形容這兩個說話者的關係？又會怎麼形容這兩段對話的氣氛？

● 答　案

你是否覺得， Conversation 1 裡面的男生聽起來有點不耐煩與不友善？好像他對這段對話不感興趣，或者不太想跟那個女生講話。這是因為他完全沒有使用 initiators。所有的 initiators 都是由女生提出，男生只有回答而已。事實上，這就是典型的「訪談模式」（Interview Structure）。舉例來說，下次各位在聽 CNN 的訪問時，注意它的對答模式，就會發現所有的問題都由訪問者提出，受訪者則是只答不問。這種對話是單向的，或是 unbalanced。西方人在和亞洲人說話時，常常有這種感覺，好像是西方人在訪問亞洲人一樣。在第二和第三章裡，各位會學到如何避免這種不平衡的 Short-turn Talk，以及要怎麼更有效地運用 Short-turn Talk。

在 Conversation 2 裡，男生完全沒回應，女生則在講她的故事。這段對話同樣是單向的，或是 unbalanced。事實上，這是典型的「演講模式」（Lecture Structure），也就是一個人在講，其他人則靜靜地聽。西方人在對亞洲人講故事時，經常會有這種感覺。他們覺得自己是在演講，而聽者連聽都不想聽！另一方面，聽者之所以沒回應，可能只是因為他們聽不太懂內容！在第四章裏，各位就會學到如何對 Long-turn Talk 適當地回應，以及要怎麼開啟自己的 long turns。

為了讓各位能同時比較平衡與不平衡的 Short-turn 與 Long-turn Talks，現在請做最後一個 Task。

Task 1.9 CD 1-05 & 1-08

請聽 Track 1.2 和 1.5 的對話，並在正確的格子中寫下對話的編號，以完成下表。請見範例。

	Balanced	Unbalanced
Short-turn Talk	*Track 1.2 Conversation 1*	
Short-turn Talk		
Long-turn Talk		
Long-turn Talk		

答 案

希望各位能確實聽出兩種版本有什麼不同。要是聽不出來，各位可以邊聽邊看下列的 CD 內容。

	Balanced	Unbalanced
Short-turn Talk	Track 1.2 Conversation 1	
Short-turn Talk		Track 1.2 Conversation 2
Long-turn Talk	Track 1.5 Conversation 1	
Long-turn Talk		Track 1.5 Conversation 2

Track 1.5

Conversation 1

She: Have you seen the new Hannibal Lecter movie?

He: Oh, yes.

She: What did you think of it?

He: I thought it was better than the others — I really liked it.

She I liked it, too. It was scary, but not disgusting. I always enjoy watching Anthony Hopkins. He's brilliant.

He: Yes.

She: What's the name of the young actor?

He: Uhm, Edward Norton, or something like that.

She: Did you like him?

He:　Yes. He was excellent. They worked well together.

She: I don't know. I think the woman was better ...

Conversation 2

She: A funny thing happened to me the other day.

(pause)

She: I was just thinking about someone I went to school with, this boy I was quite friendly with in third grade. We used to hang out together — he lived next door — but then my parents moved and I changed schools and never saw him again.

(pause)

She: I was walking down Nan Jing Dong Lu（Nan-jing E. Rd.）during my lunch break thinking about this boy — I have no idea why I was thinking about him — and suddenly I heard someone call my name. I turned around and there was this man looking at me. I didn't recognize him at all, but he obviously knew who I was.

(pause)

She: He walked up to me and said my name again and then I realized it was the boy I had been thinking about, the one from third grade!

He:　That's very interesting.

She: Yeah, isn't it!

 中 譯

對話 1

女：你看過人魔的新片了嗎？

男：哦，看過了。

女：你覺得這部片子怎麼樣？

男：我覺得它比其他幾部好看，我很喜歡。

女：我也很喜歡。它雖然恐怖，但不噁心。我一向很喜歡看安東尼‧霍普金斯演戲，
　　他很出色。

男：沒錯。

女：那位年輕的男演員叫什麼名字？

男：嗯，叫艾德華·諾頓之類的吧。

女：你喜歡他嗎？

男：是啊，他演得很棒。他們搭配得天衣無縫。

女：我不知道，我覺得裡面的女生比較棒……

對話 2

女：前幾天我碰到了一件好玩的事。

（停頓）

女：我想起一個以前跟我一起上學的人，那個男生在三年級的時候跟我很要好。他就
　　住在隔壁，我們經常玩在一起。可是後來我父母搬了家，我也轉學了，從此再也
　　沒跟他見過面。

（停頓）

女：我在午休時間走在南京東路上，心裡想到這個男孩。我不知道爲什麼會想起他。
　　我突然聽到有人叫我的名字。我回過頭去，看到有個男人在看我。我完全認不出
　　他來，他卻一副認識我的樣子。

（停頓）

女：他朝著我走過來，又叫了一次我的名字。然後我認出來了，他就是我心裡想的那
　　個三年級的男孩！

男：眞是有趣！

女：可不是嗎？

　　這章的理論多了些，但我希望各位對於談話的本質以及東西方談話的文化差異能
有新的體認。在日常生活中聽聽別人的談話，看看自己能不能判斷出它們是 long-turn
還是 short-turn ，以及他們用的是哪種 initiators 和 responses 。在看下一章之前，回
頭看一下本章的「學習目標」，確定自己已經學會。假如還有不懂的地方，也不用擔
心，過個幾天，再回到相關的章節重讀一遍，相信到時候就看得懂了。

Unit2

Short-Turn 的

談話 1：發話

引言與學習目標

在接下來兩章，我們要仔細來看 Short-turn Talk 。上一章曾經談到，社交談話包括 Short-turn 和 Long-turn Talk ，其中又以 short-turn 為多，所以能善用它是很重要的事，而且它也是個簡單的起點！各位應該記得，上一章談到，談話的 turn 多半是由 initiator「發話」和 response「回應」所組成。在本章中，我們會把重點擺在 Short-turn Initiators 上，下一章再來介紹 Short-turn Responses 。一開始先來練習聽力吧。

Task 2.1　　　　　　　　　　　　　　　　　　　　　　　　　　◉))) CD 1-09 & 1-10

請聽 Track 2.1 和 2.2 ，並回答下列問題。

Track 2.1

1. John 在週末做了什麼？

2. Joyce 做了什麼？

Track 2.2

3. Michael 的電話是在哪裡買的？

4. Janet 的電話是哪一種？

別急著找答案，在 Task 2.2 中各位就可以看到 CD 的文字內容，知道答案為何。重點是多聽幾次 CD ，訓練自己聽懂這種談話。

本章結束時，各位應達到的學習目標如下：

❏ 能夠開啟談話。

❏ 學到一些有用的話題來發問，以展開談話。

❏ 學到要怎麼以話題來延伸問題，以繼續談話。

❏ 完成一些聽力的 Task 。

❏ 完成一些發音的 Task 。

❏ 更了解 travel 、 trip 和 journey 這幾個字的差別，以及要怎麼使用。

Short-Turn 的發話

我們直接用 Task 來進入正題！在聽完 CD 之前，先別看 CD 的文字內容。

Task 2.2　　　　　　　　　　　　　　　　　　CD 1-09 & 1-10

再聽一次 Track 2.1 和 2.2，然後寫下你聽到的 Short-turn Initiators。

答　案

希望各位能從這兩段談話中聽出，最常用與最有用的一種 initiator 就是「問題」。詳讀下面的 CD 文字內容，並核對答案。

Track 2.1

John: So, did you do anything special this weekend?

Joyce: Uhm, yes, I went to Jing Shan with a friend.

John: Oh, that's nice. Did you enjoy it?

Joyce: Yes, the beach was a bit crowded, but the journey there was really super.

John: How did you get there?

Joyce: We went on my friend's motorbike, over the mountain, over Yang Ming Shan, and down the other side.

John: Wow, that's a long way!

Joyce: Yes, but great views! Have you been that way before?

John: Yes, a long time ago, but we usually go by car along the coast. How long did it take by bike?

| Word List |

super [`supɚ] *adj.* 極好的　　　　　　motorbike [`motɚ͵baɪk] *n.* 摩托車

Joyce: About two hours, but we kept stopping along the way to admire the view and take pictures. I had no idea Taiwan was so beautiful!

John: Really? Why do you say that?

Joyce: Well, I don't find the city very beautiful. I'm not really a city person. I never had the time to get out of the city before, and now I'm beginning to realize just what it is I'm missing. The landscape here is incredible.

John: Yes, I know. Maybe you need to get away more.

Joyce: I certainly do. How about you? Did you do anything nice?

John: We went to have dinner with my wife's parents.

Joyce: Oh, that sounds nice. Where do they live?

John: In Chia-yi. Have you been there?

Joyce: No, not yet. Did you drive there?

John: Yes. It took about four hours.

Joyce: So, what kind of car do you have?

John: A Toyota.

中 譯

John ： 所以，妳這個週末有沒有做什麼特別的事？

Joyce ： 呣，有，我和朋友去了金山。

John ： 喔，不錯。玩得開心嗎？

Joyce ： 開心，海灘上有點擠，不過一路上都很棒。

John ： 妳們是怎麼去的？

Joyce ： 我們騎我朋友的摩托車爬過陽明山，然後下到另一邊。

John ： 哇，好長一段路啊！

Joyce ： 是啊，可是風景不錯！你以前有走過那條路嗎？

John ： 有，很久以前，可是我們通常是沿著海岸開車去。騎車花了多少時間？

| Word List |

landscape [ˋlænskep] *n.* 景色；地貌

Joyce ： 大概兩個小時，不過我們沿路都有停下來欣賞風景與拍照。我不知道台灣竟
　　　　然這麼美！

John ： 是嗎？怎麼說？

Joyce ： 哦，我並不覺得這個城市很美，而且我根本不是個喜歡城市生活的人。以前
　　　　我從來沒有時間出市區，現在我才開始明白，是我自己沒搞懂。這裡的景觀
　　　　美極了。

John ： 是啊，我知道。也許妳需要走得更遠一點。

Joyce ： 我當然會。你呢？你有沒有做什麼開心的事？

John ： 我們去找我岳父母吃飯。

Joyce ： 噢，聽起來不錯。他們住哪兒？

John ： 嘉義。妳去過那裡嗎？

Joyce ： 沒有，還沒去過。你們是開車去嗎？

John ： 對，大概開了四個小時。

Joyce ： 你們的車是哪一種啊？

John ： Toyota。

Track 2.2

Janet: Where did you get your mobile? It's really cute.

Michael: Oh, this? I got it in Singapore. Here, do you want to take a look?

Janet: Thanks. Gee, it's really light!

Michael: Yes, it is, isn't it? A bit too light, really. What make have you got?

Janet: I've got an old Ericsson. Here. Take a look.

Michael: Wow, that's really old.

Janet: Yes, I like collecting antiques.

Michael: Why don't you get a new one?

| W o r d　L i s t |

mobile [ˋmobil] *n.* 行動電話　　　　　　make [mek] *n.* 型式
antique [ænˋtik] *n.* 古物；骨董

Janet: I don't know. I like this one, and I don't have any need for all the bells and whistles you get on the new ones.

Michael: Really, what makes you say that?

Janet: Well, I just need to make and receive calls, and it's quite reliable. I find that the more fancy stuff they put into these things, the more likely they are to break down or go wrong, you know? I mean, this camera function, for instance — how often do you use it?

Michael: Sometimes, but I guess not very often. It's more for fun. Sometimes when I'm on a trip, for example, I can take a picture and send it to my kids. Or I can send a picture of a sample back to my office and get it costed up immediately.

Janet: Well, that's nice I guess. So how many kids do you have?

Michael: Three. Two boys and a girl.

● 中 譯

Janet ： 你的手機是在哪裡買的？好可愛。

Michael ： 哦，這支嗎？我在新加坡買的。妳要看看嗎？

Janet ： 謝謝。哇，好輕！

Michael ： 是啊，它的確很輕。說眞的，它太輕了一點。妳用的是哪一款？

Janet ： 我用的是老式的 Ericsson 。你拿去看看。

Michael ： 哇，眞舊啊。

Janet ： 是啊，我喜歡收集骨董。

Michael ： 妳爲什麼不換一支新的？

Janet ： 我也不知道。我就是喜歡這支，而且你的新手機的功能五花八門，我根本用不到。

Michael ： 是哦，妳爲什麼這麼說？

| Word List |

all the bells and whistles 各式各樣的東西

Janet ： 哦，我只需要接打電話而已，這支電話在這方面很可靠。你知道嗎，我發現功能愈花俏的手機，就愈容易壞掉或故障。我的意思是，就拿這種照相的功能來說，你有多常用到？

Michael ： 有時候會用到，不過我想不會很常用，而是以好玩為主。例如有時候在旅行時，我就可以拍照，然後把它傳給我的小孩看。或者我也可以把樣品的照片傳回辦公室，以便立刻估價。

Janet ： 嗯，還不錯。你有幾個小孩呢？

Michael ： 三個，兩男一女。

　　大部分的談話都是從問題開始（開啟話題的問題：topic starter questions），而當談話一開始，說話者就會問更多的問題來延伸話題（延伸話題的問題：topic development questions）。在和別人聊天時，要注意自己可以在什麼地方問問題，以及可以問什麼問題來引導談話。接著仔細來看看這兩種問題。

開啟話題的問題

前面說過， topic starter questions 可以用來和別人「展開」談話，但當一個話題變得無聊或講完時，它也可以用來在談話中「轉換話題」。

英文問題的文法很難，而且假如鼓起勇氣和別人展開談話，你可不希望還要擔心文法，所以最好的做法就是針對自己想要用來展開談話的主題，記住幾個有用的 set-phrases。現在來做下面的 Task。完成後，再看答案和語庫小叮嚀。

Task 2.3

請看下面的類別和 set-phrases。把類別與 set-phrases 配對。請看範例。

1. Questions about someone's current lifestyle ( )
2. Questions about someone's future plans (-)
3. Questions about someone's interests and hobbies ( )
4. Questions about someone's past experiences or career ( )
5. Questions about someone's views ( )
6. Questions about something someone owns ( )
7. Questions about work ( )
8. Questions you can ask someone you are meeting for the first time (h)
9. Questions you can ask when you haven't seen someone for a while ( )

---

a)

- What have you been doing since I saw you last?
- Have you been busy?
- What did you do on the weekend?
- Did you do anything special this weekend?
- How was your holiday/weekend/trip/vacation?
- How are you?
- Are you well?
- How's it going?

- How's business?
- What happened?
- What have you been doing this week?
- Where have you been?

b)

- What are you doing this weekend?
- Are you doing anything nice this weekend?
- Where are you going for your next holiday?
- Any plans for ...?
- Are you going out later?
- Do you always want to work in ...?
- What are you thinking of doing next?
- Are you going to ...?

c)

- Where did you get your ...?
- Was your ... expensive?
- What kind of computer do you use?
- What kind of car do you drive?
- What year is your car?
- What color is your ...?
- Where can I get a ... like yours?

d)

- What did you major in?
- Where did you go to university?
- Have you been to ...?
- Where did you work before?
- Where did you live before coming here?
- Have you ever ...?

e)

- What do you think of the current economic/political situation?
- What do you think of the long-term (economic/political/business) prospects?
- What do you think of ...?
- What are your views on ...?
- Have you seen this?
- Did you read that report on ... in ...?

f)

- How is your company coping with the economic situation?
- How do you do this in your company?
- How does your company deal with ...?
- Do you get on with your boss?
- What are you working on at the moment?
- How did ... go?
- Did ... go well?

g)

- How long have you been here?
- Where do you live?
- Do you live far from the office?
- How do you get to work?
- What are you reading at the moment?
- How long does it take you to get home/get to the office/get to work?
- Do you have your family with you?
- Do your children like it here?
- Where are you sending them to school?
- How many children do you have?
- Do you miss home?
- What does your wife/husband do?
- Does she like it here?

h)

- How do you do?
- Where do you come from?
- Where are you from?
- What do you do?
- Where do you work?
- Who do you work for?
- What department do you work in?
- What does your company do?
- How long have you worked there?
- What's your job title?
- How big is your company?
- Where is it based?
- How do you find it here?
- Are you married?
- How long have you been married?
- Do you have any children?
- Can you speak Chinese?
- Where did you learn Chinese/English?

i)

- What's your handicap?
- How long have you been playing?
- Where do you play?
- Are you a (new) member?
- How long have you been a member?
- Do you do any (other) sports?
- How do you do that?
- Have you seen ...?
- What kind of music/food/books/movies do you like?
- What do you do in your free time?
- Have you ever played ...?
- Have you ever been ...?

答　案

1.	g	2.	b	3.	i	4.	d	5.	e
6.	c	7.	f	8.	h	9.	a		

有關上一個 Task 中的 set-phrases 用法與注意事項，可以參看下列的必備語庫與語庫小叮嚀。

社交必備語庫 2.1 CD 1-11

Questions You can Ask When You Haven't Seen Someone for a While	一陣子未見某人時可以問的問題
• What have you been doing since I saw you last?	• 自從我上次見到你以後，你都在幹嘛？
• Have you been busy?	• 最近忙嗎？
• What did you do on the weekend?	• 你週末的時候在幹嘛？
• Did you do anything special this weekend?	• 你這個週末有沒有做什麼特別的事？
• How was your holiday/weekend/trip/vacation?	• 你的假期 / 週末 / 旅遊 / 假期過得怎麼樣？
• How are you?	• 你好嗎？
• Are you well?	• 別來無恙？
• How's it going?	• 近來如何？
• How's business?	• 生意好嗎？
• What happened?	• 發生了什麼事？
• What have you been doing this week?	• 你這個星期都在做什麼？
• Where have you been?	• 你到哪兒去了？

★ 📂 語庫小叮嚀

◆ 注意，這些問題跟問陌生人的問題有點不一樣。
◆ 在英式英語中，假期為 holiday，而一天的國定假日則叫做 bank holiday。
◆ How was your vacation/holiday? 是指某人在國外的旅遊，而不是指一天的國定假日。
◆ How's it going? 是 How are you? 的非正式說法。

Questions about Someone's Future Plans	關於某人未來計畫的問題
• What are you doing this weekend?	• 你這個週末要做什麼？
• Are you doing anything nice this weekend?	• 你這個週末要做什麼開心的事？
• Where are you going for your next holiday?	• 你下次休假要去哪裡？
• Any plans for ...?	• 有打算要……嗎？
• Are you going out later?	• 你等一下要出去嗎？
• Do you always want to work in ...?	• 你一直想去……工作嗎？
• What are you thinking of doing next?	• 你接下來想做什麼？
• Are you going to ...?	• 你要去……嗎？

★ 📁 語庫小叮嚀

◆ 注意，這些問題都和未來有關，但都不用 will ，而是用 be going to 或 be + Ving 。

Questions about Something Someone Owns	關於某人擁有的某樣東西的問題
• Where did you get your ...?	• 你的……是在哪裡買的？
• Was your ... expensive?	• 你的……很貴嗎？
• What kind of computer do you use?	• 你用的是哪種電腦？
• What kind of car do you drive?	• 你開的是哪種車？
• What year is your car?	• 你的車是什麼年份？
• What color is your ...?	• 你的……是什麼顏色？
• Where can I get a ... like yours?	• 我在哪裡可以買到跟你一樣的……？

★ 📁 語庫小叮嚀

◆ 當你看到某人有新的電話、新的筆、新的筆記型電腦，或是新領帶、新鞋、新衣物，這些問題就可派上用場。

Questions about Someone's Past Experiences or Career	關於某人的過去經驗或生涯的問題
• What did you major in?	• 你的主修是什麼？
• Where did you go to university?	• 你唸哪裡的大學？
• Have you been to ...?	• 你有去過……嗎？
• Where did you work before?	• 你以前在哪裡工作？
• Where did you live before coming here?	• 你在來這裡以前住在哪裡？
• Have you ever ...?	• 你曾經……嗎？

★ 📁 語庫小叮嚀

◆ 在學習這些 set-phrases 時，要特別注意動詞的時態。

Questions about Someone's Views	關於某人的看法的問題
• What do you think of the current economic/political situation?	• 你對於目前的經濟／政治局勢有什麼看法？
• What do you think of the long-term (economic/political/business) prospects?	• 你對於長期的（經濟／政治／商業）展望有什麼看法？
• What do you think of ...?	• 你對於……有什麼看法？
• What are your views on ...?	• 你對於……有什麼看法？
• Have you seen this?	• 你看過這個嗎？
• Did you read that report on ... in ...?	• 你看了……的……報告嗎？

★ 📁 語庫小叮嚀

◆ 一般來說，西方人喜歡回答與本身看法有關的問題，而不喜歡回答與家人或家務有關的問題；亞洲人則相反。在和來自不同國家的人交際時，要記得這點。政治是很敏感的領域，所以在談論時要很小心。

◆ Did you read that report on ... in ...? 在 on 後面是接「主題」，在 in 後面則是接看到報告的「地方」。例如： Did you see that report on <u>the French wine industry</u> in <u>*the Economist?*</u>「你有看到經濟學人雜誌中那篇關於法國酒產業的報導嗎？」

◆ Have you seen this? 當你要談論你所閱讀的東西時，就可以用這個問題。

Questions about Work	關於工作的問題
• How is your company coping with the economic situation?	• 你們公司怎麼因應經濟情勢？
• How do you do this in your company?	• 你在公司裡怎麼做這件事？
• How does your company deal with ...?	• 你們公司怎麼處理……？
• Do you get on with your boss?	• 你跟上司處得怎麼樣？
• What are you working on at the moment?	• 你目前在做什麼？
• How did ... go?	• ……進行得怎麼樣？
• Did ... go well?	• ……進行得順利嗎？

★ 🗂 語庫小叮嚀

◆ 你可能會覺得談工作有點乏味，不過在「展開」談話時，這倒是很有效的辦法，因為它的立場很中立。此外，有些人工作之外沒什麼特別的興趣，或者是很熱愛工作，所以你還是要知道該怎麼鼓勵他們聊工作。

◆ How did ... go?、Did ... go well? 假如你知道談話的對象最近剛做了一場報告，或是開了一場會，這兩個問題就派上用場了。

Questions about Someone's Current Lifestyle	關於某人目前的生活型態的問題
• How long have you been here?	• 你來這裡多久了？
• Where do you live?	• 你住在哪兒？
• Do you live far from the office?	• 你住的地方離辦公室遠嗎？
• How do you get to work?	• 你怎麼去上班的？
• What are you reading at the moment?	• 你現在在讀些什麼？
• How long does it take you to get home/get to the office/get to work?	• 你回家／去辦公室／上班要多久？
• Do you have your family with you?	• 你跟家人住在一起嗎？
• Do your children like it here?	• 你的小孩喜歡這裡嗎？
• Where are you sending them to school?	• 你送他們去哪裡的學校？
• How many children do you have?	• 你有幾個小孩？
• Do you miss home?	• 你想家嗎？
• What does your wife/husband do?	• 你太太／先生是做哪一行的？
• Does she like it here?	• 她喜歡這裡嗎？

★ 📁 語庫小叮嚀

◆ 假如你知道對方和家人一起住在當地，這些問題就很有用。

◆ 在以某人喜歡哪些書展開話題時，What are you reading at the moment? 是很有用的問題。

Questions You can Ask Someone You are Meeting for the First Time	第一次遇到某人時可以問的問題
• How do you do?	• 你好嗎？
• Where do you come from?	• 你從哪裡來？
• Where are you from?	• 你是哪裡人？
• What do you do?	• 你是做哪一行的？
• Where do you work?	• 你在哪裡工作？
• Who do you work for?	• 你替誰工作？
• What department do you work in?	• 你在哪個部門工作？
• What does your company do?	• 你們公司是做什麼的？
• How long have you worked there?	• 你在那裡工作多久了？
• What's your job title?	• 你的工作職稱是什麼？
• How big is your company?	• 你們公司多大？
• Where is it based?	• 它在什麼地方？
• How do you find it here?	• 你是怎麼在這裡找到它的？
• Are you married?	• 你結婚了嗎？
• How long have you been married?	• 你結婚多久了？
• Do you have any children?	• 你有小孩嗎？
• Can you speak Chinese?	• 你會說中文嗎？
• Where did you learn Chinese/ English?	• 你的中文 / 英文是在哪兒學的？

★ 📁 語庫小叮嚀

◆ 這些問題跟對已經認識的人提出的問題有點不一樣。它們比較中立，並且是在對別人的生活與工作建立基本的認識。

◆ 在問 Are you married?、Do you have any children? 這些問題時要小心，因為可能會冒犯到沒有結婚但想要結婚的人，或是沒有小孩但想要小孩的人！對西方人來說，離婚不是禁忌的話題，所以假如有人提到自己離婚了，你不用覺得尷尬，但可不要再追問下去！

Questions about Someone's Interests and Hobbies	關於某人的興趣及嗜好的問題
• What's your handicap?	• 你的差點是多少？
• How long have you been playing?	• 你從事（某項運動）多久了？
• Where do you play?	• 你都在哪裡從事（某項運動）？
• Are you a (new) member?	• 你是（新）會員嗎？
• How long have you been a member?	• 你當會員多久了？
• Do you do any (other) sports?	• 你有做什麼（其他的）運動嗎？
• How do you do that?	• 你是怎麼做的？
• Have you seen ...?	• 你有看過……嗎？
• What kind of music/food/books/movies do you like?	• 你喜歡哪種音樂 / 食物 / 書 / 電影？
• What do you do in your free time?	• 你空閒時都在做什麼？
• Have you ever played ...?	• 你有沒有打過……（某項運動）？
• Have you ever been ...?	• 你有沒有在……？

★ 📁 語庫小叮嚀

◆ 一般來說，人都喜歡談論自己的嗜好與興趣。但要注意的是，在這些和嗜好與興趣有關的問題中，並不包括 What's your hobby?，因為它聽起來很幼稚。

◆ Have you ever played ...? 後面接的是「球類運動」，如：Have you ever played volleyball?「你打過排球嗎？」

◆ Have you ever been ...? 後面接的是「體能活動」如：Have you ever been hang gliding?「你有嘗試過滑翔翼嗎？」

◆ 當你在健身房或高爾夫球俱樂部和別人聊天時，Are you a (new) member? 和 How long have you been a member? 就可以派上用場了。

◆ What's your handicap? 是和高爾夫球有關的問題。打高爾夫球的人都喜歡討論差點，以顯示他們的技術水準。差點愈低，代表球打得愈好。初學者的差點可能在 30 以上，技術好的人差點可能不到 5。假如你遇到老虎伍茲，千萬不要問他的差點，因為職業選手是不用差點的。在第九章中，各位會學到更多運動方面的用語。

　　在練習這些問題的發音前，我們先來做另一項聽力 Task，看看這些問題的實際用法。

Task 2.4 　　　　　　　　　　　　　　　　　　　　　CD 1-09 &1-10

再聽一次 Track 2.1 和 2.2 。聽的時候，寫下你所聽到的 topic starter questions 。

答　案

希望各位聽得出來，兩段談話中各有兩個開啓話題的問題：一個是在展開談話，一個
是在轉換話題。假如你沒聽出來，那就再聽一遍，並邊看 CD 文字內容。

Track 2.1

開啓話題： Did you do anything special this weekend?

轉換話題： What kind of car do you have?

Track 2.2

開啓話題： Where did you get your mobile?

轉換話題： So how many kids do you have?

Task 2.5 　　　　　　　　　　　　　　　　　　　　　　CD 1-11

請聽 Track 2.3 ，聽聽語庫 2.1 中的問題，練習發音。

　　如果各位累了，現在不妨暫停一下。這章的 set-phrases 很多，所以各位可以利用
本書附錄三的「學習目標記錄表」，決定自己想鎖定哪些問題來加強。

延伸話題的問題

現在我們來看另一種問題 topic development questions。它不是那麼好學，因為你根本不知道談話會怎麼發展，所以也無法預測會用到哪個問題。不過，各位還是可以學習幾個常用的問題作為準備。現在來做下一個 Task。

Task 2.6

請研究下面的語庫與小叮嚀。

社交必備語庫 2.2

 CD 1-12

Questions to Encourage Someone to Talk More	用來鼓勵某人多說一點的問題
• Why do you say that?	• 你為什麼這麼說？
• What do you mean by that?	• 你這句話是什麼意思？
• Why is that?	• 為什麼是這樣？
• Why?	• 為什麼？
• What does that mean?	• 那是什麼意思？
• What makes you say that?	• 你這麼說的理由是什麼？

語庫小叮嚀

◆ 這些問題能鼓勵別人多說些話，自己也就能少說些話，是減輕自己壓力的好方法。還記得「社交必備本領 1」中的五大要領嗎？這些問題值得好好學習，並套用在談話中。

Task 2.7

CD 1-09 & 1-10

再聽一次 Track 2.1 和 2.2，注意說話者是怎麼運用這些問題。把所聽到的問題寫下來。

答案

假如你沒聽出這些問題，那就邊聽邊看 CD 文字內容。

Track 2.1： Why do you say that?

Track 2.2： What makes you say that?

在學習更多的 topic development questions 前，我們先來練習這些問題的發音。

Task 2.8　　　　　　　　　　　　　　　　　　　CD 1-12

請聽 Track 2.4 ，熟悉必備語庫 2.2 中的問題，並練習發音。

接著來看些其他的 topic development questions 。各位在決定使用哪個問題使談話進行下去前，需要仔細聆聽對方的談話。接下來要介紹的 set-phrases 其實只能作為參考，但我會告訴各位如何根據談話的主題來提出問題。我們來研究一些例子。

Task 2.9　　　　　　　　　　　　　　　　　　CD 1-09 & 1-10

再聽一次 Track 2.1 和 2.2 ，寫下你所聽到的 topic development questions 。

答案

Track 2.1

- Did you enjoy it?
- How did you get there?
- Have you been that way before?
- How long did it take by bike?
- Where do they live?
- Have you been there?
- Did you drive there?

Track 2.2

- What brand do you have?
- Why don't you get a new one?
- Do you use it?

各位可以回頭詳讀 CD 的文字內容，看看發問的人是如何根據前一個人所說的話來提出問題。在 Track 2.1 中， Joyce 提到她們騎摩托車去金山，於是 John 便問她：騎車要騎多久。在 Track 2.2 中， Michael 問 Janet 為什麼不買支新電話，因為他發現她拿的是舊款的手機。還要注意的是，大部分的問題都是以 wh- 開頭，這表示這些問題的答案不只是 yes 或 no ，而須提供更多訊息。這可以鼓勵對方多說些話。各位來做個關於 topic development questions 的 Task 。

Task 2.10

請閱讀下列的段落，並在下方的空格中填入一些你要延伸此話題時可能會問的問題。每個段落至少寫出四個問題。請看範例。

1. I went to Sun Moon Lake for the weekend. Wow, it was beautiful! Reminds me of the country around Lake Geneva where I grew up. We stayed in this lovely hotel and had a delicious dinner there. What a great weekend!

   Q_1 *How did you get there?*_____

   Q_2 _____

   Q_3 _____

   Q_4 _____

2. I remember when I was a student in San Francisco, we were all much more politically active in those days. Now we just care about making money. I guess that's how having a family of your own changes you: you become more aware of your responsibilities, right?

   Q_1 _____

   Q_2 _____

   Q_3 _____

   Q_4 _____

3. I used to play the piano when I was young. In fact I studied it quite seriously for about twelve years or so. Actually my first job was playing for dance classes in a dance academy! Those were the days: beautiful dancers to look at every day! I never thought I'd end up doing what I do now.

   Q_1 _____

   Q_2 _____

   Q_3 _____

   Q_4 _____

4. I swim about 1.5 kilometers every day. I find it's really good exercise, especially for my back, which I had some trouble with a few years ago, so I need to watch out with it.

Q_1 _____

Q_2 _____

Q_3 _____

Q_4 _____

● 答 案

下列的問題只是參考答案。各位所寫的問題也可能一樣有用及有趣。（可參考下列中譯）

1. Q_2: In what way is the landscape around Geneva similar to Sun Moon Lake?

Q_3: What was the name of the hotel?

Q_4: What did you have for dinner?

2. Q_1: What did you study?

Q_2: What were your politics then?

Q_3: How many kids have you got?

Q_4: Have you kept in touch with the people in your year at college?

3. Q_1: Do you still play?

Q_2: Who's your favorite composer?

Q_3: Do you still enjoy watching dance?

Q_4: Do you like what you're doing now?

4. Q_1: Where do you swim?

Q_2: What kind of stroke are you best at?

Q_3: What happened to your back?

Q_4: What's your top time for 1.5 kilometers?

● 中 譯

1. 我週末去了日月潭。哇，真漂亮！它讓我想起了日內瓦湖的鄰近地區，我就是在那裡長大的。我們住在一家很不錯的旅館，並在那裡享用了一頓美味的晚餐。這個週末真開心！

Q_1：你們是怎麼去那裡的？

Q_2：日內瓦跟日月潭的景色在哪些方面相似？

Q₃：那家旅館叫什麼名字？

Q₄：你們晚餐吃了什麼？

2. 還記得我在舊金山當學生的時候，我們都對政治很熱衷，但現在我們只顧著賺錢。我想我們是因為有了自己的家庭才變成這個樣子。我們變得更了解自己的責任，對吧？

Q₁：你讀的是什麼？

Q₂：你當時的政治立場是什麼？

Q₃：你生了幾個孩子？

Q₄：你還有跟同一屆的大學同學聯絡嗎？

3. 我年輕時有在彈鋼琴。事實上，我學得很認真，前後大概學了十二年。我的第一份工作是在舞蹈學院的舞蹈課上彈琴。在那段日子裡，每天都有美麗的舞者可看！我從來沒想過最後我會做目前的工作。

Q₁：你還在彈嗎？

Q₂：你最喜歡的作曲家是誰？

Q₃：你還喜歡看舞蹈嗎？

Q₄：你喜歡現在的工作嗎？

4. 我每天都游泳，大概游 1.5 公里。我覺得這項運動相當好，尤其是對我的背。我的背在前幾年出了點毛病，所以我得小心一點。

Q₁：你都在哪裡游泳？

Q₂：你最擅長哪種游法？

Q₃：你的背怎麼了？

Q₄：你游 1.5 公里的最快時間是多少？

重點在於，看看這些問題如何延伸第一個說話者已經提過的事。我們再做一個 Task，看看它是如何運作。

Task 2.11

再看一次上面的段落和問題，在延伸問題之後的空格，填上段落中對應的相關字。請看範例。

1. I went to Sun Moon Lake for the weekend. Wow, it was beautiful! Reminds me of the country around Lake Geneva where I grew up. We stayed in this lovely hotel and had a delicious dinner there. What a great weekend!

Q_1: How did you get there? → *Sun Moon Lake*

Q_2: In what way is the landscape around Geneva similar to Sun Moon Lake?
→ *Lake Geneva*

Q_3: What was the name of the hotel? → *lovely hotel*

Q_4: What did you have for dinner? → *a delicious dinner*

2. I remember when I was a student in San Francisco, we were all much more politically active in those days. Now we just care about making money. I guess that's how having a family of your own changes you: you become more aware of your responsibilities, right?

Q_1: What did you study? → _____

Q_2: What were your politics then? → _____

Q_3: How many kids have you got? → _____

Q_4: Have you kept in touch with the people in your year at college? → _____

3. I used to play the piano when I was young. In fact I studied it quite seriously for about twelve years or so. Actually my first job was playing for dance classes in a dance academy! Those were the days: beautiful dancers to look at every day! I never thought I'd end up doing what I do now.

Q_1: Do you still play? → _____

Q_2: Who's your favorite composer? → _____

Q_3: Do you still enjoy watching dance? → _____

Q_4: Do you like what you're doing now? → _____

4. I swim about 1.5 kilometers every day. I find it's really good exercise, especially for my back, which I had some trouble with a few years ago, so I need to watch out with it.

Q_1: Where do you swim? → _____

Q_2: What kind of stroke are you best at? → _____

Q_3: What happened to your back? → _____

Q₄: What's your top time for 1.5 kilometers? → _____

答　案

2. Q₁: student

Q₂: political active

Q₃: a family

Q₄: student

3. Q₁: used to play

Q₂: piano

Q₃: dance classes

Q₄: what I do now

4. Q₁: swim

Q₂: swim

Q₃: some trouble

Q₄: 1.5 kilometers

　　希望各位可以學會，如何提出適當的 topic development questions 來讓談話進行下去。這也取決於你的聽力，因為你要能聽懂關鍵字，才能從中提出問題。現在做下一個 Task 來練習聽力吧。

Task 2.12　　　　　　　　　　　　　　　　　　　 CD 1-13

請聽 Track 2.5（上一個 Task 中的 4 則短對話），練習在適當時機提出自己的問題。

答　案

各位可能會覺得自言自語有點奇怪，擔心萬一被別人看到，他們會懷疑你瘋了！（當我在練習中文發音時，我都把自己關在浴室裡，以免被別人聽到……）不過不用擔心，現在練習，等到有機會跟外國人洽談時，你就能從容應對，並且更有自信。所以姑且一試吧！

語感甦活區

在語庫 2.1 中，有一類問題是 Questions you can ask when you haven't seen some-one for a while ，而其中一個問題是： How was your trip?。

在這節中，我們要來看 trip 這個字，以及它的相關字 journey 和 travel 。因為有很多人都搞不清楚這些字要怎麼用。

與其思考這些字的意義有什麼差別，不如學學它們和哪些字搭配使用，以及它們是出現在哪些 MWIs 中。在商業英語中， trip 比 journey 常出現得多， travel 則是幾乎完全不用，而且通常是當作動詞。

Task 2.13

請研讀下列的 word partnership 表格，並練習造句。

• arrange • cancel • go on • organize • plan • take • make • postpone • have • be away on • come back from • return from • cut short	• business • disastrous • enjoyable • long • good • short • successful • unsuccessful • tiring • weekend • day • foreign • overseas	**trip** （註： trip 指到目的地，然後再回到出發處的旅程。）

Word List

postpone [post`pon] v. 延期

disastrous [dɪz`æstrəs] adj. 糟透的

● 答　案

可能的參考答案如下：

- Did you have a good trip to Hua-lien this weekend?
- We're planning a trip to Bali for our company outing this month.
- I've just been on a very successful but tiring business trip to Hong Kong.

Task 2.14

請研讀下列的 word partnership 表格，並練習造句。

• have • break • go on • start • finish	• safe • homeward • outward • return • terrible • comfortable	**journey** （註： journey 指的是單趟的路程）

● 答　案

可能的參考答案如下：

- Have a safe journey.
- The outward journey was OK, but the homeward journey was terrible.
- We broke our journey at Moscow and spent two nights there.

| W o r d　 L i s t |

homeward [ˈhomwəd] *adj.* 歸家的　　　　　outward [ˈaʊtwəd] *adj.* 出國的

Task 2.15

請研讀下列的 word partnership 表格,並練習造句。

travel	• by air
	• by sea
	• by road
	• on foot
	• by train
	• in style
	• in luxury
	• rough
	• extensively
	• light
	• widely
	• regularly
	• economy/first class

答 案

可能的參考答案如下:

• When I was young I traveled extensively all over Europe.

• I like to travel light, but my wife likes to travel in style.

• I think traveling by train is more romantic than traveling by air, don't you?

好了,在本章結束前,請回到本章的「學習目標」,看看自己是否了解本章的所有內容。如果各位還有不清楚的地方,請把相關章節再看一遍。

Word List

in style 豪華地
travel rough 極簡樸的旅行

in luxury 豪華地
travel light 帶極少的行李去旅行

Short-Turn 的

談話 2：回應

引言與學習目標

　　各位或許還記得，第一章曾經提到，在談話時適當地回應是很重要的事，因為這樣才能讓對方知道，你對他所說的話感興趣。本章要學的是各位在 Short-turn Talk 中的回應，先讓我們來聽一些 Short-turn Talk 的例子。

Task 3.1

　　　　　　　　　　　　　　　　　　　　　　　　CD 1-14 & 1-15

請聽 Track 3.1 和 3.2，根據對話回答下列問題。

Track 3.1

1. Jane 和 Bob 在哪裡？

2. 他們以前認識嗎？

Track 3.2

1. Sharon 和 Mike 認識對方嗎？

2. Mike 的同事發生了什麼事？

● 答　案

本章稍後會讓各位看到 CD 的文字內容，但目前只希望各位先了解大概的意思。

Track 3.1

Jane 和 Bob 並不認識對方，他們在高爾夫球會館第一次見面。注意他們是如何使談話保持相當程度的中立，他們談的是高爾夫球場和比賽。

Track 3.2

Sharon 和 Mike 認識對方。他們在談論政治、時事，他們對於這個話題的看法很不一樣。各位不應該隨便談論這種話題，除非你跟對方很熟。

本書第三部分會介紹更多安全的談話主題，但目前我們先來看 Short-turn Responses。本章結束時，各位應達成的「學習目標」如下：

❏ 適當回應別人所說的話。
❏ 表現出自己感興趣。
❏ 表達自己的意見。
❏ 表達自己是否同意別人的意見。
❏ 做完聽力練習。
❏ 做完發音練習。
❏ 侃侃而談本身的正面經驗。
❏ 輕描淡寫本身的負面經驗。

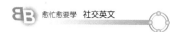
Short-Turn 的回應

我們從一個聽力 Task 開始吧。

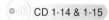
Task 3.2

再聽一次 Track 3.1 與 3.2，寫下你在這兩段對話裡所聽到的 Short-turn Responses。

答　案

這裡暫時不給各位答案，本章稍後會再回來探討這個練習。現在先保留你所記下的答案。

　　我們要來看的回應有四種：假如對方問你對某件事有什麼看法，你要能「表達自己的意見」（express your opinion）；你還要「同意」（agree）與「不同意」（disagree）對方的意見；並對他所說的話「表現出興趣」（express interest），以鼓勵他繼續說下去，這樣談話才得以繼續。請做下面的分類練習，做完後再看答案。

Task 3.3

將下列的用語分門別類，填入其後的表格中。

1. Absolutely!
2. And then?
3. But on the other hand, clause ...
4. But the problem is that + clause ...
5. Come on, you can't be serious!
6. Definitely!
7. Exactly!
8. Go on.
9. Hmm, I'll have to think about that.
10. How awful!
11. How terrible for you.

12. How wonderful.

13. I agree completely.

14. I agree with you.

15. I agree.

16. I don't see it quite like that.

17. I personally think + n. clause ...

18. I reckon + n. clause ...

19. I suspect that + clause ...

20. I think + n. clause ...

21. I'd say that + clause ...

22. I'm convinced that + clause...

23. In my experience, clause ...

24. In my opinion, clause ...

25. Indeed!

26. Many people think that + clause ... but actually ...

27. Mmm.

28. My view is that + clause ...

29. No kidding!

30. No!

31. Oh, my God, you're kidding me!

32. Oh, rubbish!

33. Oh, sure.

34. Oh, that's good.

35. Oh, yes.

36. OK.

37. Possibly, but + n. clause...

38. Really?

39. Right!

40. Right.

41. That's probably true, but + n. clause...

| Word List |

reckon [ˈrɛkən] v. 【口語】想；認爲 　　rubbish [ˈrʌbɪʃ] *interj.* 無聊！廢話！

42. To my mind, clause ...

43. Very true, but + n. clause ...

44. Well, that's exactly what I always say.

45. What bothers me is that + clause ...

46. What bothers me is the n.p. ...

47. Wow!

48. Yes, but don't forget that + clause ...

49. Yes, but don't forget the n.p. ...

50. Yes, but look at it this way: ...

51. Yes, but + n. clause ...

52. Yes, I know exactly what you mean.

53. Yes.

54. Yuck!

Expressing Your Opinion	Expressing Agreement
Expressing Disagreement	Showing Interest

答　案

┃ 請研讀下頁的必備語庫，並核對答案。

┃ W o r d　L i s t ┃

yuck [jʌk] *interj.* 表示厭惡的聲音

社交必備語庫 3.1 CD 1-16

表達意見 Expressing Your Opinion

- In my opinion, clause ...
- I personally think + n. clause ...
- To my mind, clause ...
- I think + n. clause ...
- I reckon + n. clause ...
- My view is that + clause ...
- I'm convinced that + clause ...
- I'd say that + clause ...
- I suspect that + clause ...
- Many people think that + clause ... but actually ...
- In my experience, clause ...

表示同意 Expressing Agreement

- Oh yes.
- Absolutely!
- Definitely!
- Indeed!
- Oh, sure.
- Right!
- I agree.
- I agree completely.
- I agree with you.
- Exactly!
- Well, that's exactly what I always say.
- Yes, I know exactly what you mean.
- Yes.

表示不同意 Expressing Disagreement

- Yes, but + n. clause ...
- But the problem is that + clause ...
- Possibly, but + n. clause ...
- What bothers me is that + clause ...
- What bothers me is the n.p. ...
- Yes, but don't forget that + clause ...
- Yes, but don't forget the n.p. ...
- That's probably true, but + n. clause ...
- But on the other hand, clause ...
- Yes, but look at it this way: ...
- Very true, but + n. clause ...
- Hmm, I'll have to think about that.
- Oh, rubbish!
- Come on, you can't be serious!
- I don't see it quite like that.

表現出興趣 Showing Interest

- Right.
- OK.
- And then?
- Really?
- Mmm.
- Oh, my God, you're kidding me!
- No kidding!
- Oh, that's good.
- How wonderful.
- How terrible for you.
- How awful!
- Wow!
- Yuck!
- Go on.
- No!

★ 📂 **語庫小叮嚀**

◆ 聽 CD 練習發音時，請注意在「表達意見」的 set-phrases 中，重音是在 I 或 my。如：In *MY* opinion ... 或 *I* think that ...，而不是 In my *OPINION* 或 I *THINK* that ...。

◆ I reckon 的意思跟 I think ... 一樣。

◆ 注意「表達同意」的 set-phrases 的強調方式。注意別把 I agree. 唸成 I'm agree.。

◆ 注意，在「表達不同意」的意見時，你不應該說 No.，而應該說 Yes, but ...，或是 Yes, but don't forget that ...。

◆ 有些 set-phrases 的後面可以接 n.p. 或 clause。例如：What bothers me is the possibility of attack. / What bothers me is that they might attack us.。

◆ Oh, rubbish! 和 Come on, you can't be serious! 這兩個 set-phrases 表達了很強烈的不同意。只有對很熟的人才能使用這兩個 set-phrases，而且說的時候盡量保持笑容，或是在聲音中加上一點幽默感。

◆ 在對話題「表示興趣」而有所回應時，Oh my God, you're kidding me! 和 No kidding! 這兩個 set-phrases 是用來表示驚訝；How terrible for you. 和 How awful! 這兩個 set-phrases 是用來表示你覺得反感；Oh that's good. 和 How wonderful. 這兩個 set-phrases 是用來表示你的好感；Yuck! 則是用來表示厭惡或噁心。

下一個 Task 要練習語庫中用語的發音。除了發音之外，試著模仿語調。不同的語調所表達出的情緒是不同的。

Task 3.4　　　　　　　　　　　　　　　　　　　CD 1-16

請聽 Track 3.3，練習每個 set-phrase 的發音與語調。

Task 3.5　　　　　　　　　　　　　　　　CD 1-14 & 1-15

再聽一次 Track 3.1 和 3.2，在語庫 3.1 中標示出你所聽到的 set-phrases，然後將它們和你在 Task 3.2 中所寫下的答案作個比較。

● **答　案**

▌請看下列的 CD 文字內容，並核對你的答案。

Track 3.1

Jane: Good game?

Bob: Not bad. Bit too hot for me today.

Jane: Yes, I know. Kind of hard to concentrate, isn't it?

Bob: Absolutely. Who were you playing with?

Jane: Oh, just on my own. I just joined, so I don't really have any part-
       ners.

Bob: Really? Oh, well in that case we should play together some time.
       What's your handicap?

Jane: 16. Yours?

Bob: No kidding! I'm 16, too. We should definitely play together some
       time. My name's Bob.

Jane: Jane. Nice to meet you.

Bob: Me too. So, do you like the course?

Jane: Yes, it's fine. However, I personally think the fairways between the
       greens are a bit too long, especially for such a hot climate. Don't
       they have carts?

Bob: Well, they used to, but they got rid of them because of environmen-
       tal concerns.

Jane: Oh, that's good. I guess the caddies were pleased.

Bob: Actually, in my opinion, the carts were better because you don't
       have to tip them.

Jane: Yes, but look at it this way: getting rid of the carts probably gives
       more work to local people, which is a good thing, right?

Bob: Possibly, but I still miss them! What bothers me is that the heat
       makes the caddies' life quite hard. One member's caddy fainted
       last week!

Word List

fairway [ˋfɛrˌwe] n. 美好區；平坦球路   green [grin] n. 果嶺

cart [kɑrt] n. 高爾夫球車（= golf cart）   caddy [ˋkædɪ] n. 球僮；桿弟

Jane: How awful, poor guy.

Bob: Right. Luckily it was on the eighteen hole, quite near the club-house, so he didn't have far to carry him.

Jane: Oh, my God, you're kidding me! He carried him back?

Bob: Yup.

● 中 譯

Jane： 比賽還好嗎？

Bob： 還不錯。我覺得今天太熱了一點。

Jane： 是啊，我知道。有點難以定下心來，對吧？

Bob： 沒錯。妳跟誰一起打球？

Jane： 喔，我自己打。因為我才剛加入，所以我連個球伴都沒有。

Bob： 真的嗎？噢，要是這樣的話，我們應該找個時間一起打。妳的差點是多少？

Jane： 16。你呢？

Bob： 不蓋你！我也是 16。我們一定要找個時間一起打球。我是 Bob。

Jane： 我是 Jane，很高興認識你。

Bob： 我也是。對了，妳喜歡這個球場嗎？

Jane： 喜歡，還不錯。不過，我個人覺得果嶺間的球道太長了點，尤其天氣又這麼熱。他們沒有球車嗎？

Bob： 哦，以前有，可是後來基於環保的理由就不用了。

Jane： 喔，那很好。我猜桿弟會很開心。

Bob： 其實我覺得有球車比較好，因為你不必給小費。

Jane： 是啊，可是換個角度來看，不用球車或許可以增加本地人的就業機會，這也是好事一樁，對吧？

Bob： 也許吧，可是我還是很懷念球車！我擔心的是，酷暑會使桿弟的日子變得很難過。上星期就有一位球員的桿弟昏倒了！

Jane： 太慘了，真可憐。

Bob： 的確。所幸那是在十八洞，距離會館很近，所以他不用背很遠。

Jane： 噢，天啊，你是在開玩笑吧！他背桿弟回去？

Bob： 是啊。

Track 3.2

Sharon: Have you seen this?

Mike: What?

Sharon: They killed another hostage.

Mike: Oh, how awful. What a terrible thing to do.

Sharon: I agree completely. I just don't understand what's wrong with them. Don't they have any humanity?

Mike: Well, maybe they've got a point. I mean, I suspect that they think the same about us.

Sharon: Yes, but that doesn't make them right, does it? Just because they think so?

Mike: I guess not. My view is that we should give in to their demands, so that innocent people can stop getting killed.

Sharon: Come on, you can't be serious! We should never give in to terrorist's demands, otherwise where would we be?

Mike: Well, that's probably true, but I don't think we should be dogmatic about it. A colleague of mine was kidnapped once, so perhaps I have a different view of things.

Sharon: Really? What happened?

Mike: Well, it was in the Balkans during the war. He was only held for three days, and then they simply released him. It was a case of mistaken identity, and they just let him go when they found out he was no use to them. It was lucky they didn't kill him.

Sharon: Oh, sure.

| Word List |

hostage [ˈhɑstɪdʒ] *n.* 人質

dogmatic [dɔgˈmætɪk] *adj.* 武斷的；獨斷的

terrorist [ˈtɛrərɪst] *n.* 恐怖份子

Balkans [ˈbɔlkənz] *n.* 巴爾幹半島

中 譯

Sharon：你看過這則報導了嗎？

Mike： 什麼？

Sharon：他們又殺了一個人質。

Mike： 噢，太可怕了。這種事真令人髮指。

Sharon：我完全同意。我真是搞不懂他們有什麼毛病。他們一點人性都沒有嗎？

Mike： 哦，也許他們有他們的道理。我猜他們的想法就跟我們一樣。

Sharon：是，不過這並不表示他們是對的。他們只因為想這麼做，就可以這麼做嗎？

Mike： 當然不是。我的意思是，我們應該接受他們的要求，這樣無辜的人就不會被殺了。

Sharon：拜託，你不是說真的吧？我們絕對不能接受恐怖份子的要求，否則我們要怎麼自處？

Mike： 嗯，這麼說也許沒錯，不過我覺得我們不應該固執己見。我有一位同事被綁架過，所以我對於事情的看法可能不太一樣。

Sharon：真的嗎？那是怎麼回事？

Mike： 哦，那時候巴爾幹半島在打仗。他只被挾持了三天，然後就被釋放了。他們認錯了人，所以等他們發現他沒什麼用處時，就把他給放了。所幸他們沒有殺了他。

Sharon：噢，是啊。

在下一個 Task 中，各位會聽到一些句子。聽完句子後，再用學過的回應 set-phrases 來作適當的回答。

Task 3.6

CD 1-17

請聽 Track 3.4 中的句子，並給予適當的回答。

答 案

要怎麼回答，顯然要看你的意思。我建議各位把這項練習做個幾次，練習用不同的方式來回答。此外，試著用最快的速度回答，這樣發話者和你的反應之間才不會有太大的落差。稍後各位會看到 CD 的內容文字。

Task 3.8

請聽 Track 3.5，聽聽上一個 Task 中的可能回答。

● 答 案

❚ 這些只是可能的回答。先試著聽一遍，再看 CD 的文字內容。

Track 3.5

1. A: Bach's piano music is better than his violin music.

   B: Really?

2. A: Do you think Taiwan will ever join the UN?

   B: I personally think the UN is an outdated institution.

3. A: Do you think they should build the fourth nuclear power station?

   B: My view is that it's unnecessary and unsafe.

4. A: I find hip-hop has a very negative effect on young people.

   B: Well, that's exactly what I always say.

5. A: I just heard that I'm going to be fired when I get back to the office.

   B: How terrible for you!

6. A: I really like this music.

   B: Oh, yes. Me too.

7. A: I reckon Al Pacino's latest movie is his best.

   B: Possibly, but what about *The Godfather*?

8. A: I suspect that the Yankees will win the next series.

   B: Come on. You can't be serious! They don't stand a chance!

9. A: I think Beethoven is much better than Bach.

B: Hm, I'll have to think about that.

10. A: I think Pierce Brosnan is the best actor to play James Bond.

B: I agree completely.

11. A: I think Sharon Stone looks fantastic for her age.

B: Yes, I know exactly what you mean.

12. A: I think the Americans should pull out of Iraq and leave the Iraqis to get on with it.

B: But on the other hand, if the Americans leave, the Iraqis will simply start killing each other.

13. A: I'm sure that I'm getting fatter.

B: Really?

14. A: In my opinion, cars are more of a nuisance than they're worth.

B: I don't see it quite like that.

15. A: In my opinion, Madonna should retire. She's getting too old for all that stuff.

B: I agree with you.

16. A: Most people think that Islam is a bad religion, but I personally think it's no worse than any of the others.

B: That's probably true, but I think religion is important.

17. A: My son just won the California state lottery.

B: No kidding!

| W o r d   L i s t |

nuisance [ˈnusn̩s] *n.* 麻煩的東西；討厭的東西

18. A: My wife's pregnant again.

B: How wonderful!

19. A: To my way of thinking, we should educate our children to look after their parents in old age.

B: Well, that's exactly what I always say.

20. A: What do you think about this book so far?

B: To my mind, it's very useful indeed.

21. A: What do you think of Kylie Minogue's latest album?

B: I personally think it's really boring.

22. A: What do you think of this golf course?

B: I think it's great.

23. A: What's your opinion on the situation in Iraq?

B: Many people think that they can't govern themselves, but actually I think they could, if they were given the chance.

24. A: When I was in Argentina I ate bulls' testicles.

B: Yuck!

 中 譯

1. A：巴哈的鋼琴樂比他的小提琴樂好。

B：真的嗎？

2. A：你覺得台灣有沒有可能加入聯合國？

B：我個人覺得聯合國是個過時的機構。

| W o r d   L i s t |

testicle [ˋtɛstɪkḷ] *n.* 睪丸

3. A：你覺得他們該不該建核四？
   B：我認爲核四既沒必要又不安全。

4. A：我發現嘻哈音樂對年輕人有很不好的影響。
   B：嗯，那正是我一向的主張。

5. A：我聽到消息，我回辦公室的時候就會被解雇了。
   B：你眞可憐！

6. A：我很喜歡這首音樂。
   B：噢，是啊，我也喜歡。

7. A：我覺得艾爾‧帕西諾的新電影是他最好的一部。
   B：或許吧，可是《教父》呢？

8. A：我猜洋基隊會贏得下一個系列賽。
   B：拜託，你不是說眞的吧？他們根本沒機會。

9. A：我覺得貝多芬比巴哈優秀得多。
   B：嗯，這我得想想看才行。

10. A：我覺得皮爾斯‧布洛斯南是最適合演詹姆斯‧龐德的演員。
    B：我完全同意。

11. A：我覺得莎朗‧史東就這個年紀而言還是很漂亮。
    B：是啊，我完全了解你的意思。

12. A：我覺得美國人應該撤出伊拉克，讓伊拉克人自己來接手。
    B：可是另一方面，假如美國人離開，伊拉克人就會開始自相殘殺。

13. A：我確定我變胖了。
    B：眞的嗎？

14. A：我認為車子的麻煩大於它的價值。

B：我的看法不太一樣。

15. A：我認為瑪丹娜應該退休。她太老了，不適合搞這套東西。

B：我有同感。

16. A：大部分的人都覺得回教是不好的宗教，可是我個人覺得它並不比其他任何一種宗教差。

B：這麼說或許沒錯，可是我覺得宗教很重要。

17. A：我兒子剛中了加州的樂透。

B：沒蓋我？

18. A：我太太又懷孕了。

B：太好了！

19. A：按照我的想法，我們應該教導子女照顧年邁的父母。

B：嗯，那正是我一向的主張。

20. A：到目前為止，你覺得這本書怎麼樣？

B：我覺得它真的很有用。

21. A：你覺得凱莉‧米洛的新專輯怎麼樣？

B：我個人覺得它很乏味。

22. A：你覺得這座球場怎麼樣？

B：我覺得很不錯。

23. A：你對於伊拉克的情況有什麼看法？

B：有很多人覺得他們沒辦法自治，但我覺得其實只要給他們機會，他們就做得到。

24. A：我在阿根廷時，吃過牛的睪丸。

B：嗯！

語感甦活區

　　有一個辦法可以使談話更生動──那就是在回答時使用形容詞。誇大或輕描淡寫本身的經驗。例如，你可以說： That movie was funny.，但如果你希望自己的談話更生動的話，你可以使用 funny 的同義字，並誇大地說： That movie was absolutely hilarious! 或 That movie was totally wild.。

　　要不然你也可以用同義字來輕描淡寫本身的經驗。所以你可以將 It was a boring movie. 輕描淡寫成 It wasn't the most hilarious movie I've ever seen.。

　　在「語感甦活區」中，我們要學習使用形容詞來為談話增色！記得要先做練習、再看答案。

Task 3.9

請將下列的形容詞分門別類，填入其後的表格。請見範例。

1. amazing	**12.** dull
2. appealing	**13.** eccentric
3. attractive	**14.** entertaining
4. awful	**15.** exciting
5. beautiful	**16.** fabulous
6. bizarre	**17.** fascinating
7. brilliant	**18.** ghastly
8. comical	**19.** great
9. crazy	**20.** hilarious
10. disgusting	**21.** humorous
11. dreary	**22.** lousy

| Word List |

bizarre [bɪˋzɑr] *adj.* 奇怪的；古怪的
eccentric [ɪkˋsɛntrɪk] *adj.* 古怪的；與眾不同的
hilarious [həˋlɛrɪəs] *adj.* 非常快樂的；歡鬧的

comical [ˋkɑmɪkl] *adj.* 滑稽的；可笑的
ghastly [ˋgæstlɪ] *adj.* 可怕的；糟透的

23. luxurious
24. marvelous
25. nasty
26. noteworthy
27. odd
28. peculiar
29. ridiculous
30. silly

31. stupid
32. tedious
33. terrible
34. weird
35. wearisome
36. wild
37. witty
38. wonderful

Nice	Funny	Unpleasant	Strange	Boring	Interesting
fabulous				*tedious*	

答　案

請研讀下列的必備語庫，並核對答案。

社交必備語庫 3.2 CD 1-19

Nice	Funny	Unpleasant	Strange	Boring	Interesting
• great	• entertaining	• nasty	• weird	• stupid	• fascinating
• fabulous	• hilarious	• terrible	• odd	• dull	• exciting
• marvelous	• ridiculous	• disgusting	• bizarre	• tedious	• appealing
• wonderful	• silly	• lousy	• crazy	• dreary	• noteworthy
• amazing	• wild	• awful	• peculiar	• wearisome	
• attractive	• humorous	• ghastly	• eccentric		
• brilliant	• comical				
• luxurious	• witty				
• beautiful					

Word List

nasty [ˋnæstɪ] *adj.* 令人厭惡的；骯髒的
tedious [ˋtidɪəs] *adj.* 單調乏味的

noteworthy [ˋnotˏwɝðɪ] *adj.* 值得注意的
wearisome [ˋwɪrɪsəm] *adj.* 使人疲倦的；無聊的

★ 📁 語庫小叮嚀
◆ attractive 通常是用來形容人。
◆ ridiculous 通常是負面的意思。
◆ eccentric 通常是用來形容人。

Task 3.10   ◉))) CD-1-19

請聽 Track 3.6，練習語庫中形容詞的發音。

接著來看如何使用這些形容詞來誇大和輕描淡寫。

下列為一些**誇大**的說法與規則：

• The hotel was absolutely marvelous!
• The food was totally delicious!
• It's an incredibly dull book.

規則：把 absolutely 、 totally 或 incredibly 擺在形容詞的前面。

下列為一些**輕描淡寫**的說法與規則：

• It wasn't exactly the most fabulous hotel I've ever stayed in.
  = It was a terrible hotel.
• It wasn't exactly the most interesting book I've ever read.
  = It was a boring book.
• She isn't exactly the most beautiful woman I've ever met.
  = She's not attractive.

規則：使用這個 chunk ：... isn't exactly the most ... I've ever ... 來輕描淡寫負面的
　　　　句子時，這個 chunk 就要使用正面的形容詞。這種輕描淡寫的說法不適用
　　　　於描述正面的經驗。

現在各位就來做個聽力練習，聆聽 CD 並作回應，練習完再看 CD 的文字內容。

Task 3.11

CD 1-20

請聽 Track 3.7 ，針對聽到的句子作出誇大的回應。請見下列範例。

A: He's quite an interesting man.

B: *Oh, yes, he's absolutely fascinating. We talked for hours.*

● 答　案

▌ 在公佈這部分的答案前，先來接著做下一個輕描淡寫的練習。

Task 3.12

CD 1-21

請聽 Track 3.8 ，針對聽到的句子作出輕描淡寫的回應。請見下列範例。

A: What does he look like?

B: *Well, he's not exactly the most attractive man I've ever met.*

● 答　案

▌ 請看下列 Track 3.7 和 3.8 的文字，並聽聽 Track 3.9 中提供的可能答案，拿它來和你
的答案作個比較。你可以多練習幾次，看看自己能否在發話者說完後迅速作出回應。

Track 3.9

CD 1-22

Overstatement

1. A: He's quite an interesting man.

B: *Oh, yes, he's absolutely fascinating. We talked for hours.*

2. A: Someone told me that it's a really boring book.

B: *It's totally tedious.*

3. A: Is your hotel OK?

B: *It's absolutely wonderful!*

4. A: It was such a funny movie!

B: *It was absolutely hilarious, wasn't it?*

5. A: It was a very bad trip.

B: *Sounds totally ghastly!*

6. A: She is a rather strange person, in my view.

   B: *Yes, she's totally weird.*

7. A: This ice cream is really nice.

   B: *Mmm, it's incredibly delicious.*

8. A: His presentation was quite funny, wasn't it?

   B: *Oh, man! It was totally wild!*

9. A: The climate is rather unpleasant, from what I hear.

   B: *It's absolutely lousy.*

10. A: It was a strange idea, don't you think?

    B: *Totally bizarre!*

11. A: God, that was a boring speech!

    B: *Yes, incredibly dull.*

12. A: The article in *the Economist* you showed me is rather interesting.

    B: *I thought it was incredibly exciting to read about new developments in the field.*

Understatement

1. A: What does he look like?

   B: *Well, he's not exactly the most attractive man I've ever met.*

2. A: Is it a good book?

   B: *Well, it's not exactly the most appealing book I've ever read.*

3. A: Is your hotel OK?

   B: *Well, it's not exactly the most luxurious hotel I've ever stayed in.*

4. A: Did you enjoy the film?

   B: *No, it wasn't exactly the most entertaining movie I've ever seen.*

5. A: I never want to travel with Richard again.

   B: *Sounds like it wasn't exactly the most wonderful trip you've ever been on.*

6. A: Why is she so insecure?

   B: *Mmm, she's not exactly the most attractive woman I've ever seen.*

7. A: Do you like the ice cream?

   B: *Well, it's not exactly the most delicious ice cream I've ever had.*

8. A: Why was his presentation such a failure?

   B: *Well, it wasn't exactly the most humorous presentation I've ever seen.*

9. A: The climate is rather unpleasant, from what I hear.

   B: *Yes, it's not exactly the most wonderful climate I've ever experienced.*

10. A: Did you enjoy Terence's speech?

    B: *Well, it wasn't exactly the most exciting speech he's ever given.*

 中 譯

誇大

1. A：他是個很有趣的人。

   B：噢，是啊，他真的太棒了。我們談了好幾個小時。

2. A：有人告訴我說，這本書很無聊。

   B：它簡直悶到極點。

3. A：你的旅館還好嗎？

   B：好得不得了！

4. A：這部電影真好笑！

   B：它簡直是超爆笑，對吧？

5. A：這次的旅行真糟糕。

   B：聽起來遜斃了！

6. A：在我看來，她是個挺奇怪的人。

   B：是啊，她根本是個怪胎。

7. A：這種冰淇淋真好吃。

   B：呣，它真是美味得不得了！

8. A：他的簡報真好笑，對吧？

   B：哦，老兄！是很勁爆！

9. A：我聽說天氣很不好。

   B：它的確是糟透了。

10. A：這種想法很奇怪，你不覺得嗎？

B：眞是怪到不行！

11. A：天哪，那場演講眞無聊！

B：是啊，乏味到了極點。

12. A：你給我看的那篇《經濟學人》的文章很有趣。

B：我覺得看到這個領域的新發展實在太令人興奮了。

輕描淡寫

1. A：他看起來怎麼樣？

B：哦，他絕對不是我所認識最有魅力的男人。

2. A：這本書好看嗎？

B：哦，它絕對不是我所看過最好看的書。

3. A：你的旅館還好嗎？

B：哦，它絕對不是我所住過最豪華的旅館。

4. A：你喜歡這部片子嗎？

B：不喜歡，它絕對不是我所看過最有娛樂性的電影。

5. A：我再也不想跟理察一起去旅行。

B：聽起來它絕對不是你所去過最棒的旅行。

6. A：她爲什麼這麼侷促不安？

B：唔，她絕對不是我所認識最有魅力的女人。

7. A：你喜歡這種冰淇淋嗎？

B：哦，它絕對不是我所吃過最好吃的冰淇淋。

8. A：他的簡報爲什麼這麼失敗？

B：哦，這絕對不是我所看過最幽默的簡報。

9. A：我聽說天氣很不好。

B：是啊，這絕對不是我所碰過最理想的天氣。

10. A：你喜歡泰倫斯的演講嗎？

B：哦，這絕對不是他所發表過最棒的演講。

好了，在繼續看下一章的 Long-turn Talk 前，請各位回到本章的「學習目標」，看看各位達成了多少，若還有不清楚的地方，不妨把本章的相關章節再看一遍。

假如你有機會和老外聊天，別忘了運用本章所教的用語。用你的自信和能力讓朋友刮目相看，你會驚訝地發現，原來它是這麼簡單！

Unit 4

Long-Turn

的談話

引言與學習目標

在前兩章中，我們學過 Short-turn Talk 。這章的重點則是 Long-turn Talk 。有時候在和老外洽談時，你可能有機會講笑話、說故事或是談談你所經歷的事，此時你所需要的用語和 Short-turn Talk 有點不一樣。或者，你可能有機會聽對方講笑話或說故事，此時你就得專心聆聽，以便讓對方知道，你對他所說的話感興趣。

在往下看以前，請先聽 CD ，並做下面的 Task 來暖身。

Task 4.1　　　　　　　　　　　　　　　　　　　　CD 1-23

請聽 Track 4.1 中的談話，回答下列問題。

1. John 發生了什麼事？
2. 哪個說話者說的話比較多？
3. 說話者 A 是如何開啟 long-turn 的話頭？
4. 說話者 B 是如何表示他對於 A 所說的話感興趣？
5. 對於說話者 A 所說的用語，你有沒有注意到什麼特別之處？

答案

1. 假如你想知道 John 發生了什麼事，可以多聽幾次 CD 的內容，本章稍後會提供這部分的文字內容！

2. 說話者 A 說的話比較多：這是他的 long-turn ，說話者 B 則在聆聽。

3. 說話者 A 用了下列的句子來開啟話頭： Do you remember John from head office?，本章稍後會教各位如何開啟類似的 long-turn 話頭。

4. 說話者 B 不時會發表意見，並說出下列的句子： What do you mean? 或 That's terrible.，在本章稍後，各位就會學到如何做到這點。

5. 各位可能已經注意到，這些用語的動詞時態差不多都一樣；而說話者 A 是用 Well, ... 這種 set-phrases 來鋪陳故事。各位在本章會學到更多類似的鋪陳手法。

如果你沒有答對，也不必擔心。這只是暖身而已。本章結束前，各位再回頭做一次這個 Task ，屆時你就會更有概念了。

本章結束時，各位應達成的「學習目標」如下：

❑ 認識不同類型的 long turns 。
❑ 學會如何開啓 long turns 的話頭。
❑ 鋪陳與應付 long turns 被打斷的情況。
❑ 確實了解 long turns 的語言特徵。
❑ 學會如何適當地回應別人的 long turns 。
❑ 完成聽力與發音練習。
❑ 增加字彙。

Long-Turn 的種類

Long-turn Talk 基本上有四種：

1. 笑話或幽默的故事
2. 個人的經驗或軼事
3. 發生在別人身上的故事
4. 轉述電影或書本中的故事

我們來看看，各位聽到 long turn 時能不能分辨出來。記得先不看文字內容，多聽幾次。

Task 4.2　　　　　　　　　　CD 1-23 ～ 1-27

請聽 Track 4.1 到 4.5，判斷它們是哪種 long turn。請見範例。

1. Track 4.1 ： *Type 3*
2. Track 4.2 ： _____
3. Track 4.3 ： _____
4. Track 4.4 ： _____
5. Track 4.5 ： _____

答　案

2. Type 2
3. Type 1
4. Type 4
5. Type 3

Track 4.1

A: Do you remember John from head office?
B: Yes.

A: Have you heard what happened to him?

B: No, what?

A: He had his car stolen. Actually he was kidnapped while he was in the car.

B: What do you mean?

A: Well, apparently, he was just getting into his car — he'd parked it in one of those underground multi-story things — he was just getting in and suddenly three guys with guns opened the back doors of the car and got in.

B: Crikey. Where did this happen?

A: In Taichung, I think.

B: Oh, right, I hear they have a lot of this kind of problem down there.

A: Really? Well anyway, they pointed their guns at him and said, you know, keep calm and drive out ... we don't want to hurt you ... we just want your car.

B: So what happened?

A: Well, he drove out, and when he got to the booth to pay the attendant, he pretended to have an epileptic fit, you know, to scare the thieves away. The attendant was no help at all: even though the guys were holding guns in plain view, he did nothing.

B: That's terrible.

A: Yes, makes you think, doesn't it.

B: So what happened next?

A: Well, he kept on pretending to have a fit, so they freaked out and just ran away.

B: Well, he sure was lucky.

A: I'll say.

Word List

crikey 「kraɪkɪ] *interj.* 【表示驚訝】哎呀！唷！　　booth 「buθ] *n.* 攤子；（賣票、收費、電話）亭
epileptic 「ˌɛpə`lɛptɪk] *adj.* 癲癇的

中 譯

A：你記得總公司的 John 嗎？

B：記得。

A：你有沒有聽說他出了什麼事？

B：沒有。怎麼了？

A：他的車被偷了。他等於是被綁架了，因為他當時在車裡。

B：你的意思是？

A：哦，他顯然是才剛上車。他把車停在那些多層式地下停車場的其中一層，他一上車，就有三個持槍的歹徒突然打開後車門跳進去。

B：哎喲。這件事在哪裡發生的？

A：我想是在台中。

B：喔，對，我聽說當地有很多這類的問題。

A：真的嗎？反正他們就拿槍指著他說，靜靜把車開出去就對了。我們不想傷害你，我們只是要你的車而已。

B：所以結果呢？

A：哦，他把車開出去，等開到票亭要繳錢給收費員時，便假裝羊癲瘋發作，你知道，以便把歹徒嚇跑。但收費員根本置之不理，雖然眼睜睜看著那些人拿著槍，他卻袖手旁觀。

B：太可怕了。

A：是啊，你連想都不敢想。

B：所以接下來呢？

A：哦，他一直假裝發病，於是他們便嚇得逃走了。

B：喔，他真是走運。

A：我也這麼覺得。

Track 4.2

A: I had a terrible journey back from Bangkok last week.

B: Really? Why? What happened?

A: Well, first of all, the taxi that was taking me from the client's office to the airport broke down on the freeway.

B: Oh, no.

A: Yes, and the driver didn't speak any English or Chinese and he didn't have a phone on him — can you believe it? — and his radio didn't work. So there was no way he could get in touch with the office to get them to send another taxi.

B: So what did you do?

A: Well, I actually thumbed a lift.

B: You what?

A: Yes, I stood on the side of the freeway and stuck my thumb out, and a passing truck stopped and took me to the airport.

B: Wow, good for you.

A: Yes, except he drove really slowly, and I missed my flight.

B: Oh, no!

A: Yes, so I had to wait three hours for the next one. I didn't get home till four in the morning, and when I got home I realized I'd left my house keys in my hotel in Bangkok.

B: You really have bad luck, don't you?

A: Seems like it.

中　譯

A：我上週從曼谷回來的時候，過程很驚險。

B：真的嗎？為什麼？發生什麼事了？

A：哦，首先，計程車在載我從客戶的辦公室到機場的高速公路上拋錨了。

B：噢，不會吧。

A：是啊，而且司機中英文都不會說，身上又沒電話，你能相信嗎？而且他的無線電又故障了。所以他沒辦法跟總部聯絡，以便派另一輛計程車過來。

B：那你怎麼辦？

A：哦，我只好搭便車了。

B：真的嗎？

A：是啊，我站在路邊伸出拇指，結果有一輛經過的卡車停下來載我去機場。

B：哇，真不錯。

A：是啊，只不過他開得很慢，讓我錯過了班機。

B：噢，不會吧！

A：是啊，所以我必須等三個小時才有下一班飛機。我一直到清晨四點才到家，而且到家時才發現，我把家裡的鑰匙留在曼谷的飯店裡了。

B：你真的很衰耶，對吧？

A：看起來是如此。

註：注意在對話中說話者如何描述自己的壞運氣。你在描述自己的悲慘遭遇時，並不希望把自己形容得太過正面，否則聽者可能會覺得你在炫耀。

Track 4.3

A: Do you want to hear a funny joke?

B: OK. Are you sure it's funny, though?

A: Well, you'll see.

B: OK.

A: OK, an Englishman, a Scotsman, and an Irishman were going on a trip across the desert, and they could only take one thing with them.

B: I see.

A: So they met up at the start of the journey and showed each other their equipment.

B: Oh, that's funny!

A: Hang on, I haven't finished yet.

B: Oh, sorry.

A: Well, as I was saying, they showed each other what they had decided to bring. The Englishman had brought some water. "If we get thirsty, we'll have something to drink," he said. The Scotsman brought a map. "If we get lost, we'll be able to find our way." The Irishman had brought a car door.

B: A car door? You mean just one car door?

A: Yep. A car door. "Why the door?" the others asked him. "Well," he said, "If it gets hot, we can open the window." Do you get it?

B: Well ...

中 譯

A：你想聽個好笑的笑話嗎？

B：好啊，可是你確定它好笑嗎？

A：你不妨聽聽看。

B：好。

A：好，有一個英格蘭人、一個蘇格蘭人和一個愛爾蘭人要橫越沙漠，而且每個人只能帶一樣東西。

B：我懂。

A：於是他們在行程的起點見面時，把自己的傢伙拿給其他人看。

B：喔，真好玩！

A：等等，我還沒說完。

B：喔，抱歉。

A：嗯，我說到他們把自己決定要帶的東西拿給其他人看。英格蘭人帶了一些水，他說：「假如我們口渴了，我們就有東西可以喝。」蘇格蘭人帶了一張地圖。「假如我們迷路了，我們就可以靠它來找路。」愛爾蘭人則帶了一扇車門。

B：車門？你是說一扇車門？

A：沒錯，就是車門。另外兩個人問他說：「為什麼要帶車門？」他說：「哦，假如天氣熱的話，我們就可以把車窗打開。」你聽懂了嗎？

B：呃……

註：注意這個笑話是如何鋪陳。動詞全都是過去式或過去完成式。而最後 A 說的：Do you get it?，Get a joke 是「聽懂笑話」的意思，但 B 根本不覺得這個笑話有趣。在說笑話時，你必須注意，有時候文化差異可能會使聽的人無法 get the joke。

Track 4.4

A: Have you seen the movie *Catwoman*?

B: No, not yet. Is it good?

A: Yes, it's quite amusing, actually. Good plot, and Sharon Stone's in it.

B: Oh, she's good. She must be getting on a bit now.

A: Yeah, but she looks amazing.

B: So what's the movie about?

A: Well, it's about this woman who got murdered because she discovered some company secrets about the cosmetics company she worked for. But then she got reincarnated as a cat.

B: Huh?

A: I know. Stay with me. She then decided to get her revenge by revealing the company secret and killing the boss. First, though, she had to discover her true cat nature. At the end she had a big fight with Sharon Stone, who was the real danger in the company. She had actually murdered the boss, who was her husband, and then tried to frame Catwoman for the murder, so everyone thought Catwoman was evil.

B: I see. Catwoman married the boss?

A: No. Sharon Stone was married to the boss, who treated her badly, so she killed him. So where was I? OK, so then, at the same time she fell in love with a cop, who was investigating the murder of the boss. Finally, she ditched the cop to follow her feline nature.

B: Wait a minute, I'm lost. The cop killed the boss?

A: No, Sharon Stone did.

B: And Sharon Stone is Catwoman?

A: Haven't you been listening to a word I've been saying?

中 譯

A：你看過《貓女》這部電影嗎？

B：沒有，還沒看。好看嗎？

A：好看，實際上還蠻有趣的。情節不錯，而且又有莎朗・史東。

B：喔，她不錯。她現在一定變得有點老了。

A：是啊，可是她看起來還是很漂亮。

B：所以這部電影在講什麼？

Word List

reincarnate [ˌriɪnˋkɑrnet] v. 使⋯⋯化身為⋯⋯

frame [frem] v. 陷害；誣陷

ditch [dɪtʃ] v.【俚】甩開

feline [ˋfilaɪn] adj. 像貓一樣的

118

A：哦，它是在講一個女的因為在自己所服務的化妝品公司裡發現了一些秘密而被人謀殺。但後來她化身成了一隻貓。

B：嘎？

A：我知道，聽我說。後來她決定報仇，要公佈公司的秘密並殺了老闆。不過，她必須先找出她真正的貓本性。到最後，她跟莎朗·史東大戰了一場，莎朗·史東才是公司背後真正的危險人物。老闆其實是她殺的，而且老闆還是她老公。但她試圖陷害貓女，說人是她殺的，所以每個人都覺得貓女很壞。

B：我懂了。嫁給老闆的是貓女嗎？

A：不是，嫁給老闆的是莎朗·史東。他對她很壞，所以她才殺了他。我說到哪兒了？對了，接著她同時愛上了調查老闆謀殺案的警察。最後，為了順從她的貓本性，她拋棄了那位警察。

B：等一下，我搞亂了。老闆是那個警察殺的嗎？

A：不是，是莎朗·史東殺的。

B：那莎朗·史東是貓女嗎？

A：你是不是沒有在聽我說話？

註：注意 A 是如何描述電影的情節。在第七章中，各位會更了解要怎麼談論電影。

Track 4.5

A: Did you hear what happened to Mike in Accounts?

B: No. What?

A: He got arrested on Friday night and spent the night in jail.

B: No. Really, what happened?

A: Well, it was all a big mistake, actually. He got home on Friday night really late, and apparently he'd been out drinking with some clients, so he was really drunk.

B: Was he out with the guys from the bank?

A: Yes, I think so.

B: Oh, yeah, they always get really drunk.

A: Well, anyway, he'd somehow lost his wallet and his house keys, so he couldn't get in. He lives alone, you know.

B: Oh, really. I thought he lived with his wife.

A: No, she left him last year.

B: Oh, really? Do you know why?

A: Hang on, let me finish telling you what happened. Where was I?

B: He lost his wallet and keys.

A: Oh yes, well, he tried to climb in through the bathroom window, but apparently he slipped and broke the glass with his foot. The neighbors heard him and thought a robbery was in progress, so they called the police.

B: Oh, no.

A: Yes. So when the cops arrived, they didn't believe his story: you know, he lost his wallet so he had no ID; the neighbors were new and didn't know him, so he couldn't get the police to believe his story. So they arrested him and put him in a cell until the morning.

B: So then what happened?

A: Well, when he sobered up, he called someone from work to come and bail him out.

B: Well, that's a bit of a tricky situation.

A: Yes, I know.

中　譯

A ：你有聽說財務部的 Mike 出事了嗎？

B ：不知道。他怎麼了？

A ：他星期五晚上被捕，而且被關了一個晚上。

B ：不會吧。到底是怎麼回事？

A ：哦，其實是個大誤會。他星期五晚上很晚才回家，他顯然是和幾個客戶出去喝了幾杯，而且喝得爛醉。

B ：他是跟銀行的那些人出去嗎？

| Word List |

sober [ˋsobɚ] v. 酒醒；清醒   bail [bel] v. 保釋

A：我想是吧。

B：喔，是啊，他們老是喝得爛醉。

A：哦，反正他就是弄丟了錢包跟家裡的鑰匙，所以沒辦法進門。你也知道，他是一個人住。

B：真的喔。我以為他跟老婆住在一起。

A：並沒有，她去年離開他了。

B：喔，真的嗎？你知道是為什麼嗎？

A：等等，先讓我把事情的經過說完。我說到哪兒了？

B：他弄丟了錢包跟鑰匙。

A：喔，對。他想要從浴室的窗戶爬進去，可是顯然滑了一跤，腳踢破了玻璃。鄰居聽到了聲音，以為有人闖空門，於是叫警察來。

B：噢，不會吧。

A：是啊，結果警察來了以後，並不相信他的說法。你也知道，他弄丟了錢包，所以身上沒有身分證。鄰居是新來的，也不認識他，所以他沒辦法讓警察相信他的說法。結果警察就逮捕了他，並把他關在拘留所裡，直到隔天早上。

B：結果後來又怎麼了？

A：哦，等他酒醒以後，他打電話請公司的人來保他出去。

B：哦，這種情況不太好處理。

A：是啊，我知道。

註：這個對話中所談到的是第三者所遇到的負面事件。在第六章中，各位會學到更多閒聊的用語。

現在各位對 long turn 的種類已經比較了解，那我們就更詳細地探討這種用語。

Long-Turn 的發話

第一章中介紹過,「發話」是指用來開啓話題的 set-phrases 和單字。在 Long-turn Talk 中,我們要看的「發話」有三種:「開啓」long turn 的 set-phrases、「鋪陳」這個 turn 的 set-phrases,以及被打斷時可以用來「重回」談話的 set-phrases。

現在來做下面的 Task。

Task 4.3　　　　　　　　　　　　　　　　　　　　　　　CD 1-26

請聽 Track 4.4,並把你所聽到的「開啓」、「鋪陳」或「重回」的 set-phrases 寫下來。

答 案

| 別急著找答案,先接著做下一個 Task。稍後再回來討論這個練習。

Task 4.4

將下列這些用語分門別類,填入下頁的表格。

1. A funny thing happened to me ...
2. After that, ...
3. At the end, ...
4. Do you remember ...?
5. Do you want to hear a joke?
6. Finally, ...
7. First of all, ...
8. Have you heard the one about ...?
9. Have you heard what happened to ...?
10. I had a funny experience.
11. I had a great ...
12. I had a terrible ...
13. Well, anyway, ...
14. Have you seen ...?

15. Have you read ...?

16. I heard this really funny joke the other day.

17. I've got a good joke.

18. It's about ...

19. Next, ...

20. So as I was saying, ...

21. So then, ...

22. So, ...

23. Then, ...

24. Well, ...

25. Well, apparently, ...

26. What's more ...

27. Where was I? Oh yes, ...

28. Yes, ...

Starting

Structuring

Returning

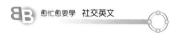
答　案

現在請研讀下列的語庫，並核對答案。

社交必備語庫 4.1

 CD 1-28

開啓 Starting
• A funny thing happened to me ...
• Do you remember ...?
• Do you want to hear a joke?
• Have you heard the one about ...?
• Have you heard what happened to ...?
• I had a funny experience ...
• I had a great ...
• I had a terrible ...
• I heard this really funny joke the other day.
• I've got a good joke.
• It's about this ...
• Have you seen ...?
• Have you read ...?
鋪陳 Structuring
• Well, apparently, ...
• First of all, ...
• Then, ...
• Next, ...
• After that ...
• Finally, ...
• At the end, ...
• So then, ...
• What's more ...

重回 Returning

- So, ...
- Well, ...
- So as I was saying, ...
- Where was I? Oh yes, ...
- Yes, ...
- Well, anyway, ...

★ 📂 語庫小叮嚀

◆ Have you heard the one about ...? 中的 The one about 指的是 the joke about。這個 set-phrase 只限定用來介紹笑話。

◆ It's about this ... 是用於開始談論電影或書本的情節。

　　還記得 Task 4.3 的練習嗎？下列的文字中，已將對話裏所運用的「開啓」、「鋪陳」或「重回」的 set-phrases 以粗體標示，各位答對了多少呢？

答　案

A: **Have you seen** *Catwoman*?

B: No, not yet. Is it good?

A: Yes, it's quite amusing actually. Good plot, and Sharon Stone's in it.

B: Oh, she's good. She must be getting on a bit now.

A: Yeah, but she looks amazing.

B: So what's the movie about?

A: Well, **it's about this** woman who got murdered because she discovered some company secrets about the cosmetics company she worked for. But then she got reincarnated as a cat.

B: Huh?

A: I know. Stay with me. She then decided to get her revenge by revealing the company secret and killing the boss. **First**, though, she had to discover her true cat nature. **At the end** she had a big fight with Sharon Stone, who was the real danger in the company. She had actually murdered the boss, who

was her husband, and then tried to frame Catwoman for the murder, so everyone thought Catwoman is evil.

B: I see. Catwoman married the boss?

A: No. Sharon Stone was married to the boss, who treated her badly, so she killed him. **So where was I? OK, so then,** at the same time she fell in love with a cop, who was investigating the murder of the boss. **Finally,** she ditched the cop to follow her feline nature.

B: Wait a minute, I'm lost. The cop killed the boss?

A: No, Sharon Stone did.

B: And Sharon Stone is Catwoman?

A: Haven't you been listening to a word I've been saying?

現在我們來做發音練習。

Task 4.5　　　　　　　　　　　　　　　　　　CD 1-28

請聽 Track 4.6 ，練習語庫 4.1 的發音。

● 答　案

練習時可以注意連音的部分，可以學會的話是最好。各位要一直練習，直到真的學會了這些 set-phrases 並且能運用自如。

練習完了發音，開始運用自身的經驗，練習 long-turn 的談話吧。

Task 4.6

花點時間準備你的 long turns ，想想自己可以分享的四種 long turns 。各位可以利用下面的表格作筆記。

第一種：我知道一個不錯的笑話

第二種：我有一個好笑的經驗

第三種：我認識的某個人有一個好笑的經驗

第四種：我最近看的一部電影的情節

Task 4.7

接著就利用你所作的筆記，並運用你所學到的用語，開始來練習說故事吧。各位可能要想像自己被打斷，這樣才能運用到「重回」的 set-phrases 。

答　案

這樣的練習方式你可能會覺得有點不自在，但別忘了第二章中談到的。自行練習的作用在於，等到實際上場交際時，你就會對自己更有自信。當然各位也可以找朋友一起練習。

　　在進入下一節之前，各位可以回頭再做一次 Task 4.3 ，看看這次你的答案是否更完整了呢。

語感甦活區

　　前面曾經提到，long turns 所用的時態通常是簡單過去式。有時候也會使用過去完成式，但由於過去完成式常常用錯，所以我會建議各位乾脆不要理它、也不要用它。各位只要專心把簡單過去式用對就好。

Task 4.8 CD 1-24

請回頭聽 Track 4.2 ，把你所聽到的動詞全部列出來。你聽到了幾個？它們是什麼時態？

答　案

如果不算助動詞的話，各位應該可以聽到 23 個動詞左右。如果你的答案比 23 個少很多，那就多聽幾次，直到可以找出更多的動詞為止。其中大部分的動詞都是簡單過去式。

Task 4.9

從下表中挑出正確的動詞，並以正確的時態填入下列空格。有些動詞可能不只用到一次。

A: I _____ a terrible journey back from Bangkok last week.

B: Really? Why, what _____?

A: Well, first of all the taxi that _____ me from the client's office to the airport on the freeway.

B: Oh, no.

A: Yes, and the driver _____ any English or Chinese and he _____ a phone on him — can you believe it? — and his radio _____, so there _____ no way he _____ get in touch with the office to get them to send another taxi.

B: So what _____ you _____?

A: Well, I actually _____ a lift.

B: You what?

A: Yes, I _____ on the side of the freeway and _____ my thumb out, and a

passing truck _____ and _____ me to the airport.

B: Wow, good for you.

A: Yes, except he _____ really slowly, and I _____ my flight.

B: Oh, no!

A: Yes, so I _____ wait three hours for the next one. I _____

home till four in the morning, and when I _____ home I _____

I'd left my house keys in my hotel in Bangkok.

B: You really have bad luck, don't you?

A: Seems like it.

• be	• have to
• break down	• miss
• can	• realize
• speak	• stand
• do	• stick
• drive	• stop
• get	• take
• happen	• thumb
• have	• work

答　案

CD 1-24

請再聽一次 Track 4.2 並以下列的文字核對答案。

A: I **had** a terrible journey back from Bangkok last week.

B: Really? Why, what **happened**?

A: Well, first of all the taxi that **was taking** me from the client's office to the air-

port **broke down** on the freeway.

B: Oh, no.

A: Yes, and the driver **didn't speak** any English or Chinese and he **didn't have**

a phone on him — can you believe it? — and his radio **didn't work**, so there

was no way he **could** get in touch with the office to get them to send another taxi.

B: So what **did** you **do**?

A: Well, I actually **thumbed** a lift.

B: You what?

A: Yes, I **stood** on the side of the freeway and **stuck** my thumb out, and a passing truck **stopped** and **took** me to the airport.

B: Wow, good for you.

A: Yes, except he **drove** really slowly, and I **missed** my flight.

B: Oh, no!

A: Yes, so I **had to** wait three hours for the next one. I **didn't get** home till four in the morning, and when I **got** home I **realized** I'd left my house keys in my hotel in Bangkok.

B: You really have bad luck, don't you?

A: Seems like it.

別忘了，有些動詞要變成否定，只要在原形動詞前面加上 didn't 即可。還可能碰到另一個問題，那就是要記住一些不規則動詞的過去式。

Task 4.10

現在回到你在 Task 4.6 中所準備的 long turns，檢查你在 long turns 中所用的動詞是否為現在簡單式。

答案

有空的時候，不妨拿字典來查查不規則動詞的過去式。花點時間再把 long turns 練習一遍，這次只看動詞就好。接著再練習一次，並把焦點從動詞的時態改為先前所學到的「發話」。一直練習，直到你有把握能正確地使用發話和時態，並能流暢、正確把事情說出來。

Long-Turn 的回應

在前三章中，我們學到了聽別人說話時可以用哪些 set-phrases 來表示自己感興趣，並鼓勵對方說下去。假如你對於自己 long turns 的會話能力或是整體的會話能力不太有把握，那就應該多學些「回應」，並鼓勵對方多開口，這樣你的壓力就會小一點。本節所要探討的就是「回應」；當對方的談話是屬於 long turns 時，這些「回應」就很有用。「回應」有三種：用來「鼓勵」對方的 set-phrases、當事情說完時加以「評論」的 set-phrases，以及概括「回應」的 set-phrases。

Task 4.11

 CD 1-27

請回頭聽 Track 4.5，把你所聽到的「鼓勵」、「評論」或「回應」的 set-phrases 寫下來。

答 案

▍別急著找答案，先做完下一個 Task，再來看答案。

Task 4.12

將下列的 Long-turn Responses 分門別類，填入下頁的表格。

1. And then?
2. He sure was (un)lucky.
3. He was really (un)lucky.
4. Mmm.
5. My god!
6. Oh, no.
7. Oh, yes?
8. OK.
9. Really.
10. That's a tricky situation. Really?
11. Right.
12. So then what happened?

13. So what did you do?

14. So what happened next?

15. So what happened?

16. That's amazing.

17. It's embarrassing when that happens.

18. That's gross!

19. That's incredible.

20. That's terrible.

21. That's weird.

22. What do you mean?

23. What happened?

24. Wow!

25. Yeah, go on.

26. Yes.

27. You're joking!

28. You're kidding!

Responding	Encouraging	Commenting

答　案

現在請研讀下列的語庫，並核對答案。各位的答案或許不太一樣，那沒關係。這三個分類的作用在於組織你記憶中的 set-phrases，而不在於釐清意義或用法上的細微差別，所以各位並不用擔心答案跟語庫有所出入。

| W o r d   L i s t |

gross [gros] *adj.* 粗劣的；下流的   weird [wɪrd] *adj.* 奇怪的

社交必備語庫 4.2　　　　 CD 1-29

回應 Responding	鼓勵 Encouraging	評論 Commenting
• Wow!	• So what happened next?	• He sure was (un)lucky.
• Yes.	• So what happened?	• He was really (un)lucky.
• Mmm.	• What happened?	• That's terrible.
• Really.	• So then what happened?	• That's amazing.
• Really?	• And then?	• That's incredible.
• OK.	• You're kidding!	• That's embarrassing
• Right.	• You're joking!	when that happens.
• Oh, no.	• My God!	• That's weird.
	• What do you mean?	• That's gross!
	• Oh, yes?	• That's a tricky situation.
	• Yeah, go on.	
	• So what did you do?	

📁 語庫小叮嚀

◆ Wow!、 You're kidding!、 You're joking!、 My God!、 That's terrible.、 That's amazing.、 That's incredible. 都是用來表示「震驚」或「驚訝」。它們也可以當作反話來用。

◆ That's weird. 適用於聽到奇怪的事情時。

◆ That's gross! 適用於聽到令人厭惡的事情時。但也可以用來表示好笑或表達諷刺之意。

◆ 注意，有很多 set-phrases 都是疑問句；在前一章談過，要回應別人所說的話，並表示你很認真地在聆聽，最好的辦法就是一直提出有趣的問題。

　　還記得 Task 4.11 嗎？請以下文來核對答案。對話中所運用到的 set-phrases 以粗體標示。

答　案

A: Did you hear what happened to Mike in Accounts?

B: No. What?

A: He got arrested on Friday night and spent the night in jail.

B: **No. Really, what happened?**

A: Well, it was all a big mistake, actually. He got home on Friday night really late,

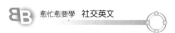

and apparently he'd been out drinking with some clients, so he was really drunk.

B: Was he out with the guys from the bank?

A: Yes, I think so.

B: **Oh, yeah,** they always get really drunk.

A: Well, anyway, he'd somehow lost his wallet and his house keys, so he couldn't get in. He lives alone, you know.

B: **Oh, really.** I thought he lived with his wife.

A: No, she left him last year.

B: **Oh, really?** Do you know why?

A: Hang on, let me finish telling you what happened. Where was I?

B: He lost his wallet and keys.

A: Oh yes, well, he tried to climb in through the bathroom window, but apparently he slipped and broke the glass with his foot. The neighbors heard him and thought a robbery was in progress, so they called the police.

B: **Oh, no.**

A: Yes. So when the cops arrived, they didn't believe his story: you know, he lost his wallet so he had no ID; the neighbors were new and didn't know him, so he couldn't get the police to believe his story. So they arrested him and put him in a cell until the morning.

B: **So then what happened?**

A: Well, when he sobered up, he called someone from work to come and bail him out.

B: Well, **that's a bit of a tricky situation.**

A: Yes, I know.

現在我們來練習發音。

Task 4.13   ◎))) CD 1-29

請聽 Track 4.7，針對語庫中的用語來練習發音。

● 答　案

確定在練習發音時，自己能重現 set-phrases 的語調與感覺。比方說，假如你要使用 Wow!，那你還得配合聲音和表情，這樣才能表現出你的震驚或驚訝。假如你在獨自練習時覺得有點蠢，不用擔心。你寧可在獨自練習時覺得蠢，而不要在和外國客戶聊天時才因為練習不夠而覺得蠢！對吧？

　　現在各位需要多些練習！在下一個 Task 中，各位會聽到一些 long turns。當各位遇到空格，試著儘快回應。為了讓各位先熟悉這種練習，第一個 long turn 是先前已經聽過的對話。在做這個 Task 時，試著先聽而不要看文字內容。如果覺得難，那就先多聽幾次，然後再看文字。

Task 4.14　　　　　　　　　　　　　　　　　　　　◉))) CD 1-30

請聽 Track 4.8，並在空格處給予適當的回應。

1.

A: A funny thing happened to me the other day.

B: ＿＿＿＿＿＿＿

A: I was just thinking about someone I went to school with, this boy I was quite friendly with in third grade. We used to hang out together — he lived next door — but then my parents moved and I changed schools and never saw him again.

B: ＿＿＿＿＿＿＿

A: Well, I was walking down Nan Jing Dong Lu（Nan-jing E. Rd.）during my lunch break thinking about this boy — I have no idea why I was thinking about him.

B: ＿＿＿＿＿＿＿

A: Yes, and suddenly I heard someone call my name. I turned around and there was this man looking at me. I didn't recognize him at all, but he obviously knew who I was.

B: ＿＿＿＿＿＿＿

A: You got it. Well, he walked up to me and said my name again and then I realized it was the boy I had been thinking about, the one from third grade!

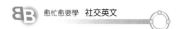

B: _____

A: Yeah, isn't it!

2.

A: Did you see *Ally McBeal* last night?

B: _____

A: Oh, it was hilarious. You know John's frog?

B: _____

A: That's right. Well, they all went out to a Chinese restaurant to celebrate and took the frog with them.

B: _____

A: Well, John thought the frog looked hungry, so he asked Ling to help him ask the waiter if they could take the frog into the kitchen to feed it. Ling asked the waiter in Chinese, and the waiter took the frog away.

B: _____

A: Well, after a while, the waiter brought a new dish to the table, which they all enjoyed. Then John started to get a bit worried about why it was taking them so long to feed the frog, so he asked the waiter about it.

B: _____

A: And the waiter told them that the dish they had just eaten was John's frog! The waiter misunderstood Ling's request and cooked the frog and served it to them.

B: _____

A: Yes, but it's also really funny, don't you think?

答　案　　　　　　　　　　　　　　　　　　　　　　CD 1-31

不用擔心自己聽不懂所有的內容，你可以根據對方的語調並適當地回應。誠如我在「社交必備本領 1」所提及，就算聽不懂對方的每一句話，也該表現出興趣並適當地回應。接著聽聽 Track 4.9 所提供的回應範例。可參考下列文字

Track 4.9

Conversation 1

見 47 頁對話 2 。

Conversation 2

A: Did you see *Ally McBeal* last night?

B: No? What happened?

A: Oh, it was hilarious. You know John's frog?

B: The one that died and then came back again?

A: That's right. Well, they all went out to a Chinese restaurant to celebrate and took the frog with them.

B: Really, how weird.

A: Well, John thought the frog looked hungry, so he asked Ling to help him ask the waiter if they could take the frog into the kitchen to feed it. Ling asked the waiter in Chinese, and the waiter took the frog away.

B: OK, so then what happened?

A: Well, after a while, the waiter brought a new dish to the table, which they all enjoyed. Then John started to get a bit worried about why it was taking them so long to feed the frog, so he asked the waiter about it.

B: And?

A: And the waiter told them that the dish they had just eaten was John's frog! The waiter misunderstood Ling's request and cooked the frog and served it to them.

B: Oh my God, that's gross!

A: Yes, but it's also really funny, don't you think?

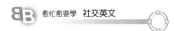

 中 譯

對話 2

A：你昨晚有看《艾莉的異想世界》嗎？

B：沒有，怎麼了？

A：喔，太有趣了，你知道 John 的青蛙嗎？

B：起死回生的那一個嗎？

A：沒錯，他們帶著青蛙一起到中國餐廳慶祝。

B：真的嗎，好奇怪！

A：嗯，John 覺得青蛙看起來有點餓，所以請 Ling 幫他請服務生帶青蛙到廚房去餵牠。Ling 用中文請服務生幫忙，服務生便把青蛙帶走了。

B：喔，然後發生了什麼事？

A：嗯，過了一會兒，服務生端一道新菜色上桌，他們都很喜歡。然後 John 開始有點擔心，為什麼餵個青蛙花了這麼久的時間，於是他問了服務生。

B：然後呢？

A：然後服務生告訴他們，他們剛用過的菜色就是 John 的青蛙！服務生誤會了 Ling 的要求，把青蛙給煮了並送上桌。

B：喔，天啊！真噁心！

A：是啊！但真的很有趣，你不覺得嗎？

語感甦活區

　　各位是否注意到，語庫 4.2 中有一個 set-phrases 使用了 tricky situation 這個 word partnership。在商用英文中，situation 是個關鍵字，但常常用得不恰當。本章的最後，我們就來看一些可以和 situation 搭配使用的 word partnerships。

Task 4.15

請研讀下列的 word partnership 表格，並練習造句。

• Sounds like a(n) • That's a(n) • What a(n) • I once found myself in a(n) • I've never been in such a(n)	• tricky • awkward • delicate • difficult • embarrassing • extraordinary • remarkable • ridiculous • risky • terrible • win-win	**situation**

答　案

可能的例句如下：

- Sounds like a delicate situation.
- What an embarrassing situation to be in!
- I've never been in such an awkward situation.

注意，表中的大部分形容詞是形容負面的情況（extraordinary 可能是正面或負面的情況）。只有 remarkable 和 win-win 是正面的。

| Word List |

delicate [ˋdɛləkɪt] *adj.* 難以處理的；脆弱的　　remarkable [rɪˋmɑrkəbl] *adj.* 令人驚訝的；非凡的
win-win *adj.* 雙贏的

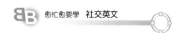
　　在看下一章之前，各位可以再聽一次 Track 4.5 ，看看和第一次做這 Task 時相較，你能多聽出幾個回應的用語。另外，請回到本章的「學習目標」，看看你達成了多少。

擴展人脈

擴展人脈 1：

餐廳

引言與學習目標

　　好的餐廳是絕佳的交際場合。吃喝會讓人放鬆，大家也可以聊聊生意以外的話題。你可以在這裡真正認識你的生意夥伴，並建立在累積人脈時不可或缺的互信。餐飲本身就是個很好的話頭，從這裡可以將話題擴展到文化差異與各國料理等不同領域。本章是以在餐廳用餐時所需的用語為重點：包括形容食物、點菜、邀請和請客作東的用語。此外，我還會介紹一些和食物以及外國用餐習慣有關的文化訊息，讓各位在交際時不會犯下嚴重的錯誤。本章頗長，建議各位拆成幾個段落來學習。

　　本章結束時，你應達成的「學習目標」如下：

❏ 邀請他人上餐館。
❏ 接受或婉拒邀請。
❏ 討論菜單內容。
❏ 和服務生應對。
❏ 知道自己是主人時該說什麼，是客人時又該說什麼。
❏ 了解東西方飲食習慣的差異。
❏ 對酒有更深的了解。
❏ 完成聽力練習。
❏ 完成發音練習。

邀請

第一節要學的是正式與非正式的邀請，以及要如何接受與拒絕邀請。

Task 5.1

CD 1-32

請聽 Track 5.1，然後完成配對。

	Formal	**Informal**
Conversation 1		
Conversation 2		

答　案

Conversation 1 為正式；Conversation 2 為非正式。

你是如何判斷「正式」與「非正式」呢？

Task 5.2

把下列的 set-phrases 分門別類，填入下頁的表格。想想哪些是正式、哪些是非正式。

1. Would you like to have dinner/lunch/breakfast?
2. Would you like something to eat?
3. Would you like dinner/lunch/breakfast/a snack?
4. We'd like to invite you to dinner.
5. We'd be very happy if you'd have dinner with us.
6. That's very kind of you. Thank you.
7. That'd be great, thanks.
8. That'd be great, thanks, but unfortunately + clause ...
9. We'd like to invite you to have dinner with us.
10. That would be lovely. Thank you.
11. That would be lovely, but unfortunately + clause ...

12. Sure, why not?

13. Shall we go get something to eat?

14. Hungry?

15. Have you eaten?

16. Could we do it another time?

17. Are you hungry?

18. Another time, perhaps. I've got to dash.

Inviting

Accepting

Rejecting

答 案

▌ 請以下頁的語庫核對答案，並仔細研讀語庫小叮嚀。

| W o r d   L i s t |

dash [dæʃ] v. 匆忙離開

社交必備語庫 5.1　　　　　　　　　　　　CD 1-33

邀請 Inviting

- Hungry?
- Are you hungry?
- Have you eaten?
- Shall we go get something to eat?
- Would you like to have dinner/lunch/breakfast?
- Would you like dinner/lunch/breakfast/a snack?
- Would you like something to eat?
- We'd like to invite you to dinner.
- We'd like to invite you to have dinner with us.
- We'd be very happy if you'd have dinner with us.

接受 Accepting

- Sure, why not?
- That'd be great, thanks.
- That would be lovely. Thank you.
- That's very kind of you. Thank you.

拒絕 Rejecting

- Another time perhaps? I've got to dash.
- Could we do it another time?
- That'd be great, thanks, but unfortunately + clause ...
- That would be lovely, but unfortunately + clause ...

⭐ 📁 語庫小叮嚀

◆ 每一個類別中的 set-phrases，都以非正式到正式的程度依序排列。亦即，第一個 set-phrase 最不正式；最後一個 set-phrase 最為正式。

◆ **Inviting**：注意，我們說的不是 eat dinner/lunch/breakfast，而是 have dinner/lunch/breakfast。另，我們會說 a snack，但不會說 a lunch/dinner/breakfast。這些小細節很重要，本章的「語感甦活區」對此會有更多的說明。

◆ **Accepting**：要接受 Shall we get something to eat? 的邀請，你應該回答 Sure, why not?；要接受 We'd like to invite you to dinner. 的邀請，你應該回答 That's very kind of you. Thank you.。

◆ **Rejecting**：注意，在拒絕邀請時，不應該直接說 no，而要先接受再婉拒。可能的理由包括：I've got another meeting.、I've got to get home to my family.、I've got a plane to catch.。

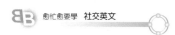
 Task 5.3　　　　　　　　　　　　　CD 1-32

再聽一次 Track 5.1，找出你在對話中所聽到的 set-phrases。

 答　案

請看下面的 CD 文字內容，粗體部分即為對話中所應用的 set-phrases。

Track 5.1

Conversation 1

A: Well, Jeff, that was a very productive meeting, I thought. You had some really great ideas in there!

B: Really? Well, thanks for saying so.

A: No, I mean it. Look, **are you hungry**? **Shall we go get something to eat?**

B: **Sure. Why not?**

A: OK, well, let me just get my coat and we'll go to the diner around the corner.

B: OK.

Conversation 2

A: That was a very interesting presentation, Ms. Wang. My colleagues and I are very impressed with your proposal.

B: Oh, no, surely. Your ideas were very interesting as well.

A: To show our appreciation for your hard work, **we'd like to invite you to have dinner with us.**

B: Oh, **that would be lovely. Thank you.**

A: Excellent. Have you had French food before?

B: Oh, yes. Marvelous!

| Word List |

diner [ˋdaɪnə] n. 簡單的速食餐廳　　　　marvelous [ˋmɑrvləs] adj. 很棒的；出色的

中　譯

對話 1

A：嘿，Jeff，我覺得這次開會的成果豐碩，你提出的那些點子真棒！

B：真的嗎？謝謝你的誇獎。

A：不，我是說真的。你餓了嗎？我們要不要去吃點東西？

B：當然好呀！

A：好，那我穿一下外套，我們去附近的館子吃飯。

B：好。

對話 2

A：王小姐，這場簡報很有趣。我跟我同事對妳的提案都印象深刻。

B：喔，真不敢當。你們的點子也很有趣。

A：為了答謝妳的辛苦付出，我們想請妳共進晚餐。

B：喔，你們真貼心，謝謝。

A：太好了。妳吃過法國菜嗎？

B：喔，吃過，味道很棒！

Task 5.4　　　　　　　　　　　　　　　　　　　　　　　CD 1-33

請聽 Track 5.2，練習語庫中 set-phrases 的發音。

　接著針對語庫中的 set-phrases 做些回應的練習。你可以找個同事一起來練習。

Task 5.5　　　　　　　　　　　　　　　　　　　　　　　CD 1-34

請聽 Track 5.3 中的邀請，並利用所學過的 set-phrases 來回應。

答　案

回應時要留意當時的情境為正式或非正式，然後再選擇適當的用語。各位可以多練習幾遍，直到自己可以很快地應答。

Task 5.6　　　　　　　　　　　　　　　　　　　　　　　CD 1-35

請聽 Track 5.4，聽聽上一個 Task 的可能回應方式。

 答 案

有二個對話情境為正式，兩個為非正式。你會分辨嗎？請對照下面的文字內容。

Track 5.4

Conversation 1 (informal)

A: Well, I'm getting really hungry. I think we should take a break and come back to this item after lunch. Shall we go get something to eat?

B: Sure. Why not? Do you know somewhere cheap and quick?

Conversation 2 (formal)

A: It's getting rather late. Can I suggest that we stop at this point and perhaps regroup tomorrow? I think we could all do with some rest. Mr. Wang, we'd like to invite you to dinner.

B: That would be lovely, but unfortunately I need to get back to my hotel as I'm expecting a call from my wife. Perhaps we could meet for breakfast?

Conversation 3 (informal)

A: My God! Will you look at the time! It's after 2:00! My wife will kill me. Joyce, are you hungry? Do you want something to eat before you go back to your hotel?

B: Could we do it another time? I'm exhausted after my flight.

Conversation 4 (formal)

A: Well, that was a very impressive presentation, Ms. Hsu. We'd like to thank you for coming all this way to explain the new concepts to us. To show our appreciation, we'd like to invite you to have dinner with us.

B: That's very kind of you. Thank you.

中　譯

對話 1 （非正式）

A：欸，我真的好餓。我想我們應該先休息一下，等吃完午飯再回來做。我們要不要去吃點東西？

B：當然好啊。你知道有什麼又便宜又快的地方嗎？

對話 2 （正式）

A：時間很晚了，我想我們能不能到此為止，也許明天再碰頭？我覺得我們可能都需要休息一下。王先生，我想請你吃個晚飯。

B：您真貼心，只可惜我要回飯店等我老婆的電話。也許我們可以一起吃早餐？

對話 3 （非正式）

A：天啊！妳看時間，已經過兩點了！我老婆會殺了我。 Joyce ，妳餓不餓？想不想在回飯店前吃點東西？

B：改天好嗎？這趟飛機讓我累壞了。

對話 4 （正式）

A：徐小姐，這場報告真精彩。我們要感謝妳遠道而來為我們解釋新概念。為了表達謝意，我們想請您共進晚餐。

B：你們真體貼，謝謝。

討論菜單

在這節中，我們要來看看菜單，以及要怎麼聊菜單。不論你是主人或客人，這裡所教的用語都很有用。

接著，先來看些中、西餐的差異。

 文化小叮嚀

- 中餐是以湯作為最後一道菜，而西餐多半是以湯作為第一道菜。
- 中餐通常是在餐後的一段時間才上甜點和茶，西餐則會在用餐的最後上甜點和咖啡，或是葡萄酒和乳酪。
- 中餐是由很多大家共用的幾道菜所組成，通常沒有特定的食用順序；西餐則是由個別的「餐」所組成，而且這些「餐」有固定的食用順序，依序是湯、沙拉、主餐、甜點。甜點通常是在吃完其他的餐後再另外單點，如此你可以有個空檔和對方交談。
- 關於「餐」的名稱和種類，歐洲的國與國之間有很大的差異。假如你對菜單上的名稱有疑問，不妨請教主人。

Task 5.7

請研究下面的兩份菜單。你能看出有哪些異同之處嗎？

Jean Pierre's Bistro

Les Hors D'evres

- *Ravioli with a Wild Mushroom Sauce*
- *A "Compresse" of Tiger Tomatoes and Langoustines flavoured with Basil*
- *Rabbit and Sage Terrine with a Fresh Apricot Coulis*
- *Soupe du jour*

Les Entrees

- *Rack of Lamb with White Beans and Rosemary*
- *Breast of Duck with Red Fruit Sauce, Sweet Corn Galette*
- *Filet of Sea Bream with Braised Fennel and Lemon Confit Jus*

Les Desserts

- *Warm Lemon Sponge flavoured with Wild Thyme*
- *Vanilla Créme Brulée*
- *Warm Chocolate Mousse with Passion Fruit Sorbet*

| W o r d   L i s t |

ravioli [ˈrævɪˋolɪ] *n.* 一種義大利點心（以麵粉皮包碎肉、乾酪等餡並以肉汁煮成）

basil [ˈbæzl] *n.* 羅勒

rosemary [ˈrozˏmɛrɪ] *n.* 迷迭香

braise [brez] *v.* 燉；蒸

thyme [taɪm] *n.* 百里香

apricot [ˈæprɪˏkɑt] *n.* 杏桃

bream [brim] *n.* 真鯛

fennel [ˈfɛnl] *n.* 茴香的果實

sorbet [ˈsɔrbɪt] *n.* 果汁冰砂；雪酪

Luigi's Trattoria

Antipasti
• *Mussels sauteed with Garlic, Cherry Tomatoes, Parsley and Black Pepper*
• *"Mozzarella di Bufala" with Tomato and Fresh Basil*
• *Zuppa del giorno*

Pasta
• *Spaghetti served with Tomato Sauce and Fresh Basil*
• *Hand-made Fettuccine with Three Sauces: Meat, Mushrooms and Peas*

Secondi Piatti
• *Grilled Tuna Filet with Fine Herbs, Olives and Capers, served with Mixed Salad*
• *Grilled Veal Chop served with Sauteed Vegetables*

Desserts
• *Tiramisu*
• *Chocolate, Almonds, and Cherries Ice Cream Cake*

答案

「bistro」是指家庭式的法國小餐館，「trattoria」則是指家庭式的義大利小餐館。這兩份菜單都是按菜別來分類，只不過義大利式的菜單上多了麵類。

Word List

mussel [ˋmʌsl̩] *n.* 淡菜
parsley [ˋpɑrslɪ] *n.* 西洋芹
filet [fɪˋle] *n.* 薄（肉）片
chop [tʃɑp] *n.* 帶骨的小肉排

sauté [soˋte] *v.* 爆炒；嫩煎
grill [grɪl] *v.* 烤
veal [vil] *n.* 小牛肉

CD 1-36

Task 5.8

請聽 Track 5.5 ，根據對話內容回答下列問題。

1. 他們在哪家餐館？是 Jean Pierre's Bistro 還是 Luigi's Trattoria ？
2. 王先生在哪段對話中是主人，在哪段對話中則是客人？

答 案

Conversation 1 ：王先生和 Mitzuko 小姐是在 Luigi's Trattoria 餐廳裡，王先生是主人。 Conversation 2 ：他們是在 Jean Pierre's Bistro 餐廳，王先生是客人， Hulot 小姐則是主人。如果你沒聽出來，就看著菜單再聽一次吧。

各位接著要學的 set-phrases 有兩種：當你是主人，你要能「推薦」與建議客人點菜；當你是客人，要知道如何向主人「請教」菜單。你可不希望吃到噁心的東西吧？

Task 5.9

將下列的用語分門別類，填入下頁的表中。

1. Can you tell me about the ...?
2. Does it have ... in it? I'm allergic to ...
3. Have you tried ...?
4. How about ...?
5. Is it low-fat?
6. Is it meat?
7. Is it oily?
8. Is it salty?
9. Is it spicy?
10. It might be too ... for you.
11. It sounds horrible, but it's actually really good.

| W o r d　 L i s t |

allergic [əˋlɝdʒɪk] *adj.* 過敏的

12. It's a little ...

13. The ... is very good here.

14. Try some ...

15. What are you having?

16. What can you recommend?

17. What does ... mean?

18. What does it come with?

19. What's good here?

20. What's the ...?

21. Why don't you just order for both of us?

22. Would you like me to order for you?

23. Would you like some ...?

24. Would you like the ...?

25. You could try ...

26. You might want to try the ... It's a local delicacy.

27. You should try the ...

Asking about Something on the Menu — the Guest
Recommending Something on the Menu — the Host

答　案

請以下列的語庫核對答案，並研讀語庫小叮嚀。

Word List

delicacy [ˈdɛləkəsɪ] *n.* 佳餚

社交必備語庫 5.2　 CD 1-37

詢問菜單上的事項—客人 Asking about Something on the Menu — the Guest

- What's the ...?
- Can you tell me about the ...?
- What does ... mean?
- Is it spicy?
- Is it oily?
- Is it meat?
- Is it low-fat?
- Is it salty?
- Does it have ... in it? I'm allergic to ...
- What are you having?
- What can you recommend?
- What's good here?
- Why don't you just order for both of us?
- What does it come with?

推薦菜單上的事項—主人 Recommending Something on the Menu — the Host

- The ... is very good here.
- You should try the ...
- Try some ...
- Have you tried ...?
- It sounds horrible, but it's actually really good.
- You might want to try the ... It's a local delicacy.
- You could try ...
- How about ...?
- Would you like the ...?
- Would you like some ...?
- Would you like me to order for you?
- It's a little ...
- It might be too ... for you.

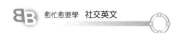
★ 📂 語庫小叮嚀

◆ Is it spicy? 也可以說成 Is it hot? 但這樣可能會讓對方搞不清楚，因為 hot 有「燙」和「辣」兩種意思。一般來說，歐洲食物沒有亞洲食物來得辣。

◆ 大部分的菜單只會告訴你主菜是肉還是魚，蔬菜和馬鈴薯算是配菜。所以你可以說 What does it come with?，問問對方主菜搭配的是哪些配菜。

◆ 假如你真的看不懂菜單，那就說 Why don't you just order for both of us?，請主人幫你點餐吧。

◆ 假如你帶外國客戶上中式餐館，客人可能不知道習慣，或看不懂菜單。此時你可說 Would you like me to order for you?，來幫對方點餐。記住，不要點太辣或太怪異的食物。

◆ 如果你覺得客人可能會誤點他不喜歡的餐，你可以說 It's a little ... 或 It might be too ... for you. 來提醒對方。

 Task 5.10   ◎))) CD 1-37

請聽 Track 5.6，練習語庫中用語的發音。

 **Task 5.11**   ◎))) CD 1-36

再聽一遍 Track 5.5，並在語庫 5.2 中勾選出你聽到的 set-phrases。

● 答 案

▌看下列的 CD 文字內容，對話中所應用的 set-phrases 以粗體標示。

◎))) **Track 5.5**

Conversation 1

Mr. Wang: Well, Mitzuko-san, I hope you like it here. This is my favourite restaurant in Taipei. It reminds me of my youth when I traveled around Europe.

Mitzuko: It looks wonderful. Very authentic.

Mr. Wang: The chef trained in Florence. **The** pasta **is very good here**.

Mitzuko: OK. So, **what can you recommend**?

Mr. Wang: Uhm ... **You should try the** mushroom fettucine. It's really good.

Mitzuko: **Is it salty?**

Mr. Wang: Not at all. It has a very delicate flavor.

Mitzuko: **What does** "Zuppa del giorno" **mean**? I'm sorry I don't know how to pronounce that.

Mr. Wang: Oh, that means soup of the day. I'll ask the waiter what they have today. **Have you tried mussels** cooked the Italian way? They're really delicious.

Mitzuko: No. I'll try them. Sounds good.

Conversation 2

Mr. Wang: This looks wonderful, Madame Hulot.

Madame Hulot: Yes, it's very nice. All our foreign visitors enjoy it. The food is wonderfully well-prepared. Let me know if you need any help with the menu.

Mr. Wang: Thank you. Mmm. **Can you tell me about** the terrine?

Madame Hulot: Yes. A terrine is a kind of meat paté. It's meat turned into a paste. **It sounds horrible but it's actually really good.**

Mr. Wang: Mmm. Maybe another time.

Madame Hulot: **You could try the** ravioli. They are rather like your Chinese dumplings, and the sauce is delicious.

Mr. Wang: Sounds good. I think I'll have the lamb for my main course. **What does it come with?**

Madame Hulot: Well, you can have frites — French fries — or simple boiled potatoes.

Mr. Wang: I'll have the potatoes. **What are you having?**

Madame Hulot: I'm having my usual. I like the fish here. **Would you like some** wine?

Mr. Wang: Oh, yes. That would be lovely.

中 譯

對話 1

王先生： 對了，Mitzuko 小姐，希望妳喜歡這裡。這是我在台北最喜歡的餐館，它
讓我想起我年輕時在歐洲的旅遊。

Mitzuko： 看起來很棒，就像真的歐洲餐廳一樣。

王先生： 大廚是在佛羅倫斯學藝，這裡的義大利麵很好吃。

Mitzuko： 好。那你可以推薦一下嗎？

王先生： 嗯，妳應該試試蘑菇麵，味道很棒。

Mitzuko： 它會很鹹嗎？

王先生： 一點都不會。它的味道很清淡。

Mitzuko： Zuppa del giorno 是什麼意思？抱歉，我不曉得要怎麼唸。

王先生： 喔，那是「每日一湯」的意思。我會問服務生今天是什麼湯。妳吃過義式
淡菜嗎？它的味道很棒。

Mitzuko： 沒吃過，那就試試看吧，聽起來不錯。

對話 2

王先生： Hulot 小姐，這裡看起來很不錯。

Hulot 小姐：是啊，的確很棒。我們的外國客人一向都很喜歡，而且它的菜餚都經過
精心烹調。假如你對菜單有不什麼不了解的地方，請告訴我。

王先生： 謝謝。嗯，可以麻煩妳介紹一下 terrine 嗎？

Hulot 小姐：好的。 Terrine 是一種肉餅，也就是把肉變成餅。它聽起來有點恐怖，不
過真的好吃極了。

王先生： 嗯，也許下次吧。

Hulot 小姐：你可以試試 ravioli。它很像是中國的水餃，而且醬料很好吃。

王先生： 聽起來不錯。我想我的主菜就吃羊肉好了。它的副餐是什麼？

Hulot 小姐：哦，你可以吃 frites，也就是薯條，或是簡單的水煮馬鈴薯。

王先生： 那我吃馬鈴薯好了。妳要吃什麼呢？

Hulot 小姐：我還是老樣子，我喜歡吃這裡的魚。你要喝點酒嗎？

王先生： 喔，好，妳真貼心。

　　各位可以用兩種方式練習這些用語。你可以根據自己的經驗或是將來可能會碰到
的情境來寫一段對話，也可以和朋友一起練習本章提供的對話。

和服務生的應對

　　本節要教各位和服務生應對的 set-phrases。各位會學到如何點餐、索取你要的東西，以及如果食物或服務不符合你的預期，要如何表達你的不滿。在開始之前，請先看下面的文化小叮嚀

文化小叮嚀

- 歐洲和美國的服務生皆是經過嚴格訓練的專業服務人員，他們對於餐廳內的食物跟酒都瞭若指掌。假如有任何疑問，不妨請教服務生。
- 當你身在國外時，應該要對服務生保持尊重和禮貌的態度。需要他們時，不要對他們彈手指，也不要喊得讓大家都聽到，只要揮幾次手就行了。即使是女性，你也要稱她們「Waiter」。
- 如果你覺得食物或服務沒有達到你的預期，最好不要在賓客面前抱怨，因為這樣會使他們很不自在。另一方面，如果點的菜很久都沒有來，你應該要讓服務生知道。
- 給小費的習慣在每個國家都不一樣，所以你應該看看菜單，上面會註明是否含服務費。假如你覺得店裡的服務很棒，公認的適當金額是帳單總額的 15%。你可以在付完帳後把小費給服務生，謝謝他的用心。

Task 5.12

CD 1-38

請聽 Track 5.7，並參照第 153、154 頁的兩份菜單。根據你聽到的兩段對話回答下列問題。

1. 王先生點了什麼？

2. 對方點了什麼？

答案

請以下面二張服務生所記錄的點菜單核對答案。要注意的是，在對話二中，Hulot 小姐改變了先前的決定，點了一道菜單上沒有的菜，也就是 a special。A special 是指根據廚師在市場上所能找到的新鮮食材而每天變換的菜色。

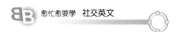

對話 1

> ### *Luigi's Trattoria*
>
> mussels (lady)
> soup <u>not too salty</u> (gentleman)
>
> fettucine (lady)
> veal (gentleman)

對話 2

> ### *Jean Pierre's Bistro*
>
> soup (lady)
> ravioli (gentleman)
> one dish of snails to share
> beef bourguignon (lady)
> lamb (gentleman)

　　接著來看在開始用餐時會使用到的 set-phrases ——索取菜單或酒單、點餐、詢問特定菜色、結帳、以及抱怨食物或服務的 set-phrases。

Task 5.13

將下列的 set-phrases 分門別類,填入下頁的表中。

1. I'll have the ...

2. Can I have the ...

3. Not too spicy/salty/sweet, please.

4. That's it.

5. I'd like the ...

6. For my starter I'll have the ...

7. For my starter I'd like the ...

8. Then I'll have the ...

9. Excuse me?

10. Can we have the menu, please?

11. Can I have the check, please?

12. Can I have the wine list, please?

13. Can you tell me what the specials are, please?

14. Can you tell me what the soup of the day is, please?

15. I'm sorry, but there's something wrong with my food.

16. I'm sorry, but this is not what I ordered.

17. I'm sorry, but we're still waiting for the ...

18. I'm sorry, can you explain this item on the bill please?

19. Can you tell me what the ... is, please?

20. I'm sorry but I don't think this is what we ordered.

Ordering Something on the Menu
Starting, Ending, Complaining and Asking

 答　案

請以下列的語庫核對答案，並研讀語庫小叮嚀。

社交必備語庫 5.3　　　　　　　　　　　　　　　　　　　　CD 1-39

點菜 Ordering Something on the Menu
• I'll have the ...
• Can I have the ...
• Not too spicy/salty/sweet, please.
• That's it.
• I'd like the ...
• For my starter I'll have the ...
• For my starter I'd like the ...
• Then I'll have the ...
開始、結束、抱怨和詢問 Starting, Ending, Complaining and Asking
• Excuse me?
• Can we have the menu, please?
• Can I have the check, please?
• Can I have the wine list, please?
• Can you tell me what the specials are, please?

- Can you tell me what the soup of the day is, please?
- Can you tell me what the ... is, please?
- I'm sorry, but there's something wrong with my food.
- I'm sorry, but this is not what I ordered.
- I'm sorry, but we're still waiting for the ...
- I'm sorry, can you explain this item on the bill, please?
- I'm sorry, but I don't think this is what we ordered.

★ 📁 語庫小叮嚀

◆ 當每個人都點完餐後，就可對服務生說 That's it.。

◆ 在英式英文裡，Excuse me? 這個 set-phrase 表示 I want your attention.。在美式英文裡，它則表示 I'm sorry, what did you say?。但，在美國、歐洲以及其他大部分的國家，你都可以用這句話引起服務生的注意。

◆ Can I have the check, please? 的英式說法是 Can I have the bill, please?

◆ 當點的菜遲遲沒有上桌，就可以說 I'm sorry, but we're still waiting for the ...。

Task 5.14　　　　　　　　　　　　　　CD 1-39

請聽 Track 5.8，練習語庫中用語的發音。

Task 5.15　　　　　　　　　　　　　　CD 1-38

再聽一次 Track 5.7，並在語庫 5.3 中勾選出你所聽到的 set-phrases。

● 答　案

▍請看下列的 CD 文字內容，對話中所應用的 set-phrases 以粗體標示。

●))) Track 5.7

Conversation 1

Mr. Wang:　**Can we have a menu, please.**

Waiter:　　Of course, sir. Here you are.

...

164

Waiter:　　　Are you ready to order, sir?

Mr. Wang:　 Yes. Mitzuko-san, please go first.

Mitzuko:　　 All right. **I'll have the** mussels, and **then I'll have the fet-tucine**.

Waiter:　　　Would you like a main course, madame?

Mitzuko:　　 No, I don't think so. I think the pasta will be enough for me.

Waiter:　　　And you, sir?

Mr. Wang:　 **Can you tell me what the soup of the day is?**

Waiter:　　　Yes. It's minestrone soup. That's a rich tomato and vegetable soup.

Mr. Wang:　 OK, I'll have that, but **not too salty,** please. And for my main course I'll have the veal. **That's it.** We might order some of your excellent tiramisu later.

Waiter:　　　Very good, sir.

Conversation 2

Waiter:　　　　　 Would you like to order some wine first, madame?

Madame Hulot: Yes. **Can I have the wine list, please?**

Waiter:　　　　　 Here you are, madame.

...

Waiter:　　　　　 Would you like to order now?

Madame Hulot: Yes. Mr. Wang, what would you like?

Mr. Wang:　　　 OK. **For my starter I'd like the** ravioli, followed by the lamb for my main course. And **can I have the** potatoes boiled, not fried, please.

Waiter:　　　　　 Of course, sir. Madame?

Madame Hulot: Mmm. **Can you tell me what the specials are, please?**

Waiter:　　　　　 Today we have beef Bourguignon and for hors d'oevres, the escargots is especially fresh.

Madame Hulot: Oh, Mr. Wang, would you like to try snails?

Mr. Wang:	Oh, yes.
Waiter:	So would you like to change the ravioli to snails, sir? Or have both?
Madame Hulot:	Why don't we have one dish of snails between us to share? Then you can try the ravioli and the snails.
Mr. Wang:	Good idea.
Waiter:	All right. And for your main course, madame?
Madame Hulot:	**I'll have the** beef, and a soup du jour to start with.
Waiter:	Very good, madame.

 中 譯

對話 1

王先生：可以麻煩你給我們菜單嗎？

服務生：沒問題，先生。請看。

……

服務生：你們要點餐了嗎，先生？

王先生：光子小姐，請妳先點。

光子：　好。我要淡菜，然後我還要麵。

服務生：小姐，您要主菜嗎？

光子：　我想不用了。我想我吃麵就夠了。

服務生：先生，您呢？

王先生：你能告訴我今天的湯是什麼嗎？

服務生：好的，是義式蔬菜濃湯，也就是有番茄和蔬菜的濃湯。

王先生：好，那我點那個，不過麻煩不要太鹹。我的主菜要小牛肉，就這樣。我們等
　　　　一下可能會點一些你們這邊很棒的提拉米蘇。

服務生：太好了，先生。

對話 2

服務生：　　小姐，您要先點杯酒嗎？

Hulot 小姐：好。可以麻煩你給我酒單嗎？

服務生：　　小姐，請過目。

......

服務生：　　您現在要點餐了嗎？

Hulot 小姐：好。王先生，你想要什麼？

王先生：　　好。開胃菜我要 ravioli，接下來的主菜則要羊肉。我可以點水煮馬鈴薯嗎？麻煩不要用炸的。

服務生：　　當然可以，先生。小姐呢？

Hulot 小姐：唔。可以麻煩你介紹一下特餐嗎？

服務生：　　今天我們有勃艮第牛肉當主菜，開胃菜則是蝸牛。

Hulot 小姐：噢，王先生，你想試試蝸牛嗎？

王先生：　　哦，好啊。

服務生：　　先生，所以您要把 ravioli 換成蝸牛，還是兩個都要？

Hulot 小姐：我們何不點一份蝸牛一起吃？這樣你就可以同時吃到 ravioli 和蝸牛了。

王先生：　　好主意。

服務生：　　好的。小姐，您的主菜要什麼？

Hulot 小姐：我要牛肉，然後先來個濃湯。

服務生：　　太好了，小姐。

　　各位可以用兩種方式練習這些用語。你可以寫一段餐廳裡的對話；也可以和朋友一起練習本章中的對話，然後去一家高檔的外國餐廳共進晚餐，並對服務生練習說英語！

語感甦活區

最後一節要學的是在聊到飲食時可以使用的實用用語。在此之前，先看些與飲食有關的文化小叮嚀。

 文化小叮嚀

東方人和西方人的餐桌禮儀有些許不同。因此，在和西方客戶用餐時，要記住一些該做與不該做的事：

- 不要在餐桌上剔牙。
- 喝湯時不要出聲，要盡量保持安靜。
- 不要大聲打嗝。假如無法克制，就用餐巾遮住嘴巴、壓低打嗝的聲音。萬一被別人察覺，要趕緊道歉。
- 咀嚼的時候不要張嘴，要緊閉雙唇。
- 不要在餐桌上擤鼻子。
- 慢慢吃，嘴裡塞滿東西時不要講話。
- 吃完時把刀叉一起放在餐盤邊緣。這也是在告訴服務生你已用餐完畢，他就會過來收拾你的餐具。
- 不要自己取用對方的食物。
- 稱讚東西好吃。但要記住的是，許多東方人重口感而不重味道，西方人則是重味道而不重口感。對東方人來說，chewy「有嚼勁」是種恭維。但對外國人來說，這就不見得了。
- 如果你不確定該怎麼做才對，可以看看同行的其他人怎麼做，然後照做就對了。
- 放輕鬆，好好吃一頓飯！

有時候客人可能會請你說明一些菜或餐點。假如你會的用語不夠，就很難解釋了。接著就來學些實用的用語。

Task 5.17

請研究下面的 word partnership 表格，並練習造句。

It's	• cooked with • made from • made with • served with • boiled • baked • roasted • fried • deep fried • stewed • rolled in • marinated	• Chinese herbs • eggs • fish • fruit • chicken • pork • beef • mutton • duck • noodles • rice • spices • vegetables

答　案

以下為一些可能的例句：

- It's rolled in bamboo leaves and baked.
- It's marinated in Chinese herbs and then roasted.

　　如果你是客人，應該對食物發表意見，不過僅限於讚美的話。學學下頁用來形容食物的形容詞吧！

Word List

marinate [ˈmærɪˌnet] v. 用滷汁醃泡　　　mutton [ˈmʌtn] n. 羊肉

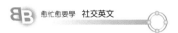

Task 5.18

研究下列的單字，想想今天中午吃了什麼，練習用下列的形容詞來描述中午的菜色。

Mmm. That's really （如果你想要挑剔一點： That's a bit too ...）	• bitter • chewy • crunchy • fatty • fruity • heavy • juicy • light • mild	• nutty • oily • rich • salty • spicy • strong • sugary • sweet • tasty

在 Track 5.3 的對話中，各位看過這個 set-phrase ： We'd like to invite you to have dinner with us. ，注意句中用的是 have dinner ，而不是 eat dinner 。在英文中，用餐的動詞是 have ，而 eat 則是指身體的動作。

Task 5.19

比較下列的二個 word partnership 表格，並練習造句。

have	• a drink • some coffee • lunch • supper • dinner • breakfast	• some tea • something to eat • something to drink • a snack • a meal

---

W o r d   L i s t

crunchy [ˋkrʌntʃɪ] *adj.* 鬆脆的

nutty [ˋnʌtɪ] *adj.* 有堅果味的；富風味的

fruity [ˋfrutɪ] *adj.* 有水果味道的

sugary [ˋʃʊgrɪ] *adj.* 糖製的；甜的

eat	• too much • too fast • a lot • slowly • well • healthily • like a horse

答　案

可能的例句如下：

- Shall we have a drink?
- Have you had breakfast?
- I'll have some coffee.
- I always eat too fast.
- It's more healthy to eat slowly.
- My son eats like a horse.

Task 5.20

請看下列幾組句子，刪掉每一組中的錯誤句子。

1. I normally don't have breakfast.
I normally don't eat breakfast.

2. Would you like to have dinner?
Would you like to eat dinner?

3. Shall we stop to eat some lunch?
Shall we stop to have some lunch?

4. Would you like to drink some coffee?
Would you like to have some coffee?

答 案

各組錯誤的句子如下：

1. I normally don't eat breakfast.

2. Would you like to eat dinner?

3. Shall we stop to eat some lunch?

4. Would you like to drink some coffee?

　　西方人習慣飲酒，所以只要跟外國人吃飯，酒就是個重要的部分。請研讀下列關於酒的文化小叮嚀。

文化小叮嚀

- 酒有紅酒和白酒二種，通常是用釀製的葡萄種類來命名。
- 最常見的酒有 Merlot、Cabernet Sauvignon、Shiraz、Zinfandel 和 Pinot Noir。紅酒適合在冬天喝，或是搭配難消化的食物，像是紅肉、醬料很重的食物或乳酪。它要在室溫下飲用，而且在飲用前通常要先開著擱置一段時間，以便讓酒「醒一下」。
- 最常見的乾白酒有：Chardonnay、Sauvignon Blanc、Reisling 和 Pinot Gris。白酒適合在夏天喝，或是搭配味道淡的食物，像是素菜、沙拉或海鮮。還有一種甜白酒是搭配甜點。白酒要冷藏後飲用，但絕對不要加冰塊。
- 雖然法國所生產的紅酒仍然被公認是世界第一，但它的白酒已經不是市場領導者。現在有很多好喝的白酒都是產自智利、加州、澳洲和南非。德國則是以甜白酒而聞名。
- 如果你在高檔的歐式餐廳用餐，主人可能會在開始用餐時點白酒，上主菜時點紅酒，上甜點和咖啡時點甜白酒或白蘭地。
- 喝酒不必喝到醉，而要以小酌的方式慢慢喝。在入喉以前，先把它在含在嘴裡幾秒，以品嚐它的味道。
- 如果你是主人，在替客人或自己倒酒時絕對不要倒到滿，只要倒一半就好了。
- 如果你想要喝醉，那就喝伏特加。如果你想要品嚐美味，那就喝葡萄酒。

　　好了，這個頗長的章節就到此結束，希望各位能找機會練習。各位不妨慰勞自己吃一頓大餐，以慶祝自己的英文社交技巧有了顯著的進步！希望各位會覺得「文化小叮嚀」既有趣又實用。結束之前，回頭看看本章的「學習目標」，你達成了多少？

Unit6

擴展人脈 2：

宴會

引言與學習目標

　　宴會大概是擴展人脈的最佳場合。你可以認識很多人、介紹別人彼此認識，幫助他們建立新的人脈。不管你是要出國洽談或開會，還是要參加婚禮或退休慶祝儀式，勢必都有機會在宴會上交際。只要有機會，就應該善加利用，不要害羞。和外國人交際的場合大部分都跟酒脫不了關係。酒可以讓人放鬆、變得健談，有助於建立人際關係。只要宴會上有外國人，酒就是不可或缺的要素。在上一章，各位已經對酒有些許了解，本章會讓各位認識宴會中的其他幾種常見的酒品。

　　許多人把參加宴會視為畏途，因為他們會遇到很多不認識的人，而他們的語言和社交技巧又有限。希望讀完本章後，各位會更有自信地去參加宴會。

　　本章結束時，各位應達成的「學習目標」如下：

❏ 自我介紹。
❏ 介紹別人彼此認識。
❏ 改變話題與中止話題。
❏ 閒聊並形容別人。
❏ 更了解外國人對酒的看法。
❏ 更了解不同宴會類型的適當穿著。
❏ 做完聽力練習。
❏ 做完發音練習。

介紹

　　我們從「介紹」開始。首先，我們得自我介紹，然後也可能得將你的談話對象介紹給別人。聆聽在這個階段也是個重要的部分，所以先來練習一下聽力吧。

Task 6.1

 CD 1-40

請聽 Track 6.1，根據對話的內容完成下表。

Conversation 1			
	Name	**Job**	**Reason for Attending Party**
Speaker 1			
Speaker 2			

Conversation 2			
	Name	**Job**	**Reason for Attending Party**
Speaker 1			
Speaker 2			

答　案

請以下表核對答案。

Conversation 1			
	Name	**Job**	**Reason for Attending Party**
Speaker 1	Paul	Finance	Conference
Speaker 2	Jane	Works for Accountancy Firm T&D	Not Known

Conversation 2			
	Name	**Job**	**Reason for Attending Party**
Speaker 1	Michael	Not Known	Invited by George
Speaker 2	Shirley	Regional Marketing Manager for IT Company	On Business, Invited to Party by Judy

Task 6.2　　　　　　　　　　　　　　　　　CD 1-40

再聽一次 Track 6.1，這次把說話者用來自我介紹的用語寫下來。

答　案

稍後會讓各位看到這二段對話的內容。目前我希望各位能聽出來，說話者是先自我介紹，提供一些個人的基本資料：在哪裏任職、從哪裏來。

　　在上面的兩段對話中，兩個說話者向對方自我介紹。接下來的對話中，說話者要向他人介紹自己的夥伴。

Task 6.3　　　　　　　　　　　　　　　　　CD 1-41

請聽 Track 6.2，這兩段對話有何相似之處？

答　案

兩段對話中都有一位說話者介紹其他二人彼此認識。在對話 1 中，Paul 把 Jane 介紹給 Alice；在對話 2 中，Michael 把 Shirley 介紹給 Gina。這兩段對話的介紹模式相同。接著來看對話 1 的介紹模式：

1. Paul 先向 Alice 介紹 Jane，因為他已經在和 Jane 談話，而 Alice 則是後來才加入。**一定要先向後來的人介紹原本的談話對象，原則上順序不要顛倒。**
2. 接著 Paul 簡單地介紹雙方的背景，包括在哪裡工作以及做什麼等等。雖然簡短，但還是很重要，因為它可使雙方有個話頭可以開始，進而延伸出新的話題。
3. 接著 Jane 和 Alice 彼此自我介紹。
4. 接著 Paul 告訴後來的 Alice 剛才他跟 Jane 在討論些什麼，這可使後來的人進入狀況並加入談話。接著這三個說話者便可決定他們要延續這個話題，還是要開啟新話題。從對話中可以發現，Alice 想要開啟新話題。

各位應該多聽幾次，確定自己可以聽出這個模式。

Task 6.4　　　　　　　　　　　　　　◎))) CD 1-41

再聽一次 Track 6.2 ，看看是否能聽出對話 2 的介紹模式。

● 答　案

1. Michael 先問 Gina 是否見過 Shirley 。接著便把 Shirley 介紹給 Gina 。

2. 接著 Michael 介紹了雙方的背景。要注意的是，他只概略地介紹 Shirley ，這大概是因為他忘了 Shirley 是做什麼的。（別忘了，他們也是剛認識）

3. 接著 Gina 和 Shirley 彼此自我介紹。

4. 接著 Michael 告訴 Gina 剛才他跟 Shirley 在聊什麼。

不必擔心自己不是每個字都聽得懂，稍後各位還有機會詳讀對話內容。希望各位在研讀第二章的 set-phrases 時有注意到談話中的轉折。現在是回頭溫習第二章和第三章的好時機。

接著來練習本章至目前為止所接觸到的用語。

Task 6.5

把下列的用語分門別類，填入其後的表格中。

1. I run my own ...

2. I work in ...

3. I work for ...

4. How do you do?

5. Hello. _____

6. Hello. I'm _____.

7. Hello, my name's _____.

8. (S)he's in ...

9. (S)he's based in ...

10. (S)he works in ...

11. (S)he works for ...

12. Pleased to meet you.

13. _____, I'd like to introduce you to _____.

14. Nice to meet you.

15. Have you met _____?

16. Do you know _____?

17. (S)he has his/her own ...

18. It's a pleasure to meet you, too.

19. _____, _____.

20. _____, this is _____.

21. _____, let me introduce you to _____.

22. _____, I want you to meet _____.

23. _____, have you met _____?

24. _____, do you know _____?

25. Pleased to meet you, too.

26. It's a pleasure.

27. It's a pleasure to meet you.

28. I'm _____, by the way.

29. I'm in ...

30. I'm based in ...

31. Nice to meet you, too.

32. Have you two met?

33. Do you two know each other?

34. I have my own ...

35. (S)he runs his/her own ...

Introducing Yourself

Introducing Someone Else

Giving Basic Information

答　案

請以下列的語庫核對答案，並研讀語庫小叮嚀。

社交必備語庫 6.1　　　　　　　　　　　　　　　　⊚))))) CD 1-42

自我介紹 Introducing Yourself
• Hello. _____   • Hello. I'm _____.   • Hello, my name's _____.   • I'm _____, by the way.   • Pleased to meet you.   • Pleased to meet you, too.   • It's a pleasure.   • It's a pleasure to meet you.   • It's a pleasure to meet you, too.   • How do you do?   • Nice to meet you.   • Nice to meet you, too.

介紹他人 Introducing Someone Else

- _____, I'd like to introduce you to _____.
- _____, let me introduce you to _____.
- _____, I want you to meet _____.
- _____, have you met _____?
- _____, do you know _____?
- _____, this is _____.
- _____, _____.
- Have you met _____?
- Have you two met?
- Do you know _____?
- Do you two know each other?

提供基本資訊 Giving Basic Information

- (S)he's in ...
- (S)he works in ...
- (S)he works for ...
- (S)he's based in ...
- (S)he works out of ...
- (S)he has his/her own ...
- (S)he runs his/her own ...
- I'm in ...
- I work in ...
- I work for ...
- I'm based in ...
- I work out of ...
- I have my own ...
- I run my own ...

★ 📁 語庫小叮嚀

Introducing Yourself

- _____ 指的是「人名」。
- 當你已經展開談話，後來才想起忘了自我介紹時，就可以說 I'm X by the way.。
- Nice to meet you./Nice to meet you too.； Pleased to meet you./Pleased to meet you too.注意，這些話是成對出現，當說話者 A 說第一句時，說話者 B 就要說第二句。這些 set-phrases 適用於任何一種介紹，無論是正式還是非正式。

180

Introducing Someone Else

- 注意，這些 set-phrases 都是先提到已經在交談的人，再提到後來的人。
- 語庫中的 set-phrases 是按照正式的程度來排列，由最正式的：_____, I'd like to introduce you to _____.；排列至最不正式的：_____, _____.（只有介紹雙方的姓名）。
- 當你想確定他們彼此是否已經見過面時，可以說：Have you met _____?/Have you two met?/Do you know _____?/Do you two know each other?。

Giving Basic Information

- (S)he's in ... /(S)he works in ... /I'm in ... /I work in ...，這些用語後面接的是「產業」、「行業」或「公司部門」。
- (S)he works for ... / I work for ...，後面接「公司名稱」。
- (S)he's based in ... /(S)he works out of ... /I'm based in ... /I work out of ...，後面接「辦公室所在城市的名稱」。
- (S)he has his/her own ... /I have my own ...，假如你是企業家的話，後面就接你所擁有的「公司類型」。

接著來看些和啤酒有關的知識吧。

 文化小叮嚀

- 葡萄酒的原料是葡萄，啤酒的原料則是穀物，通常是大麥。啤酒有兩種：下發酵啤酒（lager）和上發酵啤酒（ale）。
- Lager 的顏色和味道比較淡、泡沫比較多。大部分的大品牌啤酒都是 lager。
- Ale 的顏色比較深黃，而且味道比較重。
- 幾乎所有的外國人都覺得溫啤酒很難喝。啤酒一定要冷藏飲用，但絕對不能加冰塊。

 Task 6.6　　　　　　　　　　　　　　　　　　　　　　　CD 1-42

請聽 Track 6.3，練習語庫 6.1 中用語的發音。

答案

練習時仔細地聽連音的部分，能模仿得愈像愈好。各位應該要一直練習直到能運用自如為止。

接著把本章到目前為止的對話全部再聽一遍，並注意 set-phrases 在談話中的用法。

 Task 6.7   ◉))) CD 1-40 & 1-41

再聽一次 Track 6.1 和 6 2，在語庫 6.1 中勾選出你所聽到的 set-phrases。

 答 案

下列為對話的文字內容，其中所應用的 set-phrases 以粗體標示。

◉))) **Track 6.1**

Conversation 1

Paul: Hi. You enjoying the party?

Jane: Yes, actually. I don't really know anyone, but it's a nice place. Are you having a good time?

Paul: Yes. The drinks are very good! **I'm Paul, by the way.**

Jane: **Hello Paul. I'm Jane.** So what do you do?

Paul: **I'm in** finance. You?

Jane: Really? Me, too. **I work for** an accountancy company, T&D. Maybe you've heard of them.

Paul: T&D? Oh, yes, sure. How long have you worked there?

Jane: About two years. And you? **Are you based** here?

Paul: No. Actually, **I'm based in** Shanghai. I'm just here for the conference. So, T&D eh ...

Conversation 2

Shirley: Have we met?

Michael: I don't think so. Michael.

Shirley: **Hello, Michael. My name's Shirley. Pleased to meet you.**

Michael: **Pleased to meet you, too,** Shirley. So, what do you do?

Shirley: **I work in** marketing. I'm a regional marketing manager for an IT company. Normally, **I work out of Beijing,** but I'm here on business. My friend Judy over there, she lives here and she invited me to this party. And you? How about you?

Michael: I live here. **I was invited by** George — he's the tall guy over there. He looks a bit drunk, actually ...

 中 譯

對話 1

Paul ： 嗨，妳還喜歡這場宴會嗎？

Jane ： 嗯，很喜歡。我一個人都不認識，可是這個地方真不錯。你玩得開心嗎？

Paul ： 是啊，酒很好喝！對了，我是 Paul 。

Jane ： 哈囉，Paul ，我是 Jane 。你是做哪一行的？

Paul ： 金融業。妳呢？

Jane ： 真的嗎？我也是。我在 T&D 會計事務所服務，也許你有聽過。

Paul ： T&D ？喔，當然有。妳在那裡服務多久了？

Jane ： 兩年左右。你呢？你是在這裡工作嗎？

Paul ： 不是，其實我是在上海工作，我只是來這裡開會而已。所以， T&D ，呃……

對話 2

Shirley ： 我們見過嗎？

Michael ： 我想沒有。我叫 Michael 。

Shirley ： 哈囉，Michael 。我叫 Shirley ，很高興認識你。

Michael ： 我也是， Shirley 。妳是做哪一行的？

Shirley ： 我是做行銷的。我是一家 IT 公司的地區行銷經理。我通常在北京工作，來這裡是為了公事。我朋友 Judy 在那邊，她住在這裡，所以就邀我來參加這場宴會。你呢？你怎麼會來這裡？

Michael ： 我住在這裡，是 George 邀請我來的，就是那邊那個高個子。他看起來真的有點醉了……

 **Track 6.2**

Conversation 1

Paul: ... so it's a potentially difficult situation.

Alice: Hello, everyone.

Paul: Well, hi, Alice.

Alice: Aren't you going to introduce me, Paul?

Paul: Oh, of course. Jane, **I'd like you to meet** Alice. Alice **has her own** fashion design company here in town, and Jane **works for** T&D.

Alice: T&D, huh? Nice work. **It's a pleasure,** Jane.

Jane: **Pleased to meet you too,** Alice.

Paul: We were just discussing the new business regulations, and Jane reckons they're going to impact small businesses worst.

Alice: I never talk business after ten o'clock, Paul, as you know ...

Conversation 2

Michael: ... Well, I agree. Look, here's Gina — let's ask her about it. Hi, Gina.

Gina: Hello.

Michael: Gina, **have you met** Shirley? **Shirley, meet Gina.** Gina **has her own IT company,** and Shirley here **is** normally **based in** Beijing but is enjoying this fabulous party!

Shirley: Hello, Gina. **I'm Shirley.**

Gina: Hi, Shirley. **Nice to meet you.**

Michael: We were just talking about Judy and how she knows so many people.

Gina: Oh, yeah. She knows just about everybody. She's a great net-worker.

Shirley: So how did you meet her, Gina?

Gina: Well, I used to date her brother. Then her brother married someone else ...

中　譯

對話 1

Paul　：……所以這可能會是個麻煩的情況。

Alice：哈囉，各位。

Paul　：喔，嗨，Alice。

Alice：Paul，你不幫我介紹一下嗎？

Paul　：喔，當然要。Jane，來見見 Alice。Alice 在這裏開了一家時裝設計公司，Jane 則是在 T&D 服務。

Alice：T&D 嗎？好工作。很高興認識妳，Jane。

Jane　：Alice，很高興認識妳。

Paul　：我們剛才在討論新的商業規定，Jane 認爲它們對小企業的影響最大。

Alice：我從來不在十點過後談生意的。Paul，你知道……

對話 2

Michael：……哦，我同意。妳看，Gina 來了，我們來問問她。嗨，Gina。

Gina　：哈囉。

Michael：Gina，妳見過了 Shirley 嗎？Shirley，來認識 Gina。Gina 開了一家 IT 公司，而 Shirley 通常是在北京工作，但她現在正在享受這個很棒的宴會！

Shirley：哈囉，Gina，我是 Shirley。

Gina　：嗨，Shirley，很高興認識妳。

Michael：我們剛才在談 Judy，以及她怎麼會認識這麼多人。

Gina　：哦，對啊，她幾乎每個人都認識。她的人面很廣。

Shirley：所以妳是怎麼認識她的，Gina？

Gina　：哦，我和她哥哥交往過，後來她哥哥和別人結婚了……

好了，接著來練習這些用語吧。

Task 6.8

請由語庫 6.1 的 set-phrases 中，選出適當者填入下列空格。

Conversation 1

George: Is there any more vodka in that bottle?

Irene: Uhm. I think there's enough for one more, yes.

George: Marvelous. Pass it over. _____.

Irene: _____.

George: So Irene, what do you do?

Irene: _____. I _____ Macrohard.

George: Macrohard, eh?

Irene: What do you do?

George: _____ company designing computer programs.

Conversation 2

Donald: So it's all very complicated.

Judy: Sounds terrible. Oh, look — here comes Shirley.

Shirley: Hello.

Judy: Shirley, _____ Donald?

Shirley: No, not yet.

Judy: Donald, _____ Shirley. Shirley _____ market-ing, and Donald _____ import/export company.

Shirley: _____, Donald.

Donald: _____, Shirley.

Judy: We were just talking about George. I think he's had too much to drink. He's been having a hard time recently, and he's been hitting the vodka rather too much.

● 答 案   ◎))) CD 1-43

▌ 請聽 Track 6.4，並核對下頁的答案。

Track 6.4

Conversation 1

George: Is there any more vodka in that bottle?

Irene: Uhm, I think there's enough for one more, yes.

George: Marvelous. Pass it over. **My name's George, by the way.**

Irene: **Nice to meet you,/Pleased to meet you,/It's a pleasure,/It's a pleasure to meet you,/Nice to meet you, George. I'm/My name's Irene.**

George: So Irene, what do you do?

Irene: **I'm in computing.** I **work for** Macrohard.

George: Macrohard, eh?

Irene: What do you do?

George: **I have my own/I run my own** company that designs computer systems.

Conversation 2

Donald: So it's all very complicated.

Judy: Sounds terrible. Oh, look — here comes Shirley.

Shirley: Hello.

Judy: Shirley, **have you met/do you know** Donald?

Shirley: No, not yet.

Judy: Donald, **I want you to meet/let me introduce you to/I want you to meet/this is/meet** Shirley. Shirley **is in** marketing, and Donald **runs his own/has his own** import/export company.

Shirley: **It's a pleasure,/It's a pleasure to meet you,/Nice to meet you,** Donald.

Donald: **Pleased to meet you too,/It's a pleasure to meet you too,/Nice to meet you too,** Shirley.

Judy: We were just talking about George. I think he's had too much to

drink. He's been having a hard time recently, and he's been hit-ting the vodka rather too much.

 中 譯

對話 1

George： 那個酒瓶裡還有沒有伏特加？

Irene： 呣，有，我想一個人喝應該還夠。

George： 太好了，把它拿過來吧。對了，我叫 George。

Irene： 很高興認識你，George。我是 Irene。

George： Irene，妳是做哪一行的？

Irene： 我是電腦業的，我在 Macrohard 服務。

George： Macrohard，是嗎？

Irene： 你是做哪一行的？

George： 我自己開公司設計電腦程式。

對話 2

Donald： 所以它真的很複雜。

Judy： 聽起來真麻煩。嘿，你看，Shirley 來了。

Shirley： 哈囉。

Judy： Shirley，妳見過 Donald 嗎？

Shirley： 沒有，還沒見過。

Judy： Donald，我跟你引見一下 Shirley。Shirley 是做行銷的，Donald 則是自己開進出口公司。

Shirley： 很高興認識你，Donald。

Donald： 我也是，Shirley。

Judy： 我們剛才在聊 George。我想他喝得太多了。他最近過得不太好，所以他喝了一大堆伏特加。

語感甦活區

在 Track 6.2 中，應用了兩個 set-phrases ：一個是 *We were just discussing the* new business regulations. ，一個是 *We were just talking about* George.。當你介紹他人彼此認識後，就可以用這兩個 set-phrases 繼續談話。這類 set-phrases 有好幾種變化，請做下面的練習。

Task 6.9

研讀下列的表格，並練習造句。

We were just	• talking about n.p. • discussing n.p. • discussing whether + clause ... • wondering + 'wh-' clause ... • saying + 'wh-' clause ...
I was just	• telling ____ about n.p. • filling ____ in on n.p. • about to come and get you. • saying + 'wh-' clause • about to leave. • about to get another drink. • talking about n.p.

● 答　案

可能的例句如下：

• We were just wondering whether the merger will go ahead.
• I was just filling Judy in on the situation with T&D.
• I was just about to get another drink.
• We were just saying what a wonderful party this is.

| W o r d　L i s t |
fill in 告知某人詳細的情況

接著來看一些關於宴會穿著的小叮嚀吧。

 文化小叮嚀

宴會的正式程度經常是根據它的衣著規定來評斷。邀請函上通常會註明得體的衣著規定。
以下是各位在職場生涯中常見的衣著規定：

- **極正式（參與正式的活動）**：男生應該穿晚禮服或黑色西裝、正式的白襯衫，以及黑色的蝶形領結。女生應該穿高跟鞋加短禮服或亮絲質套裝，並且要吹整頭髮。
- **正式（日常上班服）**：男生應該穿夾克或深色西裝、深色領帶，以及白色或藍色襯衫。女生應該穿套裝加高跟鞋。
- **上班便服（適合輕鬆的星期五）**：男生可以穿淡顏色的長褲，以及扣領衫或是沒有領子的 polo 衫。女生可以穿長褲、短上衣和平底鞋。牛仔褲不宜當作上班便服來穿。
- **非正式**：喜歡什麼就穿什麼，只要整齊乾淨就好！

閒聊

　　本節要教各位如何閒聊。雖然閒聊是取得資訊以及擴展人脈的好方法，但注意：不要流於八卦。好的閒聊者知道如何讓別人多說一點，而且絕對不會太多嘴！本節也需要做些聽力練習，先練習聽，之後再看文字內容喔。

Task 6.10　　　　　　　　　　　　　　　　　　　　　　CD 1-44

請聽 Track 6.5，針對這兩段對話回答下列問題。

1. 他們在聊誰？
2. 他們談了關於他的什麼事？

● 答　案

在 Conversation 1 中，他們在聊 George，以及他跟公司之間的問題；在 Conversation 2 中，他們在聊 Alice，以及和她前任老闆有關的性醜聞。多聽幾次，直到可以聽懂為止。

　　現在來學些閒聊時可以使用的用語。我們要看的 set-phrases 有兩組。第一組是用來讓對方明白你所說的話不代表自己的意見，你只是在「轉述」（passing on）從別人那裡聽來的消息。第二組是用來告知對方你不希望別人知道這段談話的內容，希望他「保密」（keep it secret）。

Task 6.11

將下列這些用語分門別類，填入其後的表格中。

1. According to sb. , ...
2. According to the grapevine, ...

| Word List |

grapevine [ˋgrep͵vaɪn] *n.* 八卦消息管道

3. Aren't they supposed to be Ving

4. Aren't you supposed to be Ving

5. Don't tell anyone, but + clause ...

6. From what I hear, clause ...

7. From what I heard, clause ...

8. Haven't you heard?

9. I don't want this to get out.

10. I hear that + clause ...

11. I hear you're thinking of Ving

12. I heard on the grapevine that + clause ...

13. I heard that + clause ...

14. I read somewhere that + clause ...

15. I thought everyone knew.

16. I thought it was common knowledge.

17. I understand + n. clause ...

18. I won't mention any names, but ...

19. If word gets out that + clause ...

20. It appears that + clause ...

21. It seems that + clause ...

22. It sounds as if + clause ...

23. It's all a big secret.

24. Just between ourselves, ...

25. Just between us, ...

26. Off the record, ...

27. Rumor has it that + clause ...

28. Someone told me + clause ...

29. I'm not one to gossip, but ...

30. They say + n. clause ...

31. This is just between ourselves, of course.

32. This is just between you and me, of course.

33. This is not to go any further, of course.

34. This is not to go outside this room.

35. Well, apparently, ...

36. You didn't hear this from me.

Passing It On
Keeping It Secret

 答　案

請以下列語庫核對答案，並研讀語庫小叮嚀。

社交必備語庫 6.2 CD 1-45

轉述 Passing It On
• According to sb. , ...
• According to the grapevine, ...
• Aren't they supposed to be Ving
• Aren't you supposed to be Ving
• From what I hear, clause ...
• From what I heard, clause ...
• Haven't you heard?
• I hear that + clause ...
• I hear you're thinking of Ving
• I heard it from the grapevine that + clause ...

- I heard that + clause ...
- I read somewhere that + clause ...
- I thought everyone knew.
- I thought it was common knowledge.
- I understand + n. clause ...
- I'm not one to gossip, but ...
- It appears that + clause ...
- It seems that + clause ...
- It sounds as if + n. clause ...
- Rumor has it that + clause ...
- Someone told me + clause ...
- They say + n. clause ...

保密 Keeping It Secret

- Don't tell anyone, but + clause ...
- I don't want this to get out.
- I won't mention any names, but ...
- If word gets out that + clause ...
- It's all a big secret.
- Just between ourselves, ...
- Just between us, ...
- Off the record, ...
- This is just between ourselves, of course.
- This is just between you and me, of course.
- This is not to go any further, of course.
- This is not to go outside the room.
- Well, apparently, ...
- You didn't hear this from me.

★ 📁 語庫小叮嚀

◆ 注意 Passing It On 中 set-phrases 的動詞是如何使用，hear、think、read、seem、appear、be supposed to、sound、say 和 tell。這些動詞都是在說明：你所說的話不代表你的意見，只是轉述其他來源的訊息。

◆ Grapevine 指的是一種「傳播謠言的管道」。

Task 6.12

CD 1-45

請聽 Track 6.6，練習語庫 6.2 中用語的發音。

● 答 案

練習這些 set-phrases 時，應該模仿 CD 中的語調。你必須聽起來像是低聲細語，而不是大聲嚷嚷使得整間屋子的人都聽得到你的談話！

Task 6.13

CD 1-44

再聽一次 Track 6.5，從語庫 6.2 中勾選出你所聽到的 set-phrases。

● 答 案

對話中所應用的 set-phrases 如下。此處暫時先不提供對話的完整內容。假如你沒有聽到這些 set-phrases，那就多聽幾次，直到你可以聽出來為止。

Conversation 1
- From what I hear, ...
- Off the record, ...
- I hear that + clause ...

Conversation 2
- I'm not one to gossip, but ...
- Rumor has it that + clause ...
- This is just between ourselves, of course.

接著來看一些關於酒的介紹。

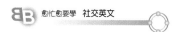
 文化小叮嚀

- 小心，酒很容易讓人失去理性，你可能在酒後說出悔不當初的話。有一句古老的拉丁諺語：*in vino veritas*，它的意思是「酒後吐真言」。在社交場合，說實話不一定是好事，所以還是小心點好！
- 除了葡萄酒和啤酒，酒精類飲料還可分為兩種：烈酒（spirits）和香甜酒（liqueurs）。
- 香甜酒是由草藥、香料、水果和核果所釀成的甜酒。其中有許多都有數百年之久，而且是由僧侶所發明。最著名的香甜酒包括由橘子釀成的 Cointreau、在 1510 年首次推出的 Benedictine，以及有 130 種不同成分的 Chartreuse。還有很多新的香甜酒則是加了一些味道，像是咖啡、巧克力或奶油。香甜酒可以當作飯後酒，也可以當作餐前酒，或是用來調製雞尾酒。
- 六種最常見的烈酒包括 gin、vodka、whisky、brandy、rum 和 tequila。
- Gin 和 vodka 是透明的烈酒。Gin 來自英格蘭，原料是杜松子；Vodka 來自俄羅斯，是最純的烈酒。Whiskey 的原料是麥芽，味道很重。Brandy 是由蒸餾過的葡萄酒所製成，15 年以上的最容易讓人喝醉。Rum 來自加勒比海，原料是糖，是海盜的傳統飲料！Tequila 來自墨西哥，原料是 blue agave（一種仙人掌）。

轉換或中止話題

現在來學習如何在談話中「轉換話題」（change the topic），以及要如何「中止談話」（break off a conversation）。

Task 6.14　　　　　　　　　　　　　　　　　　　　　CD 1-44

再聽一次 Track 6.5，針對對話內容回答下列問題。

1. 開啓的新話題是什麼？
2. 談話是如何結束？

答　案

Conversation 1：Susan 開啓的新話題是她的新筆記型電腦。Mary 並不想談筆記型電腦，於是藉故再去喝一杯。

Conversation 2：Karen 提及 Henry 和秘書的事。這使得 Henry 很不自在，於是藉故去打電話。

如果沒有完全聽懂，就多聽幾遍吧。

Task 6.15

將下列這些用語分門別類，填入其後的表格。

1. Can I just change the subject before I forget?
2. Could you excuse me a moment?
3. Good talking to you.
4. I have to be off.
5. I have to make a phone call.
6. I must just go and say hello to someone.
7. I need another drink.
8. I need to get some fresh air.
9. I want a cigarette.
10. I'll be back in a sec.

11. I'll be right back.

12. I'll catch you later.

13. I'm just going to the bar/the buffet.

14. If you'll excuse me a moment.

15. It's been nice talking to you.

16. It's getting late.

17. Oh, before I forget, ...

18. Oh, by the way, ...

19. Oh, I meant to tell you earlier.

20. Oh, incidentally, ...

21. Oh, that reminds me.

22. Oh, while we're on the subject, ...

23. Oh, you reminded me of something.

24. On the subject of n.p. ...

25. Talking of n.p. ...

26. That reminds me of n.p. ...

27. There's someone I want to/need to talk to.

28. Would you excuse me a moment?

Changing the Topic

Breaking off the Conversation

 答　案

以下頁的語庫核對答案，並研讀語庫小叮嚀。

社交必備語庫 6.3

 CD 1-46

轉換話題 Changing the Topic

- Can I just change the subject before I forget?
- Oh, by the way, ...
- Oh, before I forget, ...
- Oh, I meant to tell you earlier.
- Oh, incidentally, ...
- Oh, that reminds me.
- Oh, while we're on the subject, ...
- Oh, you reminded me of something.
- That reminds me of n.p. ...
- On the subject of n.p. ...
- Talking of n.p. ...

中止談話 Breaking off the Conversation

- Could you excuse me a moment?
- Good talking to you.
- I have to be off.
- I have to make a phone call.
- I must just go and say hello to someone.
- I need another drink.
- I need to get some fresh air.
- I want a cigarette.
- I'll be back in a sec.
- I'll be right back.
- I'll catch you later.
- I'm just going to the bar/the buffet.
- If you'll excuse me a moment.
- It's been nice talking to you.
- It's getting late.
- There's someone I want to/need to talk to.
- Would you excuse me a moment?

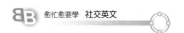

★ 📁 語庫小叮嚀

Changing the Topic

◆ 注意，許多 set-phrases 是以 Oh 為開頭，目的是在喚起對方的注意：你有個想法要告訴對方。

Breaking off the Conversation

◆ 當你覺得無聊、想找別人說話，或是話題或對方讓你覺得不自在，可以用這些 set-phrases 來中止談話。其實，這些 set-phrases 大部分只是藉口。

◆ I'll be back in a sec.（Sec 是 second 的縮寫。）

◆ I have to be off. 是「我必須離席」之意。

▌Task 6.16　　　　　　　　　　　　　　　　◉)))） CD 1-46

請聽 Track 6.7，練習語庫 6.3 中用語的發音。

◉ 答　案

▌ 練習時注意連音和語調的掌握。各位要多練習幾遍，直到能運用自如為止。

▌Task 6.17　　　　　　　　　　　　　　　　◉)))） CD 1-44

再聽一次 Track 6.5，在語庫 6.3 中勾選出你所聽到的 set-phrases。

◉ 答　案

對話中所應用的 set-phrases 如下所示。此處暫不提供對話內容。如果你沒有聽出這些 set-phrases，就多聽幾次。

Conversation 1

- Oh, that reminds me.
- I need another drink.
- I'll be back in a sec.

Conversation 2

- Oh, while we're on the subject, clause ...
- Could you excuse me a moment?
- I have to make a phone call.

好了，現在來練習一下這些用語吧。

| Task 6.18

請看下列的對話，由語庫 6.2 和 6.3 找出適當的 set-phrase 填入下列空格。

Alice:　Who's that man over there talking to James?

Judy:　Where? Oh, that's Henry.

Alice:　He's very handsome, isn't he? What's he like?

Judy:　He's very nice, actually, but rather eccentric.

Alice:　Really? I love eccentric people.

Judy:　Yes, but he may be too eccentric even for you.

Alice:　Why? What do you mean by that?

Judy:　Well, haven't you heard?

Alice:　Heard what? No one ever tells me anything.

Judy:　_____, he's been having an affair with his secretary.

Alice:　Really! How fascinating.

Judy:　_____ Mary, he's divorcing his wife and there's a big fight going on about the children. _____

Alice:　Well, what can I say? I didn't know. _____, your blouse doesn't really match your skirt. Those colors don't really suit you either.

Judy:　Oh. Thanks. Look, _____.

● 答　案　　　　　　　　　　　　　　　　　　　　　(o)))) CD 1-47

請聽 Track 6.8，答案當然不只 CD 中所提供的版本，語庫中提供的用語都是可以應用到對話中的。接著以下列的 CD 內容核對答案。

Track 6.8

Alice: Who's that man over there talking to James?

Judy: Where? Oh, that's Henry.

Alice: He's very handsome, isn't he? What's he like?

Judy: He's very nice, actually, but rather eccentric.

Alice: Really? I love eccentric people.

Judy: Yes, but he may be too eccentric even for you.

Alice: Why? What do you mean by that?

Judy: Well, haven't you heard?

Alice: Heard what? No one ever tells me anything.

Judy: **Well, apparently**, he's been having an affair with his secretary.

Alice: Really! How fascinating.

Judy: **According to** Mary, he's divorcing his wife and there's a big fight going on about the children. **I thought everyone knew.**

Alice: Well, what can I say? I didn't know. **Oh, I meant to tell you earlier,** your blouse doesn't really match your skirt. Those colors don't really suit you either.

Judy: Oh. Thanks. Look, **I must just go and say hello to someone. I'll be right back.**

中 譯

Alice：在那邊跟 James 講話的男士是誰？

Judy：在哪兒？噢，那是 Henry。

Alice：他真帥，對吧？他為人怎麼樣？

Judy：說真的，他人很好，可是很古怪。

Alice：是嗎，我喜歡古怪的人。

Judy：是啊，可是連妳都可能會覺得他太古怪了。

Alice：為什麼？妳這話是什麼意思？

Judy：哦，妳沒有聽說過嗎？

Alice：聽說什麼？從來沒人跟我說過什麼。

Judy：哦，他好像跟他的秘書有過一腿。

Alice：哇塞！太精彩了。

Judy　：Mary 說他正在和太太鬧離婚，而且為了小孩的事吵得很兇。我以為大家都知道。

Alice：哦，說真的，我不知道。對了，我剛才就想告訴妳，妳的衣服跟妳的裙子不太配。這些顏色也不太適合妳。

Judy　：哦，謝謝。對了，我得去跟別人打個招呼，等下就回來。

　　現在不妨回頭溫習一下本章的所有對話，加強各位在本章學到的用語。

Task 6.19

看看下列 Track 6.5 的對話內容，練習找出到目前為止所學過的用語。

Track 6.5

Conversation 1

Mary: Who's that tall guy over there?

Susan: Oh, that's George. He looks very drunk.

Mary: What's he like normally?

Susan: Oh, he's really reserved, normally. But, from what I hear, he's got lots of problems?

Mary: Really? What kind of problems?

Susan: Well, off the record, of course, but I hear that he's got terrible debts. He has his own company, and it's not going very well.

Mary: Really? Well, I hate to say this, but I'm not surprised.

Susan: Really? What makes you say that?

Mary: Well, he doesn't look very honest.

Susan: I know, that's the problem. He can't find any customers. It's a pity, really, because his products are very good. Oh, that reminds me. Did I tell you about my new laptop?

Mary: Oh, don't talk to me about laptops. Mine crashed on Friday and I lost everything. I hate them.

Susan: Oh, really?

Mary: Look, I need another drink. Do you want one?

Susan: Yes, I'll have another cocktail.

Mary: Vodka martini?

Susan: Absolutely.

Mary: I'll be back in a sec.

Susan: OK. I'll wait for you here.

Conversation 2

Henry: Who's that striking woman over there?

Karen: Hm? Oh, that's Alice. She's totally mad. Don't get yourself in a room alone with her.

Henry: Really? Why not? She looks great.

Karen: Yes, I know, but she's dangerous.

Henry: Really? Tell me more.

Karen: Well, I'm not one to gossip, as you know, but rumor has it that she sued her former boss for sexual harassment.

Henry: Wow, crikey. So what happened?

Karen: Well, this is just between ourselves, of course, but he was her lover and he wanted to leave her, so she got revenge. I heard him say she was a dangerous woman.

Henry: Wow.

Karen: Oh, while we're on the subject, what happened to you and your secretary?

Henry: I have no idea what you're talking about.

Karen: Oh, come on. Everybody knows.

Henry: Could you excuse me a moment? I have to make a phone call.

Karen: Oh, sure.

中 譯

對話 1

Mary　：那邊那個高個子是誰？

Susan　：哦，那是 George。他看起來醉得很厲害。

Mary　：他平常為人怎麼樣？

Susan　：哦，他平常很拘謹。可是據我所知，他似乎有很多問題。

Mary　：是嗎？什麼樣的問題？

Susan　：哦，別告訴別人，我聽說他負債累累。他自己開公司，但經營得不太好。

Mary　：真的嗎？我很不想這麼說，不過我並不覺得意外。

Susan　：中是嗎，妳為什麼會這麼說？

Mary　：呃……他似乎不太老實。

Susan　：我知道，問題就出在這裡。他根本找不到客戶。這真的很可惜，因為他的產品很好。對了，我突然想到，我有沒有跟妳提過我的新筆記型電腦？

Mary　：拜託，別跟我提到筆記型電腦。我的筆記型電腦星期五掛了，資料全都不見。氣死我了。

Susan　：哦，是嗎？

Mary　：對了，我要再喝一杯。妳要嗎？

Susan　：好，我還要一杯雞尾酒。

Mary　：伏特加馬丁尼是嗎？

Susan　：沒錯。

Mary　：我等下就回來。

Susan　：好，我在這裡等妳。

對話 2

Henry　：那邊那個大美女是誰？

Karen　：嘎？哦，那是 Alice。她根本是個瘋子，千萬不要跟她獨處一室。

Henry　：是嗎，為什麼？她看起來很不錯啊。

Karen　：是啊，我知道，可是她很危險。

Henry　：是嗎，再說多一點。

Karen　：哦，你也知道我不愛說長道短，不過有傳聞說，她告她的前任老闆性騷擾。

Henry　：哇塞，結果呢？

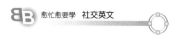
Karen：這個嘛，千萬不要說出去，他們兩個是一對，而他想要離開她，於是她就報
　　　　復。我聽他說，她是個危險的女人。

Henry：哇。

Karen：對了，既然我們聊到了這件事，你跟你的秘書怎麼樣了？

Henry：我不知道妳在說什麼。

Karen：你得了吧，大家都知道。

Henry：容我告辭一下好嗎？我得打個電話。

Karen：哦，當然好。

答　案

可以本章的各個語庫來核對答案，重點是學會如何將這些用語應用到你的談話當中。

接著來看些關於雞尾酒的介紹吧。

　文化小叮嚀

- 雞尾酒是 1920 年代在美國所發明。當時賣酒跟喝酒是違法的，所以酒必須偽裝成水果或蘇打飲料。
- 大部分的雞尾酒都包含三種不同的酒：基酒（gin、vodka、whisky、tequila、rum和 brandy）加上主調料（葡萄酒、苦艾酒、果汁、蛋或奶油）再加上特殊調料（香甜酒、有色香甜酒）。這些成分可以放在調酒器裡一起搖、用筷子攪拌混合，或是一層層仔細地堆疊起來。
- 裝雞尾酒的玻璃杯有很多不同的種類，而且雞尾酒的名稱往往既花俏又有想像力。好的調酒師要經過好幾個月的訓練，而且多半必須通過很嚴格的考試。

語感甦活區

在上一章學過了動詞 eat 和 have 的用法。在本章，我們要來學的動詞是 drink 。這個動詞通常都跟酒脫不了關係。

Task 6.20

將下列的 set-phrases 分門別類，填入下表。

1. Drink?
2. Can I get you a drink of something?
3. Would you like a drink of something?
4. Would you like a drink?
5. Can I get you a drink?
6. Would you like something to drink?
7. Would anyone like another drink?
8. I'd like a nice stiff drink.
9. I need a drink.
10. Can you get me a/another drink?

Offering to Get a Drink	Asking for a Drink

| Word List |

stiff [stɪf] *adj.* 烈的；多酒精的

答案

以下列的語庫來核對答案。要注意的是，這些 set-phrases 都是關於酒類。如果你想喝茶或咖啡，就要把 drink 這個字改成 cup of tea 或 coffee，例： Would you like a coffee?、 Would anyone like another cup of tea?

社交必備語庫 6.4

CD 1-48

詢問是否需要飲料 Offering to Get a Drink	要求飲料 Asking for a Drink
• Drink? • Can I get you a drink of something? • Would you like a drink of something? • Would you like a drink? • Can I get you a drink? • Would you like something to drink? • Would anyone like another drink?	• I'd like a nice stiff drink. • I need a drink. • Can you get me a/another drink?

Task 6.21

研讀下面的 word partnership 表格，並練習造句。

drink	• like a fish • up • and drive • in moderation • sensibly • too much • moderately

答案

可能的句子如下：

• My boss drinks like a fish.

• My doctor told me to only drink in moderation.

• I have a rule never to drink and drive.

注意：drink like a fish 是指「經常喝很多酒的人」。

drink up 是指「喝完」。

drink in moderation/drink sensibly/drink moderately 是指「偶爾喝酒而且只喝少量」。

在 Track 6.5 和 6.8 的對話中，有一些使用了 say、tell 和 talk 的 set-phrases。這些動詞的意思很相近，所以經常讓人搞不清楚。接著就來研究一下這些動詞吧。

Task 6.22

研讀下列三個表格。

Say	
• I was about to say ...	• 我要説的是……
• I was just going to say ...	• 我只是想説……
• I hate to say this, but ...	• 我很不想這麼説，不過……
• It's fair to say that + clause ...	• 憑良心説……
• I heard him say + clause ...	• 我聽他説……
• He was quoted as saying that + clause ...	• 有人引述他的話説……
• That was a nasty thing to say.	• 那麼説真是惡劣。
• And I said, ...	• 然後我説……
• So I said, ...	• 於是我説……
• What was I going to say? Oh, yes.	• 我是要説什麼？哦，對了。
• What can I say?	• 我能説什麼？

Tell	
• I'll tell you what.	• 我會告訴你怎麼回事。
• Did I tell you about n.p.?	• 我有沒有跟你提過……？
• Did I tell you what happened to n.p.?	• 我有沒有跟你説過……發生了什麼事？
• So I told him to V	• 於是我叫他……
• No one ever tells me anything.	• 根本沒人跟我提過任何事。
• Why didn't you tell me this?	• 你為什麼不跟我説？
• Tell me more.	• 多説一點。

Tell	
• What are you guys talking about?	• 你們幾個在聊什麼？
• Do you know what I'm talking about?	• 你知道我在說什麼嗎？
• I don't know what you are talking about.	• 我不知道你在說什麼。
• I have no idea what you're talking about.	• 我聽不懂你在說什麼。
• He talks a load of rubbish.	• 他講的都是一堆廢話。
• Don't talk to me about n.p.	• 別跟我提……
• We were just talking about you.	• 我們剛才在聊你。

　　在本章的對話中，各位也可以看到對於人的形容，如：Henry is rather eccentric.。下面的 Task 要教各位許多可以用來形容人的形容詞。

Task 6.23

研讀下列的 word partnership 表格，並練習造句。

What's (s)he like?		正面的形容詞	負面的形容詞
(S)he's	• rather • kind of • sort of • very • really • terribly • incredibly • totally	• hard-working • interesting • good to work with • easy to talk to • witty • reliable • eccentric • mad	• big-headed • obstinate • moody • bossy • absent-minded • reserved • arrogant • rude

| Word List |

big-headed [ˋbɪgˋhɛdɪd] *adj.* 自以為了不起
moody [ˋmudɪ] *adj.* 心情不穩定的；情緒壞的

obstinate [ˋɑbstənɪt] *adj.* 頑固的

答　案

可能的例句如下：

- He's totally mad.
- She's kind of moody.
- He's rather arrogant.

也可回頭看看 Track 6.5 和 6.8 的內容，練習找出這些 word partnerships 以加深印象。

　　好了，結束之前，請回到本章的「學習目標」看看你達成了多少。如果還有不清楚的地方，把相關章節再讀一遍。

　　祝赴宴愉快！

聊天的主題

社交必備本領 2
四個如何「談論話題」的必備本領

金言語錄

Great people talk about ideas, average people talk about things, and small people talk about wine.
　　　　　　　　　　　　　　　　　　　　　— *Fran Lebowitz*
偉人談想法，凡人談事情，小人談酒。
　　　　　　　　　　　　　　　　　—— 芙蘭‧雷伯維茲

人物檔案

芙蘭‧雷伯維茲是紐約的女作家，她以損人式的幽默以及如上一句式的點語而聞名。各位如果想多了解她一點，可以上網查些她所說過的話。如果各位能將它們加入你的談話中，會產生詼諧與風趣的效果。

　　詳讀以下四個「必備本領」，在研讀本書的第三部分時想想它們是如何運用。

四個如何「談論話題」的必備本領

如何：
1. 選一個你有把握談論的話題，或是讓對方選擇話題，然後積極參與談話
2. 不要害怕表達自己的意見
3. 記住外國名人的英文名字
4. 掌握自己的嗜好或興趣的相關字彙

1 選一個你有把握談論的話題，或是讓對方選擇話題，然後積極參與談話

🔑 假如你對於對方所談的話題一無所知，那就請他解釋給你聽，從基本項目開始談起。

🔑 不妨針對幾個話題準備相關字彙，並設法把談話引導到這些話題上。只要拿第二章所教的 topic starter questions 來發問，就可以做到這點。

🔑 你所選擇的話題應該取決於你對談話對象的熟悉度，以及他的文化背景。

🔑 安全又有趣的話題包括：運動、嗜好和興趣、下榻旅館、衣服、飲食、渡假計畫、共同的經驗。安全但可能乏味的話題包括：天氣、樂透、工作、手邊的案子、生涯規畫。

🔑 應避免的話題有：政治、性、宗教、健康。談論時應謹慎的話題有：家庭、雙方都認識的人、時事。

2 不要害怕表達自己的意見

🔑 西方人習慣於先表達自己的看法，然後再聽別人的意見。如果他們表達完自己的看法，你卻沒有表示意見，他們會覺得很奇怪。

🔑 外國人很樂於發表看法，即使不是針對自己專長的領域，所以當他們問你有什麼看法時，盡量不要說：「我不知道。」因為這樣會使談話無法進行。

🔑 假如你對於所討論的話題沒有意見，編也要編一個出來！

🔑 你的意見不一定得和對方一致，但如果你的意見完全對立，也不須表現出強硬的態度，只要適度地表示即可。

3 記住外國名人的英文名字

🔑 遺憾的是，你不能指望外國人記住中文名字。

🔑 要讓社交談話變得比較容易，很重要的一點在於：記住名人的英文名字。不管是歷史人物、新聞中的現代人物、運動員，還是名流。在你的談話中這些都可以派上用場。

🔑 盡量記住一些最近讀過的英文書名，即使你讀的是中譯本也一樣。

🔑 記住你喜歡或最近看過的電影的英文片名，以及片中主要演員的英文名字。

🔑 練習這些名字的發音，以便能把它們清楚、正確地唸出來。

4 掌握自己的嗜好或興趣的相關字彙

🔑 如果你有某項興趣，確定自己能夠談論它的細節。可以在浴室裡對著鏡子練習解說。你也可以找個同伴或是網路聊天室，練習或是觀察別人如何談論自己的興趣。

🔑 舉例來說，當對方的嗜好是收集與品嚐法國紅酒，你就可以告訴他，你一直想要了解法國紅酒，可是從來不知道該問誰。接著請他談些相關的基本訊息，並對他所說的話表現出興趣。

🔑 平時應該針對本身的嗜好或興趣吸取相關知識，這可以幫助你增進字彙，也讓你有話可聊。

🔑 如果你沒有嗜好或興趣，那就去找一個！

話題 1：電影

引言與學習目標

　　本章把重點擺在談論電影的字彙上。電影是個很有趣的話題，因為大部分的人都喜歡看電影，而且對於自己最喜歡的電影或演員都有一套看法。意見相同的感覺很好，而意見相左也無妨，因為這個話題並沒有那麼嚴肅。不過，還記得我在「社交必備本領」中提過，要記住演員和電影的英文名字嗎？這點很重要：如果你記不得英文名字，對方就不知道你談的是哪部電影，你也就無法參與這個有趣的話題。

　　在本章中，各位會學到很多關於電影的 word partnerships 和 chunks ，以及要如何靠閱讀來增加你的字彙量。

　　研讀完本章，各位應達成的「學習目標」如下：

❏ 能夠談論不同類型的電影。
❏ 能夠談論拍電影的人。
❏ 能夠表達對電影的好惡。
❏ 增加電影方面的字彙。

電影的種類

一開始先來想想你最喜歡的五部電影。

Task 7.1

寫下你最喜歡的五部電影的中文和英文片名。

	中文片名	英文片名
1		
2		
3		
4		
5		

● 答　案

本章結束前，我們會再回來看看這個 Task 。如果你不知道英文片名，可以上網查，或是問問朋友和同事。

Task 7.2

◉))) CD 2-01

請聽 Track 7.1 ， John 跟 Mary 在談論電影，根據對話回答下列問題。

1. 他們喜歡的是同一類電影嗎？
2. 他們所討論的電影叫什麼名字？
3. John 跟 Mary 談到了關於這部電影的什麼事？

● 答　案

　1. 不是。
　2. 談論的片名是 *The Business Godfather* （這不是一部真的電影）。
　3. John 跟 Mary 談到了這部電影在拍攝時所遇到的問題。
　稍後各位會看到對話的內容，如果聽不出答案，就多聽幾遍。

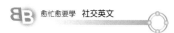
接著來學學 John 跟 Mary 在談話中所使用的用語，一開始先談談不同類型的電影。電影可以根據類型（genres）來分類，而且每種類型都有它的特徵。

Task 7.3

把下列的類型和下頁中的敘述配對。請見範例。

1. animated movie/cartoon

2. art movie

3. biopic

4. blue movie

5. cable movie

6. costume drama

7. documentary

8. epic

9. gangster movie

10. ghost movie

11. horror movie

12. kung fu movie

13. musical

14. prequel

15. road movie

16. romantic comedy

17. sequel

18. spy movie

19. straight-to-video movie/straight-to-DVD movie/B movie

20. thriller

21. war movie

22. western

| Word List |

animated [ˋænəˌmetɪd] movie 動畫　　biopic [ˋbaɪoˌpɪk] n. 傳紀影片
blue movie 色情電影　　documentary [ˌdɑkjəˋmɛntərɪ] n. 記錄片
epic [ˋɛpɪk] n. 史詩　　kung fu 功夫
prequel [ˋprikwəl] n. 前篇　　road movie n. 公路電影
sequel [ˋsikwəl] n. 續集　　thriller [ˋθrɪləˋ] n. 驚悚片

220

	A movie which is so bad that it never gets general release in the theater, but goes straight to DVD or video distribution
	A movie specially made for cable TV
	A movie which tells what happened after the story of a previous movie
	A movie which tells what happened before the story of a previous movie
	A movie about real events, with real people, not actors
	A movie made of drawings, like Walt Disney or Japanese manga
biopic	A movie about a famous person's life
	A pornographic movie
	A movie about cowboys and Indians
	A movie about the supernatural, usually involving lots of blood
	A scary movie about ghosts
	An exciting or suspenseful movie in which the main character is in danger
	A movie about spies and secret agents
	A movie about the old days when ladies wore long dresses
	A funny movie about falling in love
	A movie in which people start singing
	A movie about the mafia, triads, or yakuza
	A movie about war
	A movie about a long journey
	A movie in which there is a lot of kung fu fighting
	A long movie with a huge cast and thousands of extras
	A slow, beautifully-filmed movie

答 案

▌請以下頁的語庫核對答案。

▌Word List▌

mafia [ˋmɑfɪə] *n.* 黑手黨　　　　　　　　triad [ˋtraɪæd] *n.* 西方傳媒所泛指的中國黑社會
yakuza *n.* 日本黑社會

社交必備語庫 7.1

straight-to-video movie/straight-to-DVD movie/B movie	A movie which is so bad that it never gets general release in the theater, but goes straight to DVD or video distribution
cable movie	A movie specially made for cable TV
sequel	A movie which tells what happened after the story of a previous movie
prequel	A movie which tells what happened before the story of a previous movie
documentary	A movie about real events, with real people, not actors
animated movie/ cartoon	A movie made of drawings, like Walt Disney or Japanese manga
biopic	A movie about a famous person's life
blue movie	A pornographic movie
western	A movie about cowboys and Indians
horror movie	A movie about the supernatural, usually involving lots of blood
ghost movie	A scary movie about ghosts
thriller	An exciting or suspenseful movie in which the main character is in danger
spy movie	A movie about spies and secret agents
costume drama	A movie about the old days when ladies wore long dresses
romantic comedy	A funny movie about falling in love
musical	A movie in which people start singing
gangster movie	A movie about the mafia, triads, or yakuza
war movie	A movie about war
road movie	A movie about a long journey
kung fu movie	A movie in which there is a lot of kung fu fighting
epic	A long movie with a huge cast and thousands of extras
art movie	A slow, beautifully-filmed movie

Task 7.4

請聽 Track 7.2，練習語庫 7.1 的發音。

Task 7.5

想想你所知道的電影，它們分別是屬於哪一個種類，將它們的片名填入下表。

straight-to-video movie/straight-to-DVD movie/B movie	
cable movie	
sequel	
prequel	
documentary	
animated movie/ cartoon	
biopic	
blue movie	
western	
horror movie	
ghost movie	
thriller	
spy movie	
costume drama	
romantic comedy	
musical	
gangster movie	
war movie	
road movie	
kung fu movie	
epic	
art movie	

答 案

各位或許覺得有點難。不必擔心表填得不完整，只要鎖定你較熟悉的種類即可。如果你只記得中文片名，可以上網或問問朋友它的英文片名，然後把它記起來！

223

各位可能會遇到的另一個問題是，有些電影不只屬於一個類型。○○七電影算是哪一類？它屬於喜劇、驚悚還是間諜電影？這種討論可能就是下次社交談話的主題！

Task 7.6　　　　　　　　　　　　　　　　　　　　　　　　CD 2-01

再聽一次 Track 7.1 ，John 和 Mary 喜歡的是哪種類型的電影？

● 答　案

John 喜歡的是 gangster movies ； Mary 喜歡的是 cartoons 。

談論電影的用語

你喜歡的是哪種類型的電影呢？接著就來學「表達好惡」的用語吧。

Task 7.7

將下列的 set-phrases 分門別類，填入下表。

1. I really like n.p. ...
2. I don't really like n.p. ...
3. I quite like n.p. ...
4. I love n.p. ...
5. ... n.p. is OK.
6. ... n.p. is really good.
7. I'm crazy about n.p. ...
8. I can't bear n.p. ...
9. I can't stand n.p. ...
10. I'm rather keen on n.p. ...
11. I'm not so keen on n.p. ...
12. I really don't like n.p. ...

Positive	Negative

● 答　案

❘ 請以下頁的語庫核對答案。要注意的是，它們是按照喜惡的強弱，由上而下排列。

社交必備語庫 7.2

正面 Positive	負面 Negative
• I'm crazy about n.p. ... • I love n.p. ... • I really like n.p. ... • ... n.p. is really good. • I quite like n.p. ... • I'm rather keen on n.p. ... • ... n.p. is OK.	• I can't stand n.p. ... • I can't bear n.p. ... • I really don't like n.p. ... • I don't really like n.p. ... • I'm not so keen on n.p. ...

Task 7.8

再聽一次 Track 7.1 ，John 和 Mary 使用了語庫中的哪些 set-phrases 呢？

答 案

John : I don't really like cartoons.

Mary : I love them!、 I really don't like gangster movies.

Task 7.9

現在以 Task 7.5 中你所寫下的電影為對象，利用語庫 7.2 的用語來練習造句。

注意，有時候 movie 又稱為 picture ，在英國又稱為 film 。

Task 7.10

研讀下列的 word partnership 表格，並練習造句。

• shoot • appear in • make • release • finance • be cast in • watch • see	**a movie/ a picture/ a film**

Word List

finance [ˈfaɪnæns] v. 資助　　　　　　be cast in 參與演出（cast 過去分詞同型）

可能的例句如下：

- They're shooting a movie in my street this week.
- That film hasn't been released yet.
- My company is financing a picture.

接著來看些關於電影的介紹吧。

文化小叮嚀

- 奧斯卡金像獎創始於西元 1928 年。
- 該獎的正式名稱是 The Academy Award of Merit ，而 Oscar 則是小金人的名字。它之所以稱作 Oscar ，是因為它讓 Bette Davis （好萊塢的早期巨星）想起了丈夫裸體的樣子，而他的名字就叫作 Oscar 。
- 這個獎項是由位於洛杉磯的美國影藝學院（Academy of Motion Picture Arts and Sciences）所頒發。該學院有 5,600 位投票會員，其中大部分都是在洛杉磯從事電影業。
- 首先，提名會由同儕所決定（演員投票決定提名的演員、導演投給導演，依此類推），名單確定後，接著再由所有獎項的所有會員來選出得獎者。
- 目前有 25 類獎項。
- 贏得最多奧斯卡獎項的電影包括 1959 年的《賓漢》(*Ben Hur*)、 1997 年的《鐵達尼號》(*Titanic*)，以及 2003 年的《魔戒第三集》(*The Lord of the Rings Part 3*)。它們都贏得了 11 座奧斯卡金像獎。

現在來學一些關於電影從業人員的用語。

Task 7.11

把下列的工作和下頁的敘述配對。請見範例。

1. stuntman

2. art director

3. stand in/double

4. casting director

5. distributor

6. female lead

Word List

stuntman [ˈstʌntˌmæn] *n.* 特技替身　　　　stand in/double 替身

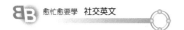

7. cast

8. composer

9. male lead

10. executive producer

11. screenwriter

12. supporting role

13. director

14. sound director

15. editor

16. camera man

17. star

18. assistant director

	The person responsible for how the movie looks; what shapes, colors, interiors, and exteriors are used; and what period is recreated.
	The person or people who help the director to make the movie.
	The person who shoots the movie using the movie camera. This person is also responsible for the lighting.
	The group of actors and stars in the movie.
	The person responsible for choosing which actors are going to appear in the movie.
	The person responsible for composing and performing the music used in the movie.
	The person with overall responsibility for making the movie.
distributor	The person or company responsible for releasing the movie to the theaters and collecting box office receipts.
	The person responsible for taking all the footage that has been shot and linking it together so that it tells a good story.
	The person responsible for financing the movie, and making sure it is made within budget and on schedule, not over budget or behind schedule.
	The main actress, who plays the part of the main female character, the one which the story is about.
	The main actor, who plays the part of the main male character, the one which the story is about.

| Word List |

footage [ˈfutɪdʒ] *n.* （影片的）呎數

	The person responsible for writing or adapting the screenplay which the actors, director, and cameraman use.
	The person responsible for recording all the sound effects and dialogue.
	The person who looks similar to the star and is used to replace the star in shots where the star's face is not seen.
	A famous actor or actress who is cast to help attract more people to watch the movie.
	The person who does all of the dangerous shots like falling off buildings or jumping into rivers.
	A person in the story who is not one of the main characters.

● 答　案

▌ 請以下列的語庫核對答案。

■ 社交必備語庫 7.3　　　　　　　　　　 CD 2-04

art director	The person responsible for how the movie looks; what shapes, colors, interiors, and exteriors are used; and what period is recreated.
assistant director	The person or people who help the director to make the movie.
camera man	The person who shoots the movie using the movie camera. This person is also responsible for the lighting.
cast	The group of actors and stars in the movie.
casting director	The person responsible for choosing which actors are going to appear in the movie.
composer	The person responsible for composing and performing the music used in the movie.
director	The person with overall responsibility for making the movie.
distributor	The person or company responsible for releasing the movie to the theaters and collecting box office receipts.
editor	The person responsible for taking all the footage that has been shot and linking it together so that it tells a good story.

executive producer	The person responsible for financing the movie, and making sure it is made within budget and on schedule, not over budget or behind schedule.
female lead	The main actress, who plays the part of the main female character, the one which the story is about.
male lead	The main actor, who plays the part of the main male character, the one which the story is about.
screenwriter	The person responsible for writing or adapting the screenplay which the actors, director, and cameraman use.
sound director	The person responsible for recording all the sound effects and dialogue.
stand in/double	The person who looks similar to the star and is used to replace the star in shots where the star's face is not seen.
star	A famous actor or actress who is cast to help attract more people to watch the movie.
stuntman	The person who does all of the dangerous shots like falling off buildings or jumping into rivers.
supporting role	A person in the story who is not one of the main characters.

Task 7.12   CD 2-04

請聽 Track 7.4，練習語庫 7.3 中這些名稱的發音。

　　在上列語庫的工作描述中，有一些很實用的 word partnerships 可以用來談論電影。

Task 7.13

把兩欄中的字配對，以形成 word partnerships。請見範例。利用語庫 7.3 和 7.1 的工作敘述及電影類型來幫忙。

___d___ **1.** be over   a) a character
_____ **2.** be within   b) a part
_____ **3.** box-office   c) release
_____ **4.** movie   d) budget

_____	**5.** play	e)	budget
_____	**6.** play	f)	romance
_____	**7.** shoot	g)	camera
_____	**8.** off-screen	h)	receipts
_____	**9.** general	i)	some footage
_____	**10.** be	j)	on schedule
_____	**11.** be	k)	behind schedule
_____	**12.** be	l)	ahead of schedule
_____	**13.** write	m)	violence
_____	**14.** adapt	n)	a screenplay
_____	**15.** sound	o)	a screenplay
_____	**16.** take	p)	effects
_m_	**17.** on-screen	q)	a shot

答案

請以下列的語庫核對答案。

社交必備語庫 7.4　　　　CD 2-05

• adapt a screenplay	• 改編劇本
• be ahead of schedule	• 進度超前
• be behind schedule	• 進度落後
• be on schedule	• 按照進度
• be over budget	• 超出預算
• be within budget	• 預算之內
• box-office receipts	• 票房收入
• general release	• 全面上映
• movie camera	• 電影攝影機
• off-screen romance	• 戲外緋聞
• on-screen violence	• 銀幕暴力
• play a character	• 飾演角色
• play a part	• 軋一角
• shoot some footage	• 拍一些畫面

• sound effects	• 音效
• take a shot	• 拍攝
• write a screenplay	• 寫劇本

接著來學一些 be 開頭的 chunks。它們在談論電影時很實用。

Task 7.14

把左邊的 chunks 和右邊的例句配對。

__g__	**1.** be in	a) It's not out yet.
_____	**2.** be out	b) I think it's on at Warner Village.
_____	**3.** be on at	c) It's by Steven Spielberg.
_____	**4.** be by	d) It's about a fish.
_____	**5.** be about	e) It's from Hong Kong.
_____	**6.** be from	f) It was made in London.
_____	**7.** be made in	g) Julia Roberts is in it.

答　案

請以下列的語庫核對答案。

社交必備語庫 7.5　　　　　　　　　　　　CD 2-06

• be in	有演	Julia Roberts is in it.
• be out	推出	It's not out yet.
• be on at	在……上映	I think it's on at Warner Village.
• be by	由……執導	It's by Steven Spielberg.
• be about	描述	It's about a fish.
• be from	產自	It's from Hong Kong.
• be made in	拍攝於	It was made in London.

現在從文章中來看看這些 chunks 如何運用。

Task 7.15

詳讀下列這篇報導，找出語庫 7.5 中的 chunks 並畫上底線。

Robert Neare Stars in New Socriss Picture!

G-spot Studio's new movie has now been completed and is out on December 12. *Kill 'em All* is the twenty-seventh movie by Michael Socriss. It stars Robert Neare, and other Hollywood luminaries are in it, too. The movie is about an Italian-born gangster who takes over a violent New York neighborhood in the early nineteenth century. Although it's from America, the movie was actually made in Amsterdam, because the director said that city resembled the New York of that historical period. Critics have said the movie is very like the same director's previous movie, *Gals of New York*. *Kill 'em All* is on at Warner Village and selected movie theaters around town.

答案

Robert Neare Stars in New Socriss Picture!

G-spot Studio's new movie has now been completed and <u>*is out*</u> on December 12. *Kill 'em All* is the twenty-seventh movie by Michael Socriss. It stars Robert Neare, and other Hollywood luminaries <u>*are in*</u> it, too. The movie <u>*is about*</u> an Italian-born gangster who takes over a violent New York neighborhood in the early nineteenth century. Although <u>*it's from*</u> America, the movie <u>*was actually made in*</u> Amsterdam, because the director said that city resembled the New York of that historical period. Critics have said the movie is very like the same director's previous movie, *Gals of New York*. *Kill 'em All* <u>*is on at*</u> Warner Village and selected movie theaters around town.

Word List

luminary [ˈlumə͵nɛrɪ] *n.* 名人

resemble [rɪˈzɛml̩] *v.* 像……

Amsterdam [ˈæmstɚ͵dæm] *n.* 阿姆斯特丹

gal [gæl] *n.* 【口語】女孩；少女

233

中 譯

G 點製片廠的新電影現已殺青,預計在 12 月 12 日推出。《片甲不留》是麥可‧蘇格里斯的第 27 部電影,由勞勃‧尼迪洛主演,裡面還有其他的好萊塢明星。本片描述一個在義大利出生的幫派份子在 19 世紀初接管了紐約的鄰近地區。本片雖然是產自美國,但其實是在阿姆斯特丹所拍攝,因爲導演説該城很像過去那個時代的紐約。影評説,本片跟該導演的前一部片子《紐約姑娘》很類似。《片甲不留》將在華納影城以及選擇一些市區附近的電影院上映。

Task 7.16

將正確的字詞填入下列空格,接著找出完整的 chunks。

Julie Tolbert in New Spielberg Picture!

Watson Sister's new movie has now been completed and is _____ on December 12. *The Return of ET* is the eighteenth movie _____ Stephen Spielberg. It stars Julie Tolbert, and other Hollywood luminaries are _____ it, too. The movie is _____ the mother of the alien from the first ET picture who comes to earth looking for her son, and who falls in love with a doctor. Although it's _____ Hollywood, the movie was actually made _____ Argentina, because the director said filming in that country was much cheaper than filming in LA. Critics have said the movie is like the previous ET movie. *The Return of ET* is _____ _____ Warner Village and selected movie theaters around town.

答 案

Julie Tolbert in New Spielberg Picture!

Watson Sister's new movie has now been completed and *is out* on December 12. *The Return of ET is* the eighteenth movie *by* Stephen Spielberg. It stars Julie Tolbert, and other Hollywood luminaries *are in* it, too. The movie *is about* the mother of the alien from the first ET picture who comes to earth looking for her son, and who falls in love with a doctor. Although it*'s from* Hollywood, the movie *was* actually *made in* Argentina, because the director said filming in that country was much cheaper than filming in LA. Critics have said the movie is like the previous ET movie. *The Return of ET is on at* Warner Village and selected movie theaters around town.

中　譯

華森姐妹的新電影目前已經殺青，預計在 12 月 12 日推出。《ET 再現》是史提芬・史匹柏的第 18 部電影，由茉莉・塔勃茲主演，裡面還有其他的好萊塢明星。本片是在描述第一部《ET》電影中的外星人媽媽來地球找兒子，並和一位醫生墜入愛河。本片雖然是產自好萊塢，但其實是在阿根廷所拍攝，因為導演說在該國拍片比在加州拍片便宜得多。影評說，本片跟前一部《ET》電影很類似。《ET 再現》將在華納影城以及選擇一些市區附近的電影院上映。

現在來溫習一下到目前為止所學過的用語。

Task 7.17　　　　　　　　　　　　　　　CD 2-01

現在再聽一次 Track 7.1 ，在對話中找出本章中教過的用語。

答　案

▌ 請以下列的對話內容核對答案，本章教過的用語以粗體標示。

Track 7.1

Mary: Have you seen the new Robert Neare movie?

John: Is that the animated one?

Mary: Yeah, it's really good.

John: I don't really like cartoons.

Mary: Really? I love them! They're so cute!

John: I find them boring. I prefer gangster movies.

Mary: Oh, yeah? I really don't like gangster movies. I don't like **on screen violence.** What's your favorite movie?

John: I think *The Business Godfather* is the best one. You?

Mary: Part 1 or 2?

John: Actually Part 2 is better.

Mary: Yes, I agree. Part 3 is terrible. Randy Gracias **is in** it, right?

John: Yes, that's right, and it **was made in** Rome. It's not so good. You

know it took ages to make, and **was behind schedule** and **over budget.**

Mary: Really?

John: Yes. And they had problems with the **cast.** Most of them didn't like the star, and the **male and female leads** had an **off-screen romance.** The **female lead** got pregnant, which made **shooting the movie** difficult. I also heard that the **director** and **cameraman** kept fighting.

Mary: Wow. It must be so difficult to **make a move**, actually, if you think about it: so many people to manage, and so many things to organize.

John: Yes. My company is **financing a movie** at the moment.

Mary: Really?

John: Yes, a low budget art house movie, but our CEO believes in supporting the arts.

Mary: Oh, so do I.

● 中　譯

Mary： 你看了勞勃・尼迪洛的新電影嗎？

John： 是那部動畫片嗎？

Mary： 是啊，那部片很好看。

John： 我不太喜歡看卡通。

Mary： 是嗎？我愛死了！它們實在好可愛！

John： 我覺得它們很無聊。我寧可去看幫派電影。

Mary： 是哦？我不太喜歡幫派電影，因為我不喜歡銀幕暴力。你最喜歡什麼電影？

John： 我覺得最棒的是《The Business Godfather》。妳呢？

Mary： 第一集還是第二集？

John： 說實話，第二集比較好。

Mary： 沒錯，我同意。第三部就很差了，藍迪・格瑞西斯有演，對吧？

John： 對，沒錯，而且它是在羅馬拍攝，只是拍得不怎麼樣。妳知道，它可是拍了好久，進度落後又超出預算。

Mary： 是嗎？

John： 是啊，而且他們的卡司也有問題。他們大部分的人都不喜歡那個明星，而且男女主角又鬧出戲外緋聞。結果女主角懷孕了，而這也提高了電影拍攝的難度。我還聽說，導演和攝影師從頭吵到尾。

Mary： 哇，說真的，拍電影一定很難。你想想看，有這麼多人要管理，又有這麼多事要安排。

John： 是啊。我公司目前就在出資拍電影。

Mary： 真的嗎？

John： 真的，是一部低預算的藝術電影，可是我們老闆認為要支持藝術。

Mary： 喔，我有同感。

 文化小叮嚀

- 除了好萊塢以外，全世界最龐大的電影工業是在印度，集中在孟買城，所以才會有孟萊塢（Bollywood）這個名字。它是世界上產量最大的電影工業，每年推出的片子大約有 1,000 部。
- 其中有 65% 的片子不敷成本，25% 打平，但有 10% 可以大撈一票。
- 印度最紅的電影 Solay（印度話）幫它的製作人賺進 2,000 萬美元的票房收入。
- 印度電影大部分都是歡樂與極具娛樂性的浪漫音樂喜劇，並有大陣仗的臨時演員唱歌跳舞。
- 印度的電影明星都紅得不得了，無論走到哪裡都是萬人空巷。寫歌的作曲家也會很紅，歌曲是每部孟萊塢電影的主要元素。
- 每週大概會有 7,500 萬個印度人去看電影，平均的消費金額則是 35 美分。

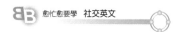
提升字彙量

我想很多人都是空有想法，但缺乏英文「字」來表達這些「想法」。切記：文字就是想法，想法就是文字。因此，多記些 word partnerships 真的很重要，可使你更容易表達出想法。本節要教各位，如何靠自修來加強本身的電影字彙。

Task 7.18

請看下列關於《教父》電影的報導。把下頁的敘述和報導的段落配對。

From beginning to end, The Godfather trilogy ranks as one of the United States' most accomplished and most highly regarded motion picture productions. *The Godfather* is often seen as the ultimate "guy" movie, so it is perhaps surprising how many women also count this among their cinematic favorites. This film appears on so many "top 10" lists because of its widespread appeal and its wonderfully realistic production quality.

The Godfather was a three-film collaboration between Francis Ford Coppola, the director, and Mario Puzo, the writer. Many people believe that *The Godfather Part 1* is better written than *The Godfather Part 2*, that it is more tightly edited, and has more emotional resonance than its sequel. Both are great films, and of course you need to see both of them to get the full impact of the story. However, as independent pieces of cinema, they both stand alone. There is also *The Godfather Part 3*, but not very many people take that one seriously. Even Al Pacino, the star, appears not to have taken it too seriously!

| W o r d   L i s t |

trilogy [ˈtrɪlədʒɪ] *n.* 三部曲　　　　　　cinematic [ˌsɪnəˈmætɪk] *adj.* 電影的

collaboration [kəˌlæbəˈreʃən] *n.* 協力；合作　　resonance [ˈrɛznəns] *n.* 回響

It's not just gangsters, guns, and great quotable lines that make the movies memorable, but it's also the fact that the story is an American tragedy. This is the kind of screenplay Shakespeare would have written if he had been writing in Hollywood today.

Paragraph _____ The reasons why it's so highly regarded.
Paragraph _____ *The Godfather* is one of the most popular American movies ever made.
Paragraph _____ The three parts of the movie can be seen together or separately.

答案

段落 ___3___ 它備受好評的原因。
段落 ___1___ 《教父》是美國歷來最紅的片子之一。
段落 ___2___ 這三集電影可以一起看，也可以分開看。

可參考下列的譯文。

中譯

從開頭到結尾，《教父》三部曲都是美國最有成就與評價最高的電影之一。《教父》經常被視爲「男性」電影的極致，所以有這麼多女性也把它列爲最喜愛的電影頗令人意外。這部片子出現在不計其數的「十大」排行榜中，因爲它具有廣泛的吸引力，以及十分務實的製作品質。

《教父》的這三部電影都是由導演法蘭西斯‧福特‧哥普拉和馬里歐‧普佐編劇攜手合作。有很多人認爲，《教父》第一集寫得比第二集好，因爲它的剪輯比較緊湊，而且情緒共鳴也比續集來得強。它們都是好片子，你當然兩部片都要看，才能了解故事的完整意義。不過，如果分開來看，它們也都是獨立的片子。《教父》還有第三集，可是並沒有很多人看重它，連影星艾爾‧帕西諾似乎也不太看重它！

這部電影令人難忘的地方不只在於幫派、槍枝和經典名句，更在於它的故事是美國式的悲劇。假如莎士比亞在現今的好萊塢編劇，這正是他會寫出的劇本。

在這篇報導中，有很多 word partnerships 可以用來談論電影。各位可以針對喜歡的電影，在電影雜誌、報紙或網路上找出相關的報導。詳讀這些報導，並把 word partnerships 找出來。然後把它們做成表格，印出來隨身攜帶。只要一有空，就記些 word partnerships ，這是個提升你字彙能力的好方法。現在，我們來找出上面這篇報導中的 word partnerships 。

Task 7.19

參考上面的報導，在下列的空格中填上適當的字，使它們成為完整的 word partnerships 。請見範例。

1. most highly *regarded*
2. _____ picture
3. the ultimate _____ _____
4. _____ favorite
5. widespread _____
6. _____ _____ production quality
7. three-film _____
8. _____ written
9. tightly _____
10. _____ resonance
11. full _____
12. _____ pieces
13. stand _____
14. _____ lines
15. American _____

答案

請以下頁的語庫核對答案。注意，有些 word partnerships 是三個字，有些則是四個字。

社交必備語庫 7.6　　　　　　　　　　　　CD 2-07

- most highly regarded
- motion picture
- the ultimate "guy" movie
- cinematic favorite
- widespread appeal
- wonderfully realistic production quality
- three-film collaboration
- better written
- tightly edited
- emotional resonance
- full impact
- independent pieces
- stand alone
- quotable lines
- American tragedy

Task 7.20　　　　　　　　　　　　　　 CD 2-07

請聽 Track 7.7，練習語庫中 word partnerships 的發音，然後利用這些用語來練習談論《教父》。

● 答　案

▍ 練習發音、試著運用這些用語是很重要的，記住，熟能生巧喔！

　　本章到此結束。希望各位現在都能盡情暢談電影！如果各位還沒有看過《教父》，不妨去看看，因為它真的很好看！

　　別忘了回到本章的「學習目標」，看看你達成了多少。

Unit 8

話題 2：文化

引言與學習目標

東西方的文化有很大的差異，這種差異可以是很有趣的談話主題。本章要學的是關於「文化產品」的字彙，如：書籍、音樂。在學習本章時，可以配合第二、三章中 Short-turn Talk 發話的用語，也可以配合第七章中談論好惡的 set-phrases。本章也會提供許多文化方面的訊息，增加各位在談論這個話題時的信心。如果遇到不了解的部分，不用害怕發問，對方應該會很樂於解釋。只要你也向他介紹一些本地的文化即可。

本章結束時，各位應達成的「學習目標」如下：

❏ 能夠談論書籍。
❏ 能夠談論音樂。
❏ 完成聽力與發音練習。
❏ 對西方文化的進程與人物有更通盤的了解。
❏ 提升文化方面的字彙量。

談論書籍

書籍通常分為兩大類：小說（fiction，想像的作品）與非小說（non-fiction，描述現實的作品）。首先，想想自己最喜歡的三本書。

Task 8.1

想想你最喜歡的三本書，在下表中寫下它們的中文和英文書名。

	中文書名	英文書名
1		
2		
3		

答 案

本章結束前，我們會回頭來看這個練習。如果你不知道英文書名，可以上網查，或是問朋友和同事。

Task 8.2

 CD 2-08

請聽 Track 8.1，根據對話回答下列問題。

1. Janice 在看什麼書？
2. Stephen 在看什麼書？

答 案

稍後會提供對話的內容。目前希望各位能聽得出來： Janice 正在看一本談兩性與購物的小說； Stephen 則在看火車之旅方面的書。如果沒聽出來，不妨多聽幾次。

接著來看看書的種類。

Task 8.3

將下頁的種類名稱和表格中的敘述配對。請見範例。

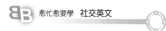

1. modern classic
2. philosophy
3. authorized biography
4. thriller
5. criticism
6. short story
7. detective story
8. pulp fiction
9. history
10. ghost story
11. unauthorized biography
12. horror story
13. play
14. novella
15. poetry anthology
16. autobiography
17. self-development manual/self-help book
18. classic novel
19. travel book

	A story written to be acted in a theater
	The story of a real person's life written by someone else with the cooperation of the subject or the subject's family
	The story of a real person's life written by that person
classic novel	A work of fiction which has become very famous and important
	Non-fiction books written about other books
	A story involving a crime and how it is solved
	A story about ghosts
	A non-fiction book about real events in the past

▎ W o r d   L i s t ▎

pulp [pʌlp] *adj.* 低俗的

anthology [æn`θɑlədʒɪ] *n.* 選集

novella [no`vɛlə] *n.* 中篇小說

	A story involving the supernatural and lots of blood
	A work of fiction written in the last 100 years which has become famous and important
	A short novel, or a long short story
	A non-fiction book about ideas and their relationship to real life
	A collection of poems by one or more poets
	Cheap books of fiction, usually involving crime
	A non-fiction book teaching you how to live a better life or how to be a happier, more successful person
	A work of fiction of only a few thousand words
	An exciting work of fiction, usually involving crime or war
	A non-fiction book about journeys to far-away places
	The story of a real person's life written by someone else without the cooperation of the subject's family

 答 案

請以下列的語庫核對答案。

社交必備語庫 8.1 CD 2-09

a play	A story written to be acted in a theater
authorized biography	The story of a real person's life written by someone else with the cooperation of the subject or the subject's family
autobiography	The story of a real person's life written by that person
classic novel	A work of fiction which has become very famous and important
criticism	Non-fiction books written about other books
detective story	A story involving a crime and how it is solved
ghost story	A story about ghosts
history	A non-fiction book about real events in the past
horror story	A story involving the supernatural and lots of blood

modern classic	A work of fiction written in the last 100 years which has become famous and important
novella	A short novel, or a long short story
philosophy	A non-fiction book about ideas and their relationship to real life
poetry anthology	A collection of poems by one or more poets
pulp fiction	Cheap books of fiction, usually involving crime
self development manual/ self help manual	A non-fiction book teaching you how to live a better life or how to be a happier, more successful person
short story	A work of fiction of only a few thousand words
thriller	An exciting work of fiction, usually involving crime or war
travel book	A non-fiction book about journeys to far-away places
unauthorized biography	The story of a real person's life written by someone else without the cooperation of the subject's family

Task 8.4   ◉)))) CD 2-09

請聽 Track 8.2，練習「書的種類」的發音。

　　現在回頭看看 Task 8.1。你喜歡的三本書是屬於哪個種類呢？你還喜歡其他哪些種類？

Task 8.5

在各個種類中，你知道的書有多少，試著將它們寫下來，並記住它們的英文書名。

　　各位或許有注意到，在語庫 8.1 中，有個種類是 modern classic。 Classic 是個很妙的字，它常和 classical 混為一談，但二者意思不同。 Classical 是在談論歷史的時候使用，在談論概括的歷史時，它是指古希臘或古羅馬；在談論音樂史時，它是指 18 世紀末。 Classic 則是在談論歷史之外的東西時使用，它的意思是「著名且重要的東西」或「經典」。它可以當作名詞，也可以當作形容詞。在談論文化產品時，它是常用的字。在談論行銷時，它也很好用。

Task 8.6

研讀下列的 word partnership 表格，並練習造句。

• 1950s • Shakespeare's • Science fiction • non-fiction • great • modern • nineteenth-century	**classic (*n.*)**
classic (*adj.*)	• brand • case of • example of • film • movie

答　案

可能的例句如下：

- It's a 1950s classic.
- It's one of the great classics of Chinese literature.
- It's a classic case of corruption.
- It's a classic brand.

現在來學一些字，你在描述「書籍」時它們可以派上用場。

Task 8.7

把下列這些字分門別類，填入下表。

1. binding	裝訂	**7.** message	主旨
2. blurb	內容簡介	**8.** period	時代
3. characterization	性格描述	**9.** plot	情節
4. cover	封面	**10.** review	書評
5. dialogue	對白	**11.** setting	場景
6. jacket	書衣	**12.** description	描述

249

The Book As Story	The Book As Object

答　案

請以下列的語庫核對答案。

社交必備語庫 8.2

 CD 2-10

書的內容 The Book As Story	書的物件 The Book As Object
• characterization • dialogue • setting • period • description • message • plot	• cover • jacket • blurb • review • binding

Task 8.8

把下列的 word partnerships 分門別類，填入其後的表格。

1. flat descriptions
2. gripping plot
3. implausible events
4. important message
5. plausible events
6. predictable plot

7. trivial message
8. vivid descriptions
9. witty dialogue
10. wooden dialogue
11. fully drawn characters
12. two-dimensional characters

Word List

gripping [ˋgrɪpɪŋ] *adj.* 緊湊的
trivial [ˋtrɪvjəl] *adj.* 瑣碎的；不重要的

implausible [ɪmˋplɔzəbḷ] *adj.* 難以相信的

Positive	Negative

答　案

請以下列的語庫核對答案。注意，這些用語大部分都是在談論小說作品時使用。

社交必備語庫 8.3　 CD 2-11

正面 Positive	負面 Negative
• fully drawn characters • gripping plot • important message • plausible events • vivid descriptions • witty dialogue	• flat descriptions • implausible events • predictable plot • trivial message • two-dimensional characters • wooden dialogue

Task 8.9　 CD 2-11

請聽 Track 8.4，練習語庫中 word partnerships 的發音。

　　下列的 chunks 在談論書籍時非常實用，值得各位學習。

Task 8.10

研讀下列語庫中的 chunks 和例句。

社交必備語庫 8.4　 CD 2-12

• bring sth. out • sth. comes out	• BETA is bringing out its new book in the fall. • His new book is coming out in the fall.
• get across sth.	• He didn't know how to get across all of the emotions he was feeling.
• get sth. across • sth. comes across	• Her new book really gets her message across. • Her message really comes across in her new book.

251

Task 8.11

在語庫 8.4 中挑出適當的用語，填入下列空格。

1. Penguin is soon _____ a new anthology of modern Taiwanese poetry.
2. There's a new anthology of modern Taiwanese poetry _____ soon.
3. It really _____ the feeling of being young.
4. The feeling of being young really _____.

 答　案

    1. Penguin is soon _bringing out_ a new anthology of modern Taiwanese poetry.

    2. There's a new anthology of modern Taiwanese poetry _coming out_ soon.

    3. It really _gets across_ the feeling of being young.

    4. The feeling of being young really _comes across_.

Task 8.12

根據下列提示，利用語庫 8.4 中的 chunks 造句。

1. Beta ... new dictionary
2. new dictionary
3. The book ... the dangers of environmental pollution
4. The dangers of environmental pollution

答　案

    1. Beta is bringing out a new dictionary.

    2. Beta's new dictionary is coming out soon.

    3. The book really gets across the dangers of environmental pollution.

    4. The dangers of environmental pollution really come across.

希望各位能看出這兩組 chunks 在用法上的差異。它們在談論電影時也很好用。

來複習一下各位到目前爲止所學過的內容。

Task 8.13　　　　　　　　　　　　　　　　　　　　　　　◦))) CD 2-08

再聽一次 Track 8.1 ，把你所聽到語庫 8.1 到 8.4 中的用語寫下來。

● 答　案

▌看看下列的對話內容，對話中所應用的用語以粗體標示。

◦))) **Track 8.1**

Stephen: What's that you're reading?

Janice:　This? Oh, it's the latest **novel** by Pam Wheeler.

Stephen: Oh, right. Any good?

Janice:　Yes, it's not bad. It got a **gripping plot**, and the **dialogue** is quite **witty**.

Stephen: What's it about?

Janice:　It's about sex and shopping, really. It really **gets across** the mood of the 1980s.

Stephen: Yes, I read her first book.

Janice:　Oh, yes, that's a classic of its kind. Did you like it?

Stephen: It was certainly a page-turner.

Janice:　So what are you reading?

Stephen: I'm reading this **travel book**, about a train journey across Mongolia.

Janice:　Wow, sounds good.

Stephen: Yes, it's really interesting, full of wonderfully **vivid descriptions** of landscapes. The only trouble is it's taking me ages to read.

Janice:　Oh, why's that?

Stephen: Well, it's a really heavy book, and the **binding's** broken, so I can't carry it around with me.

中　譯

Stephen：妳在看的那本是什麼書？

Janice：　這本嗎？哦，這是帕恩‧惠勒最新的小說。

Stephen：原來如此。好看嗎？

Janice：　嗯，還不錯。它的情節不賴，對白也寫得很好。

Stephen：它在講什麼？

Janice：　它其實是在談兩性與購物。它很能反映出 1980 年代的心情。

Stephen：的確，我看過她的第一本書。

Janice：　喔，對啊，它可說是同類的經典之作。你喜歡嗎？

Stephen：它絕對是一本引人入勝的書。

Janice：　那你在看什麼？

Stephen：我在看這本旅遊書，它談的是橫跨蒙古的火車之旅。

Janice：　哇，聽起來不錯。

Stephen：是啊，有趣得很，裡面充滿了對景色極為生動的描述。唯一的麻煩是，我得花很長的時間來看完。

Janice：　哦，為什麼會這樣？

Stephen：這本書好重，而且裝訂的地方又散了，所以我沒辦法隨身攜帶。

接著，來看些西方文化的介紹。

文化小叮嚀

Quentin's

- 請看看下表，但不必背誦！它只是為了讓各位對西方文化有個大概的了解，以及熟悉其中的一些名詞。
- 各位可以針對感興趣的部分，上網查查相關資料，進一步地了解它們。
- 當你在閱讀下表時，可將其中的一些 word partnerships 做成表格，增加記憶。如此一來，下次洽談時，你才能用一些 word partnerships 來談論其中的某些事項，讓對方留下深刻的印象！

時期名稱	古典時期（Classical Period）	羅馬時期（Roman Period）	中古時代（Middle Ages）	文藝復興（The Renaissance）
世紀	西元前 6 世紀與 5 世紀	西元前 1 世紀到西元 4 世紀	4 世紀到 1400 年	1400 年到 1600 年
歷史事件	波斯戰爭（Persian Wars）、伯羅奔尼薩戰爭（Peloponnesian War）	耶穌誕生、羅馬垮台	瘟疫（Plague）、英法百年戰爭（100 Years War between England & France）	發現美洲、宗教改革（Protestant Reformation）、印刷革命
文學戲劇	希臘悲劇：沙孚克理斯（Sophocles）	維吉爾（Virgil）的《伊尼亞德》（Aeneid）、普羅托斯（Plautus）、特倫斯（Terence）	但丁（Dante）、喬叟（Chaucer）	莎士比亞（Shakespeare）、史賓塞（Spenser）
科學工程	希波克拉底（Hippocrates）：醫學之父	導水管、道路	煉金術、星盤	伽利略（Galileo）、培根（Bacon）、哥白尼（Copernicus）
藝術建築	雅典衛城（Acropolis）、巴森農神殿（Parthenon）、希臘雕像	羅馬競技場（Col-osseum）、萬神殿（Pantheon）	大教堂	達文西（Leonardo da Vinci）、米開朗基羅（Michelangelo）
音樂			單旋律聖歌（plainsong）和格里高里聖詠（Gregorian chant）	蒙台威爾第（Monteverdi）、帕萊斯特理納（Palestrina）、拜爾德（Byrd）、杜蘭（Dowland）
哲學	柏拉圖（Plato）、亞理斯多德（Aristotle）	塞尼加（Seneca）	阿圭奈（Aquinas）、歐坎（Ockham）	伊拉斯（Erasmus）、蒙田（Montaigne）

談論音樂

本節不打算對音樂類型著墨太多，而將重點放在如何談論音樂類型與音樂產業。西方音樂可以分為兩種：古典（classical）音樂，其中的偉大音樂家有巴哈（Bach）、莫扎特（Mozart）、舒伯特（Schubert）與史特拉汶斯基（Stravinsky）等；以及非古典（non-classical）音樂，它所包含的音樂有爵士（jazz）、搖滾（rock）、龐克（punk）和各式各樣的流行（pop）音樂。

Classical 這個字容易讓人混淆。它有兩個意思：第一個意思是指整個藝術音樂的範疇（「非」爵士、搖滾、龐克或流行）。第二個意思是指整個古典音樂史的特定期間，從 1770 年到 1827 年左右，當時的作曲家包括了海頓（Hayden）、莫扎特和貝多芬（Beethoven）。但在談論音樂時，這個字通常是指第一個意思。

首先，想想自己最喜歡的三首樂曲。

Task 8.14

將你所想到的三首樂曲的相關資料填入下表。

	名稱	作曲者	演奏者
1			
2			
3			

● 答　案

本章結束前，我們會回頭來看這項練習。但現在請記住它們的英文名稱，這樣在談論時會比較容易。

Task 8.15　　　　　　　　　　　　　　　　　　　CD 1-13

請聽 Track 8.6 ，根據對話回答下列問題。

1. Michael 喜歡哪種音樂？

2. Sally 喜歡哪種音樂？

答　案

1. 爵士樂。

2. 古典樂與大樂團（big band）。（大樂團指的是由超過 20 個銅管樂手所組成，演奏爵士樂的樂團。）

稍後各位還有機會練習聽這段對話。接著先來學一些談論音樂的字彙。

Task 8.16

將下列的字彙與其後表格中的敘述配對。請見範例。

1. chamber music

2. quartet

3. trio

4. quintet

5. duo

6. symphony

7. sonata

8. album

9. concerto

10. choral music

11. gospel choir

12. soprano

13. alto

14. tenor

15. baritone

16. bass

17. lead singer

18. opera

Word List

quartet [kwɔr`tɛt] *n.* 四重奏

quintet [kwɪn`tɛt] *n.* 五重奏

sonata [sə`natə] *n.* 奏鳴曲

choral [`kɔrəl] *adj.* 合唱團的

soprano [sə`præno] *n.* 女高音

tenor [`tɛnə] *n.* 男高音

trio [`trio] *n.* 三重奏

duo [`duo] *n.* 二重奏

concerto [kən`tʃɛrto] *n.* 協奏曲

gospel [`gɑspl] *n.* 福音

alto [`ælto] *n.* 次高音

baritone [`bærə͵ton] *n.* 男中音

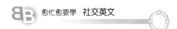

19. backing vocals

20. band

21. rock star

22. opera *diva*

23. composer

24. conductor

25. song writer

26. hit single

27. pop group

28. keyboard

29. jingle

30. string instrument

31. wind instrument

32. brass instrument

33. record company

34. record label

35. concert

36. live recording

	A CD of jazz or pop music
	A low female voice
	The singing performed in the background behind a main singer
	A group of jazz players or brass instrument players
	A male voice that is not too high or too low. Most men's voices are like this.
	A low man's voice, a low tune
	The family of instruments made of metal pipes which you blow
	Music written to be played at home by one, two or a maximum of six players
	Music written for a large choir
composer	A person who writes music
	A live performance of any kind of music
	A piece of classical music for one main instrument accompanied by an orchestra
	The person who shows the orchestra how to play by waving his arms
	Two people playing jazz or classical music together
	A large choir that sings popular religious songs
	A recording of a song by a famous pop star which makes it to the top ten

| W o r d   L i s t |

diva [ˈdivə] *n.* 歌劇中首席女角

	A piece of music written for a TV commercial
	The family of instruments which has a row of black and white keys which the player presses
	The main singer in a pop group
	A recording made of a concert
	A play in which the actors sing, accompanied all the way through by an orchestra
	A great female opera singer
	A group of people who play pop music together
	Four people playing jazz or classical music together
	Five people playing jazz or classical music together
	A company whose business is making and selling music CDs
	A brand name used by a record company to market a particular kind of music
	A great male or female singer of rock music
	A piece of music that has a three-part structure and is played on one instrument
	A person who writes pop or jazz songs
	The highest female voice
	The family of instruments made of wood and wire which you play with a bow
	A piece of music structured into three parts played by an orchestra
	A high male voice
	Three people playing jazz or classical music together
	The family of instruments made of wooden pipes and wire which you blow

答　案

┃ 請以下頁的語庫核對答案。

社交必備語庫 8.5　　　　　　　　　　　　CD 2-14

album	A CD of jazz or pop music
alto	A low female voice
backing vocals	The singing performed in the background behind a main singer
band	A group of jazz players or brass instrument players
baritone	A male voice that is not too high or too low. Most men's voices are like this.
bass	A low man's voice, a low tune
brass instruments	The family of instruments made of metal pipes which you blow
chamber music	Music written to be played at home by one, two or a maximum of six players
choral music	Music written for a large choir
composer	A person who writes music
concert	A live performance of any kind of music
concerto	A piece of classical music for one main instrument accompanied by an orchestra
conductor	The person who shows the orchestra how to play by waving his arms
duo	Two people playing jazz or classical music together
gospel choir	A large choir that sings popular religious songs
hit single	A recording of a song by a famous pop star which makes it to the top ten
jingle	A piece of music written for a TV commercial
keyboard instrument	The family of instruments which has a row of black and white keys which the player presses
lead singer	The main singer in a pop group
live recording	A recording made of a concert
opera	A play in which the actors sing, accompanied all the way through by an orchestra
opera diva	A great female opera singer
pop group	A group of people who play pop music together
quartet	Four people playing jazz or classical music together

quintet	Five people playing jazz or classical music together
record company	A company whose business is making and selling music CDs
record label	A brand name used by a record company to market a particular kind of music
rock star	A great male or female singer of rock music
sonata	A piece of music that has a three-part structure and is played on one instrument
song writer	A person who writes pop or jazz songs
soprano	The highest female voice
string instrument	The family of instruments made of wood and wire which you play with a bow
symphony	A piece of music structured into three parts played by an orchestra
tenor	A high male voice
trio	Three people playing jazz or classical music together
wind instrument	The family of instruments made of wooden pipes and wire which you blow

　　知道這些字彙的意思後，來做一些關於這些字彙的練習，加深各位對這些字彙的記憶。

Task 8.17　　　　　　　　　　　　　　　　　　　　CD 2-14

請聽 Track 8.7，練習語庫 8.5 中字彙的發音。

Task 8.18

如果要將下列的字彙分類，你會怎麼做呢。

1. chamber music
2. quartet
3. trio
4. quintet
5. duo
6. symphony
7. sonata
8. album
9. concerto
10. choral music
11. gospel choir
12. soprano
13. alto
14. tenor

15. baritone
16. bass
17. lead singer
18. opera
19. backing vocals
20. band
21. rock star
22. opera diva
23. composer
24. conductor
25. songwriter

26. hit single
27. pop group
28. keyboard
29. jingle
30. string instrument
31. wind instrument
32. brass instrument
33. record company
34. record label
35. concert
36. live recording

答 案

我不知道各位會怎麼分類，下表是我的分類方式。重點在於，分類方式應該對自己有意義，這樣才能幫助自己了解並記住這些用語。如果你不知如何分類，那也沒關係，就利用下表來幫助你記憶吧！

古典音樂 Classical Music	二者皆適用 Both	非古典音樂 Non-classical Music
• chamber music	• quartet	• album
• symphony	• trio	• gospel choir
• sonata	• quintet	• lead singer
• concerto	• duo	• backing vocals
• choral music	• soprano	• band
• opera	• alto	• rock star
• opera diva	• tenor	• songwriter
• conductor	• baritone	• hit single
• composer	• bass	• pop group
	• keyboard	• jingle
	• wind instrument	
	• brass instrument	
	• record company	
	• record label	
	• concert	
	• live recording	
	• string instrument	

現在來學學如何談論演奏樂器的人。

Task 8.19

研讀例句，然後從下列的字彙中，選出適當者並做適當的變化，試著自己造句。

piano	flute
organ	clarinet
violin	saxophone
cello	oboe
guitar	accordion

1. A person who _makes music_ is a musician.

2. A person who _plays the piano_ is a pianist.

3. A person who _plays the violin_ is a violinist.

4. A person who plays _____

5. A person who _____

6. A person _____

7. A _____

8. _____

◉ 答　案

注意，各位應該要在樂器名稱前加上 the ；通常只要在樂器的後面加上 -ist ，就是指演奏者。但也要注意以下這些例外：

- drums → drummer
- double bass/bass guitar → bassist/bass player
- horn → horn player
- trumpet → trumpet player

　　有時候你也會想談談談音樂帶給你的感受。這並不容易，因為情緒很難用言語來表達。下面這項練習會教各位一些有用的字彙，各位可以用它們來描述音樂的不同類型。

Word List

organ [`ɔrgən] *n.* 風琴

clarinet [͵klærə`nɛt] *n.* 豎笛；單簧管

accordion [ə`kɔrdɪən] *n.* 手風琴

flute [flut] *n.* 笛

oboe [`obo] *n.* 雙簧管

trumpet [`trʌmpɪt] *n.* 小喇叭

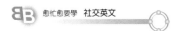

Task 8.20

將下列的形容詞分門別類，填入下表。

1. calming	**11.** light-hearted
2. cheerful	**12.** lulling
3. consoling	**13.** nostalgic
4. ecstatic	**14.** peaceful
5. exhilarating	**15.** playful
6. full of longing	**16.** soothing
7. funky	**17.** thrilling
8. gloomy	**18.** triumphant
9. heartbroken	**19.** uplifting
10. introspective	**20.** wild

Happy	Sad
Energetic	**Relaxing**

| Word List |

ecstatic [ɪk`stætɪk] *adj.* 欣喜若狂的；忘形的
funky [`fʌŋkɪ] *adj.* 【俚】極好的
introspective [ˌɪntrə`spɛktɪv] *adj.* 省思的
nostalgic [nɑ`stældʒɪk] *adj.* 懷舊的；鄉愁的
uplifting [ʌp`lɪftɪŋ] *adj.* 振奮精神的

exhilarating [ɪg`zɪləˌretɪŋ] *adj.* 興高采烈的
gloomy [`glumɪ] *adj.* 憂鬱的；悶悶不樂的
lulling [`lʌlɪŋ] *adj.* 緩緩吸引人的
triumphant [traɪ`ʌmfənt] *adj.* 歡欣鼓舞的

○ 答　案

▌ 請以下列的語庫核對答案。

社交必備語庫 8.6 CD 2-15

快樂的 Happy	悲傷的 Sad
• cheerful	• nostalgic
• triumphant	• full of longing
• ecstatic	• introspective
• light-hearted	• heartbroken
• playful	• gloomy
振奮的 Energetic	放鬆的 Relaxing
• funky	• calming
• thrilling	• soothing
• exhilarating	• lulling
• wild	• consoling
• uplifting	• peaceful

Task 8.21 CD 2-15

請聽 Track 8.8，練習語庫 8.6 中字彙的發音。

　　當這些形容詞無法精確地傳達你的感受時，你就需要使用一些「模糊」的用語，做完下面的練習你就會明白我的意思。

Task 8.22

研讀語庫 8.7，並練習造句。

社交必備語庫 8.7 CD 2-16

「模糊」的用語 Being Vague
• sort of ...
• ... kind of ...
• ... or anything
• ... like ...

- ... or something ...
- It's hard to describe, but ...
- It's difficult to say, but ...
- It's not easy to put into words, but ...
- I can't really describe it, but ...
- I'm not sure how to put it, but ...
- ... do you know what I mean?

★ 📁 語庫小叮嚀

◆ 注意，... or anything 一定要搭配否定動詞。
◆ ... like ... 後面所接的例子一定是被拿來和所談的主題做比較（明喻）。

● 答 案

以下為可能的例句：

- It's hard to describe, but it's kind of consoling, very slow and sweet, do you know what I mean?
- It's difficult to say, but it sounds sort of light-hearted.
- It's not easy to put into words, but it makes me think of the sea, or something.
- I can't really describe it, but it seems like it doesn't have any happiness in it or anything.
- I'm not sure how to put it, but it's like honey all over me!

Task 8.23　　　　　　　　　　　　　　　　　　　　　◎))) CD 2-16

請聽 Track 8.9，練習語庫 8.7 中用語的發音。

現在來複習一下本章所學過的用語。

Task 8.24　　　　　　　　　　　　　　　　　　　　　◎))) CD 2-13

再聽一次 Track 8.6，對話中應用了哪些本章教過的用語，請寫下來。

● 答 案

▌各位可以詳讀下頁的對話內容，對話中應用的用語以粗體標示。

Track 8.6

Sally:　Hi, Michael. What's that you're listening to?

Michael:　Hm? Oh, this? It's Miles Davis. His last **album**.

Sally:　Oh. You like **jazz**, do you?

Michael:　Oh, yeah, in a big way. You?

Sally:　Well, I like some kinds of jazz. I like **big band** music, for example. But **classical music**'s more my thing. I like going to **chamber music concerts.**

Michael:　Oh, me, too, but I like going to listen to jazz trumpet.

Sally:　Oh, yes? Do you play?

Michael:　Yes, a bit, unfortunately for my neighbors! You?

Sally:　I **played the violin** when I was a kid, but I stopped when I left school.

Michael:　Oh, right. Oh, listen to this.

...

Sally:　Wow, it's really **exciting!**

Michael:　Isn't it? Just listen to that **bass**.

Sally:　Oh, yes. I like it. It's hard to describe, but it's **kind of** … **uplifting**?

Michael:　It's **funky**, man! Funky!

中 譯

Sally：　嗨，Michael。你在聽的是什麼音樂？

Michael：　嗯？這個嗎？這是邁爾斯‧戴維斯的上一張專輯。

Sally：　哦。你挺喜歡爵士樂的。

Michael：　對啊，相當喜歡。妳呢？

Sally：　嗯，有幾種爵士樂我還滿喜歡的，像我就蠻喜歡大樂團音樂。不過，古典樂就不太合我的意了。我喜歡聽室內音樂會。

Michael：　喔，我也是。不過我喜歡聽的是爵士喇叭。

Sally：　喔，是嗎？你會吹嗎？

Michael：　會一點，不過鄰居就倒楣了。妳呢？

Sally：　我小時候會拉小提琴，不過離開校園生活以後就沒在拉了。

Michael：我了解。喔，天哪，妳聽聽這個。

……

Sally：　哇，真令人興奮！

Michael：可不是嗎，聽聽裡面的低音。

Sally：　喔，聽到了，我喜歡。它很難形容，不過讓我覺得很舒服？

Michael：那是放克音樂，嘿！放克！

接著再來看看西方文化進程的介紹。

文化小叮嚀

- 請看看下列的表格。在上一個「文化小叮嚀」中已提過，表格中的介紹只是讓各位對西方文化的發展有點概念。各位可針對感興趣的部分，上網查詢更詳盡的資料。

時期名稱	早期現代時期（Early Modern Period）	啟蒙時代（The Age of Enlightenment）	浪漫時代（The Romantic Age）	維多利亞極盛時代（The High Victorian Age）	現代時期（The Modern Period）
世紀	1600 年到 1699 年	1700 年到 1790 年代	1790 年代到 1850 年代	1850 年代到 1900 年	1900 年到 1945 年
社會事件	歐洲三十年戰爭（the Thirty Years War）、英國內戰（English Civil War）	法國大革命及美國革命	拿破崙戰爭（Napoleonic Wars）	都市社會的成長、工業革命、美國南北戰爭	第一及第二次世界大戰、俄國與中國革命
文學	密爾頓（Milton）、莫里哀（Moliere）	歌德（Goethe）、盧梭（Rousseau）、約翰生（Johnson）的英文字典	華滋華斯（Wordsworth）、柯勒芝（Coleridge）、濟慈（Keats）、普希金（Pushkin）、巴爾扎克（Balzac）、奧斯汀（Austen）	狄更斯（Dickens）、喬治·艾略特（George Eliot）、左拉（Zola）、托爾斯泰（Tolstoy）、杜斯妥也夫斯基（Dostoevsky）	吳爾芙（Woolf）、福斯特（E.M. Forster）、喬伊斯（James Joyce）、普魯斯特（Proust）

科學	牛頓（New-ton）、虎克（Hooke）	富蘭克林（Franklin）	法拉第（Fara-day）、拉瓦謝（Lavoisier）	達爾文（Darwin）、孟德爾（Mendel）	愛因斯坦（Einstein）
藝術	林布蘭（Rembrandt）、維米爾（Vermeer）	根茲巴羅（Gainsborough）、華鐸（Wat-teau）	卡斯伯・大衛・佛列德利赫（Caspar David Friedrich）、康斯塔伯（Cons-table）、泰納（Turner）	莫內（Monet）、竇加（Deg-as）、塞尚（Cezanne）、梵谷（Van Gogh）	畢卡索（Pica-sso）、馬諦斯（Matisse）、美國現代主義
音樂	普賽爾（Purcell）、巴哈（Bach）、韓德爾（Handel）〔又稱爲巴洛克（Baroque）時期〕	海頓（Hayd-en）、貝多芬（Beethoven）、莫扎特（Mo-zart）〔又稱爲古典（Classi-cal）時期〕	舒伯特（Schu-bert）、孟德爾頌（Mendel-ssohn）	艾爾加（Elgar）、白遼士（Ber-lioz）、華格納（Wagner）	荀白克（Schoenberg）、馬勒（Mahler）、史特拉汶斯基（Stravinsky）、爵士的誕生
哲學	巴斯卡（Pas-cal）、霍布斯（Hobbes）、洛克（Locke）	伏爾泰（Volt-aire）、亞當・斯密（Adam Smith）、康德（Kant）	愛默生（Emer-son）、齊克果（Kierkegaard）、叔本華（Schopenhauer）	馬克斯（Marx）和恩格斯（En-gels）、尼采（Nietzsche）	羅素（Russell）、維根斯坦（Wittgenstein）、艾爾（Ayer）、羅逖（Rorty）

提升字彙量

　　在最後一節中，我要教各位如何提升談論書籍與音樂的字彙量。方法和上一章相去不遠。先看一篇書評或樂評，找出其中的 word partnerships。各位可以上網或是在雜誌、報紙上找到書評和樂評。花點時間研究當中的字彙，之後你會發現花這些時間是很值得的！

Task 8.25

請閱讀下列對於《達文西密碼》（*The Da Vinci Code*）的評論。然後將下列敘述和段落配對。

This is a good book about a secret society and the search for the Holy Grail. A fun book to read, and very well written, with fast-pacing, quick-editing, and an engrossing tale. The book is truly hard to put down and it's very difficult to resist the temptation to read ahead. However, I was disappointed that the ending wasn't better, and the author's own religious views seem to spoil what is otherwise a great fictional mystery.

In spite of the skill of the writer in keeping the reader involved, the historical research on which it is based could have been done by anyone with half an hour to spare and a good Internet connection. In spite of the note at the beginning making claims to historical precision, the book is full of descriptive errors and historical inaccuracies. For example, the secret society described in the novel, the Priory of Sion, was in fact a complete hoax invented in the late 1950s by Pierre Plantard and not dating from 1099 as Brown wants us to believe.

Paragraph _____ What the reviewer didn't like about it
Paragraph _____ The reasons why the reviewer enjoyed it

| Word List |

grail [grel] *n.* 杯　　　　　　　　　　engrossing [ɪnˋgrosɪŋ] *adj.* 吸引人的
hoax [hoks] *n.* 騙局

答　案

段落 ___2___ 書評不喜歡它的地方
段落 ___1___ 書評欣賞它的原因

可參考下列的譯文。

中　譯

這是本談論秘密會社與尋找聖杯的好書。本書讀來有趣、筆觸十分流暢，步調明快、編輯迅速、故事引人入勝。讓人一看就手不釋卷，無法抗拒想一直讀下去的的誘惑。但令我失望的是，結局不夠好，而且作者本身的宗教觀點似乎破壞了原本應該會很棒的虛構之謎。

雖然作者吸引讀者的本領出眾，但書中作為立足點的歷史研究，只要花個半小時再加上良好的網路連線，任何人都可以做到。儘管本書在開頭的註釋中強調，它的歷史考據很嚴謹，但書中卻充滿了敘述上的錯誤與史實上的偏差。比方說，小説中所描述的秘密會社「錫安會」其實根本是個騙局。它是在 1950 年代末期由皮耶・普蘭塔德所杜撰，而不是布朗要大家相信的始於 1099 年。

Task 8.26

從 Task 8.25 的文章中找出下列所缺少的字，填入下列空格使其成為完整的 word partner-ships。請見範例。

1. good _____
2. _____ book
3. very well _____
4. fast - _pacing_
5. quick - _____
6. _____ tale
7. hard to _____ _____
8. _____ the temptation to
9. read _____

10. _____ views
11. great fictional _____
12. _____ research
13. making _____ _____
14. _____ precision
15. descriptive _____
16. _____ inaccuracies
17. complete _____

● 答　案

請以下列的語庫核對答案。注意，有些 word partnerships 是三個字，有些則是四個字。

■ 社交必備語庫 8.8　　　　　　　　　　　　　 CD 2-17

- good book
- fun book
- very well written
- fast-pacing
- quick-editing
- engrossing tale
- hard to put down
- resist the temptation to
- read ahead

- religious views
- great fictional mystery
- historical research
- making claims to
- historical precision
- descriptive errors
- historical inaccuracies
- complete hoax

現在各位應該能夠運用其中一些字彙來談論書籍了。各位應該以同樣的方式來增加音樂方面的字彙。

本章結束之前，請回頭看看「學習目標」，你達成了多少呢？

話題 3 ：運動

引言與學習目標

　　本章要學的是關於運動方面的用語。談論運動不是件易事，因為每種比賽都有其專業的用語，除非熟悉相關的規則或技術，否則很難了解它們。舉例來說，雖然我是英國人，但當我的同胞談論板球時，我完全聽不懂。對我來說，它就像外星話一樣。本章以三種運動為重點，包括足球、網球和高爾夫球。

　　如果各位已經熟悉這些運動，你會發現本章有助於增加字彙與相關的會話能力。如果各位不了解這些運動，也可學學這些運動的器材和相關字彙，作為入門的開始。我還會教各位如何談論自己的健身之道，這對各位也很實用。

　　本章結束時，各位應達成的「學習目標」如下：

❏ 能夠談論足球、網球和高爾夫球。
❏ 能夠談論自己的健身之道。
❏ 做完聽力與發音練習。
❏ 更加了解足球、網球和高爾夫球的歷史。
❏ 增加運動方面的字彙。

談論運動

我們先來想想你會做哪些運動，或者曾經做過哪些運動。

Task 9.1

看看下列這些運動和活動的名稱，哪些是你做過的運動？哪些是你看過的比賽？

1. 25 laps
2. a workout
3. aerobics
4. athletics
5. backgammon
6. basketball
7. chess
8. climbing
9. diving
10. exercise
11. football
12. golf
13. hiking
14. jogging
15. mahjong
16. martial arts
17. ping-pong
18. rugby
19. running
20. sailing
21. skiing
22. soccer
23. swimming
24. tai chi
25. tennis
26. volleyball
27. yoga

答 案

熟悉一下這些運動和活動的名稱，若對方談及這些項目，你就能了解他所指為何了。

Word List

aerobics [ˌeəˋrobɪks] *n.* 有氧運動

backgammon [ˋbækˌgæmən] *n.* 西洋雙陸棋戲

martial [ˋmɑrʃəl] *art* 武術

tai chi *n.* 太極

athletics [æθˋlɛtɪks] *n.*【英】田徑運動

mahjong *n.* 麻將

rugby [ˋrʌgbɪ] *n.* 橄欖球

yoga *n.* 瑜珈

Task 9.2

研讀下列語庫，並練習造句。

社交必備語庫 9.1

 CD 2-19

• It makes me feel really + adj. • Afterwards I feel so + adj. • While I'm doing it I feel so + adj.	• It does me good. • I really get a kick out of it. • It helps (me) to V

語庫小叮嚀

◆ 表格左邊的 set-phrases 後面是接形容詞。

◆ It helps me to ... 後面要接動詞。

答 案

可能的例句如下：

* While I'm doing it I feel so focused.
* It helps me to unwind after a hard day at the office.

現在來仔細看看這些運動與活動。

Task 9.3

看看下列這些項目應該搭配哪個動詞，將它們分門別類，填入下表。

1. 25 laps
2. a workout
3. aerobics
4. athletics
5. backgammon
6. basketball
7. chess
8. climbing
9. diving
10. exercise
11. football
12. golf
13. hiking
14. jogging
15. mahjong
16. martial arts
17. ping-pong
18. rugby

19. running
20. sailing
21. skiing
22. soccer
23. swimming

24. tai chi
25. tennis
26. volleyball
27. yoga

play			do	25 laps	go	

答　案

請以下列語庫核對答案，然後研讀例句。

社交必備語庫 9.2　　　　　　　　　　　　CD 2-20

play		do		go	
	• soccer		• a workout		• climbing
	• football		• exercise		• jogging
	• basketball		• athletics		• swimming
	• volleyball		• aerobics		• running
	• golf		• yoga		• hiking
play	• tennis	**do**	• tai chi	**go**	• sailing
	• ping-pong		• martial arts		• diving
	• rugby		• 25 laps		• skiing
	• backgammon				
	• mahjong				
	• chess				

例句：

- I play mahjong with my parents every Saturday night.
- A: I've started doing yoga.

  B: No wonder you look so relaxed!
- A: I'm going diving this weekend.

  B: Really! Wow, where?

Task 9.4　　　　　　　　　　　　　　　CD 2-20

請聽 Track 9.2，練習語庫 9.2 的發音。

在談論運動時，play 這個動詞非常實用。我們來仔細看看它的用法。

Task 9.5

研讀下列的 word partnership 表格，並練習造句。

play	• a good game (of) • a pretty good game (of) • a mean game (of) • a rough game (of) • a good round (of) • a mean round (of)
	• excellently • superbly • brilliantly • well • badly • sometimes • with a handicap of • with friends • with my local team • against sb.

答　案

可能的例句如下：

* A: You play excellently.

  B: Well, thanks! You play a pretty good game yourself!
* A: Manchester United are playing against Everton tonight. Do you want to watch it with me?

  B: I'd love to but I'm playing with my local team tonight.

現在我們進一步來看這三種運動：網球、高爾夫球和足球。

Task 9.6

請將這三種運動與下列各組器材和場地的字彙配對。

1. golf　**2.** tennis　**3.** soccer/football

_____	• pitch/field • team • game • goal • match • referee • player • stadium

_____	• course • player • caddie • cart • club • iron • ball • game

Word List

pitch [pɪtʃ] *n.*【英】足球的比賽場地　　referee [ˌrɛfəˋri] *n.* 裁判員

stadium [ˋstedɪəm] *n.* 運動場

_____	• court • ball • match • player • racket • umpire • net • doubles partner

答案

以下列語庫核對答案，並研讀語庫小叮嚀。

社交必備語庫 9.3

CD 2-21

soccer/football	• pitch/field • team • game • goal • match • referee • player • stadium
golf	• course • player • caddie • cart • club • iron • ball • game

Word List

umpire [ˈʌmpaɪr] _n._ 裁判

tennis	• court • ball • match • player • racket • umpire • net • doubles partner

★ 📁 語庫小叮嚀

◆ **Football** ： Pitch 是舉行比賽的場地； stadium 則是指整個建築，包括觀眾席在內。 Game 這個字可以指一般的活動，也可以指特定的比賽（美式英文的用法）；而 match 則是指舉行比賽的特定場合。

◆ **Golf** ： iron「鐵桿」是 club「球桿」的一種（另一種球桿是木桿）。 Club 也可以指擁有高爾夫球場的組織。如果要在高爾夫球場打球，通常必須加入 club 。

◆ **Tennis** ： doubles partner 是指雙打比賽中跟你搭檔的人。負責監看比賽並防止有人違反規則的人叫做 umpire ，這種角色在足球場上則叫做 referee 。

Task 9.7   🔊 CD 2-21

請聽 Track 9.3 ，練習語庫中用語的發音。

接著來個別看看這三種運動的介紹。此部分的專業術語較多，所以提供了較多的中文輔助。

高爾夫球

Task 9.8   🔊 CD 2-22

請聽 Track 9.4 ，他們在談論什麼比賽？你是如何知道的？寫下你所聽到的關鍵單字和用語。

● 答　案

▎他們在談論高爾夫球。稍後各位可看到對話的內容。

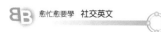
Task 9.9

研讀下列的語庫。

社交必備語庫 9.4　　　　　　　　　　　　　　　CD 2-23

	on the range	Range「練習場」是指練習的地方；那裡有網子可以讓你把球打進去。
	on the course	Course 是指你和其他人一起比賽的地方。
	play a shot	輪到你打球。
	feel your tempo	當打高爾夫球的人談及良好的揮桿時，他們就會這麼說。
	selecting a club	打高爾夫球的人會在球袋裡放一些不同的球桿；它們的重量都不一樣，而且適合不同類型的揮桿。選擇適當的球桿來打球是件重要的事。
	line of putt	Putt 是指沿著地面輕推，以便把球打入洞中。 line of putt 是指球要進洞的行進方向。
	early holes	比賽的前幾洞。總共有 18 個洞。
	finishing holes	比賽的最後幾洞。
	practice tee	Tee 是指在該洞第一次揮擊時的小台子（開球區域）。
	smooth backswing	高爾夫球的揮桿包含兩個部分，一是把球桿後移的向後揮擊（backswing），一是把球打出去的向下揮擊（downswing）。
1	shoot in the 70s	在 18 洞的球場中，70 桿以下的成績對職業選手來說算是很好的成績。成績的算法是選手揮擊的總桿數加上罰桿。
	on the green	Green 是一塊很平順的短草地，上面有洞。中文慣稱為「果嶺」。

Task 9.10　　　　　　　　　　　　　　　　　　　CD 2-22

再聽一次 Track 9.4 ，按照你所聽到的順序在上列的語庫中標號。請見範例。

 答　案

你填下的號碼依序應為： 2 → 4 → 9 → 11 → 10 → 8 → 5 → 6 → 3 → 12 → 1 → 7 。各位可以參考下列的對話內容。

Track 9.4

Sandy: You play golf, don't you?

Roger: Yep. Twenty years, on golf courses all over the world.

Sandy: Well, my handicap is fourteen, but I still dream of **shooting in the 70s** someday. My boss is disgusted with the way I play. Any tips?

Roger: Well, it's all a question of mindset. What do you think your strengths are?

Sandy: Well, I'm pretty good **on the range** and the **practice tee**, but when I get **on the course**, it all goes to pieces.

Roger: Well, that's a pretty common problem. Are your **early holes** better than your **finishing holes**?

Sandy: Hm, yes, actually they are.

Roger: Well, my advice is this: when you're **on the greens**, choose the **line of putt** carefully and stroke the ball. When you're **playing a shot**, **select your club** carefully, **feel your tempo**, and try to get a **smooth backswing**.

Sandy: Well, thanks! Can I get you a drink?

中 譯

Sandy： 你打高爾球吧，是不是？

Roger： 是啊！２０年了，世界各地的球場都去過了。

Sandy： 嗯，我的差點是１４，但我還是夢想有一天能有７０桿以下的成績。我老闆很厭惡我的打球方式，有任何訣竅嗎？

Roger： 呃，這全是心態的問題。妳認為妳有什麼優勢？

Sandy： 嗯，我在練習場打得很好，開球也不錯，但開始比賽時，這些都消失殆盡了。

Roger： 嗯，這是個很常見的問題。妳前幾洞的成績是不是比後幾洞的成績好？

Sandy： 呃……，沒錯，正是如此。

Roger： 嗯，我的建議是這樣的：當妳在果嶺時，謹慎挑選一個路徑，然後擊球。輪到妳打球時，謹慎挑選球桿，感受身體的律動，做好球桿向後拉的揮擊動作。

Sandy： 嗯，謝謝！要我拿杯飲料給你嗎？

Task 9.11　　　　　　　　　　　　　　　　　　　　CD 2-23

請聽 Track 9.5，練習語庫中用語的發音。

　　把你覺得有用的用語學起來。假如你對高爾夫球不感興趣、連一個高爾夫球選手也不認識，或者從來不打高爾夫球，那就讀過有個大概的了解即可。

　　接著來看些關於高爾夫球歷史的介紹，增加你對高爾夫球的認識。

 文化小叮嚀

- 高爾夫球起源於蘇格蘭東岸，大約是 15 世紀後期。雖然有許多古老的運動都需要球和桿子，但一直到球洞出現後，高爾夫球的歷史才算開始。
- 這項運動變得很受歡迎，大家都沈迷於打高爾夫球，疏於練習戰技，導致高爾夫球被蘇格蘭國王禁了 15 年。
- 蘇格蘭的瑪莉女王把這項運動引進了法國，而在旁邊幫她背球桿的男孩都是軍校生，於是有了 caddie「桿弟」的名稱。
- 在大英帝國的顛峰期，印度和愛爾蘭設立了英國境外第一批的高爾夫球會。
- 這項運動隨著鐵路的發展而很快地流行起來，因為它把更多人送到高爾夫球場上。另高爾夫球流行的另一個因素則是 gutta percha（一種橡膠）和量產鐵桿的發明。高爾夫球在 1900 年成了奧運項目。
- 全球各地的高爾夫球是由 R&A（皇家古典高爾夫球俱樂部：Royal and Ancient Golf Club）和 USGA（美國高爾夫協會：United States Golf Association）共同管理。它們每四年開一次高峰會，共同修改正式頒行的高爾夫球規則。

網球

Task 9.12　CD 2-24

請聽 Track 9.6，他們談論的是什麼比賽？你是如何知道的？寫下關鍵的單字和用語。

答　案

他們談論的是網球。稍後各位會看到對話內容。

Task 9.13

研讀下列的語庫。

社交必備語庫 9.5　CD 2-25

1	tied thirty-thirty	網球的分數是從 love（0 分）算起，然後 15、30、40 分，最後則是 game。假如兩個球員都拿到 40 分，就稱爲 deuce，而接下來的那分則叫做 advantage。此時必須超前兩分，才能贏得該局。
	match point	決定贏球或輸球的那一分。
	game, set, and match	贏得比賽時，裁判會説的話。
	be up in the first set	Set 最少是由六個 games 所組成。先贏得六局的人就算贏得該盤。若對方已經贏了五局，此時你必須贏他兩局來阻止他獲勝，並要增加局數來決定誰勝誰負。Match 所包含的 set 從二到五個不等。
	go through to the semi-finals	如果你贏了 semi-finals，你就有機會在 finals 與另一個 semi-finalist 交手。如果贏了 finals，你就是冠軍。
	clipped the net	觸網。
	superb volley	Volley「截擊」是指球還沒落地就把它打回去。其他的揮擊包括高壓扣殺（smash）和發球（serve）。
	lost her serve	指輸掉擁有發球權的那一局。擁有發球權對打者是有利的，所以能否贏得擁有發球權的那一局是很重要的。

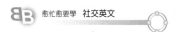
change sides	每一盤的第一局結束後，球員須在球場上換邊，而接下來也有固定的換邊間隔。
rain stopped play	當下雨的時候，比賽就會中止，草地也會被覆蓋起來保護。
a formidable backhand	Backhand「反手拍」是指把右手移到身體的左邊來打球，或是左撇子的球員把左手移到身體的右邊來打球。
be seeded fourth	被認爲是錦標賽中第四頂尖的選手才會被 be seeded fourth，通常運動協會或是錦標賽的舉辦單位會將選手分組，讓頂尖的選手在後幾輪時才會相遇比賽。
ace	發球得分。

Task 9.14　　　　　　　　　　　　　　　　CD 2-24

再聽一次 Track 9.6，並按照你所聽到的順序在語庫中標號。請見範例。

答　案

你寫下的號碼依序應為：1 → 11 → 13 → 2 → 9 → 8 → 6 → 3 → 5 → 4 → 7 → 10 → 12。各位可以參考下列的對話內容。

Track 9.6

Susie: What's the score?

Irene: Fisher is up five games to four, but it's **tied thirty-thirty** now. Martina **was up in the first set** but she **lost her serve.** Then **rain stopped play,** and when they came back and **changed sides** she never recovered.

Susie: Hm. English weather, typical. Wow, that was a **superb volley.**

Irene: I know, Fisher's got the most **formidable backhand.** Oooooh, Fisher **clipped the net** but it still went over!

Susie: Oh, dear. Fisher has pulled ahead. Who do you want to win?

Irene: Well, if Martina wins she'll **go through to the semi-finals,** but Fisher **is seeded fourth**, so it's going to be hard for her. Oh my goodness, it's **match point** already! Hush.

...

Irene: **Ace**! **Game, set, and match**! She's won! Fantastic!

● 中　譯

Susie： 現在比數多少？

Irene： Fisher 五局領先 Martina 的四局。現在比數是二比二。 Martina 在第一盤原本領先，但她輪掉了擁有發球權的那一局。後來雨中斷了比賽，當她們再度回到場上，換邊比賽後，她就每況愈下。

Susie： 嗯，真是典型的英國氣候，哇！那真是一個精彩的截擊

Irene： 沒錯，她的反手拍無人能比。哦！她觸網了，但球還是過了。

Susie： 哦！ Fisher 領先了。妳希望誰贏？

Irene： 嗯，如果 Martina 贏了，她就可以進入準決賽，不過 Fisher 是排名第四的種子選手，所以對她而言並不是件易事。喔，天啊！已經是決定勝負關鍵的一分了，安靜！

……

Irene： 發球得分！比賽終了！她贏了，真是太棒了！

▌Task 9.15　　　　　　　　　　　　　　　　　●))) CD 2-25

請聽 Track 9.7 ，練習語庫中網球語彙的發音。

　　把你覺得有用的用語學起來。假如你對網球不感興趣、連一個網球選手也不認識，或者從來不打網球，那就讀過有個大概的了解即可。下頁關於網球的歷史介紹，也可增加你對網球的了解。

Quentin's 文化小叮嚀

- 雖然從早期的埃及開始,就已經有人拿桿子或拍子互相擊球,但我們所知道的網球賽是源於 16 世紀的法國王室宮廷。打球的人在開始前會互相喊一聲「tenez」(也就是法語的「play」),所以才會有 tennis 這個名稱。
- 早期的網球是在英國和法國的王室宮廷裡舉行,和現今的比賽有很大的不同。它是在長形的室內舉行,並讓球彈到周圍的牆上。
- 只有在維多利亞時代,網球是移到室外舉行。這是因為後來發明的橡膠球不會破壞草地!
- 溫布頓網球俱樂部(Wimbledon Tennis Club)成立於 1877 年,1927 出現了首次的收音機轉播。早期的球員都是巨星,他們的名字如今更成了大廠的流行品牌,像是 Fred Perry 和 Henri Lacoste。

足球

Task 9.16

 CD 2-26

請聽 Track 9.8,他們在談論什麼比賽?你如何知道?寫下關鍵的單字或用語。

● 答　案

| 他們在談論的是足球。稍後各位會看到對話內容。

Task 9.17

研讀下列的語庫。

社交必備語庫 9.6

 CD 2-27

	a penalty kick	在十八碼禁區內判的罰球。罰球員從罰球點踢球,除罰球者與對方的守門員,其他球員都得待在禁區外和罰球點之後。
	penalty area	禁區。離球門很近的區域,假如防守隊伍在這個區域犯規,對方就可得到 penalty kick。

	injury time	裁判延長比賽的時間，以彌補球員受傷所耗損的時間。
	foul sb.	Foul 是指球員犯規，或使其他球員受傷。
	an equalizer	指球隊進球，使雙方的比數相同。
	full time	全場比賽有 90 分鐘，上下半場各 45 分。
	decided on penalties	在錦標賽中，假如比賽到正規時間結束時還是不分勝負，兩隊就要各踢五罰球來決定誰勝誰負。
	end in a draw	指在 90 分鐘的比賽結束後，雙方的比數一樣。
1	leads one-nil/leads one-nothing	Nil 是英式英語，在談論足球時為「零」的意思。 Leads one-nothing 為美式說法。
	yellow card	當球員粗暴地對別人作出犯規動作或故意犯規時，裁判就會對他舉 yellow card「黃牌」。假如球員在同一場比賽出現兩次這種情形，他就會被舉紅牌並驅逐出場。

Task 9.18　　　　　　　　　　　　　　　CD 2-26

再聽一次 Track 9.8 ，並按照你聽到的順序在語庫中標號。請見範例。

● 答　案

你所填的號碼依序應為： 2 → 4 → 8 → 3 → 6 → 9 → 10 → 8 → 1 → 5 。各位可參考下列的對話內容。

Track 9.8

Jane:　　What's the score?

George: United **leading one-nil.**

Jane:　　Crikey!

George: The other side have got **a penalty kick** now because Becky **fouled someone** inside the **penalty area**.

Jane:　　Oh.

George: It's tense, man. The referee's been handing out **yellow cards** all over the place.

Jane:　　Yes, but don't worry, if it's one-nil, United will hold on to win.

George: Yes, but I want the other side to win! Take the ball!! Take the ball!! Ooooooh! He's a lousy player!

Jane: I think the best you can hope for is **an equalizer** during **injury time**.

George: If the other team scores, I reckon it will **end in a draw** at **full time**. It's too bad only tournament matches are **decided on penalties**.

● 中 譯

Jane： 比數是多少？

George： United 以一比零領先。

Jane： 哎呀！

George： 由於 Becky 在禁區內犯規，對方得到一個罰球的機會。

Jane： 哦！

George： 天呀！真緊張！裁判到處舉黃牌！

Jane： 是呀，但不用擔心，如果比數是一比零，United 會繼續領先。

George： 是呀！但我希望另一方會贏。搶球！搶球！呃！他真是個差勁的球員。

Jane： 我想你最多只能期望在延長比賽時能來個同分。

George： 如果對方得分，我認為在比賽終了時雙方比數會相同。太可惜了，只有錦標賽會以二隊各踢五罰球來決定勝負。

Task 9.19　　　　　　　　　　　　　　　◉))) CD 2-27

請聽 Track 9.9，練習語庫中足球相關用語的發音。

　　把你覺得有用的用語學起來。假如你對足球不感興趣、連一個足球選手也不認識，或者從來不踢足球，就讀過有個大概的了解即可。接著來看看足球歷史的介紹吧。

文化小叮嚀

- 證據顯示，在中國的漢朝時代，把球踢到網子裡的遊戲已經被軍隊用來訓練士兵，日本也有類似的做法。古代的希臘人和羅馬人也有一種與足球類似的遊戲。
- 現今所熟知的足球賽是源於八世紀的英格蘭，一開始跟暴力脫不了關係。根據傳說，有些村民曾經在打勝仗後，拿丹麥王子的頭來當足球踢，
- 中古時代，各個城鎮和村落會舉行比賽互相較量，一比就是一整天。各種暴力行為都不受限，所以這項運動和暴動無異。因此女王伊莉莎白一世頒布一條法律，規定踢足球為違法，須入獄服刑一個星期。但根本沒人注意到這件事。
- 1815 年，英格蘭的伊頓公校（Eton School）建立了一套規則，獲得其他公校與大學同意採用。這就是後來所謂的「劍橋規則」（Cambridge Rules），它也是現今足球比賽的準則。
- 1863 年，足球協會（Football Association）成立。它在規則中規定：手不可以觸球。有些會員不同意，於是自辦比賽，並成立橄欖球協會（Rugby Association）。在橄欖球比賽中，你可以拿著球並帶著它跑。
- 在英格蘭，足球稱做 football ；在美國 football 則是指「橄欖球」。

健身

　　接著要學的是談論健身時所使用的語言。我們先看一些 chunks ，再看一些 word partnerships 。

Task 9.20　　　　　　　　　　　　　　　　　🔊)) CD 2-28

請聽 Track 9.10 ，依據對話內容回答下列問題。

1. Kelly 通常是做哪項運動？
2. Brad 通常是做哪項運動？

答　案

1. Kelly 通常會鍛鍊腹肌和大腿、在墊子上做一些伸展運動，然後慢跑半小時。
2. Brad 通常是練舉重以及踩跑步機。

不必擔心自己聽不懂，稍後各位會看到對話內容。

Task 9.21

把下列的 chunks 和例句配對，請見範例。

___f___ **1.** work out 做運動

a) She forgot to warm up before her exercise class and she injured her back.

_____ **2.** burn off 消耗

b) My routine is quite hard but I want to stick to it so I look good for my vacation.

_____ **3.** work off 發洩

c) I didn't cool down after my run, and, because I was all sweaty, I caught a cold.

_____ **4.** warm up 熱身

d) I want to burn off some of those calories I ate last night.

_____ **5.** cool down 緩和

e) Even when I feel exhausted after twenty minutes of jogging, I never give up. I always try to make thirty.

_____ **6.** give up 放棄

f) I always work out in the morning because the gym is quieter at that time.

_____ **7.** stick to it 堅持

g) I'm really into my gym instructor. He's so cool!

_____ **8.** be into it 著迷

h) I have a lot of stress from my job, so the gym is a good place to work it off.

答 案

2. ___d___ **3.** ___h___ **4.** ___a___ **5.** ___c___ **6.** ___e___ **7.** ___b___ **8.** ___g___

接著聽聽 Track 9.11，練習下列語庫的發音。

社交必備語庫 9.7

CD 2-29

• work out	I always work out in the morning because the gym is quieter at that time.
• burn off	I want to burn off some of those calories I ate last night.
• work off	I have a lot of stress from my job, so the gym is a good place to work it off.
• warm up	She forgot to warm up before her exercise class and, she injured her back.
• cool down	I didn't cool down after my run, and, because I was all sweaty, I caught a cold.
• give up	Even when I feel exhausted after twenty minutes of jogging, I never give up. I always try to make thirty.
• stick to it	My routine is quite hard but I want to stick to it so I look good for my vacation.
• be into	I'm really into my gym instructor. He's so cool!

Task 9.22

把下列的 word partnerships 配對，請見範例。

_d_　**1.** work up
_____ **2.** add on
_____ **3.** get into
_____ **4.** follow
_____ **5.** number of
_____ **6.** maintain

a) reps
b) motivation
c) a routine
d) a good sweat
e) more weights
f) shape

● 答　案
2. __e__　**3.** __f__　**4.** __c__　**5.** __a__　**6.** __b__

接著聽聽 Track 9.12，練習下列語庫的發音。

社交必備語庫 9.8

 CD 2-30

• work up a good sweat
• add on more weights
• get into shape
• follow a routine
• number of reps
• maintain motivation

Task 9.23

由語庫 9.7 和 9.8 的用語中挑選適當者，填入下列空格。

Kelly: Hi, Brad. I haven't seen you here before!

Brad: Hi, Kelly. Oh, yeah? I come here regularly every other morning.

Kelly: Oh, right. I usually come in the evening, but I just joined a few weeks ago.
I'm trying to _____ for the summer.

Brad: Oh, good. Are you _____ a routine?

Kelly: Yes, I'm doing abs and thighs, and some work on the mats, then I do half an hour of jogging to ＿＿＿＿＿＿＿ sweat. What about you? You look pretty buff.

Brad: Oh, really? Thanks. Well, I'm just doing my normal workout. I'm trying to increase the ＿＿＿＿＿＿＿ reps I'm doing on this machine, as I want to strengthen my lower back. I've added some ＿＿＿＿＿＿＿, so it's kind of hard at the moment because I'm not used to it. I also need to ＿＿＿＿＿ some of last night's beer, so I'm going to run a couple of miles on the treadmill.

Kelly: Wow, you're really ＿＿＿＿＿＿＿ it. It's really good for ＿＿＿＿＿＿＿ stress, isn't it, coming here?

Brad: Well, sometimes it's hard to maintain ＿＿＿＿＿＿＿, especially if you're really busy, but it's important to find a routine that works for you and ＿＿＿＿＿＿＿.

Kelly: Yeah, don't ＿＿＿＿＿＿＿, right.

Brad: You got it. Also, don't forget to ＿＿＿＿＿＿＿ properly; otherwise you'll hurt yourself, and ＿＿＿＿＿＿＿ afterwards, too.

Kelly: That's good advice. Well, catch you later.

Brad: You too. Enjoy your workout.

Kelly: You too.

答　案

各位可以再聽一次 Track 9.10，並以下列的對話內容核對答案。

────────────────────────────

| W o r d   L i s t |

abs [æbz] *n.* 腹肌
buff [bʌf] *adj.* 肌肉鼓起的；肌肉發達的

thigh [θaɪ] *n.* 大腿
treadmill [ˈtrɛdˌmɪl] *n.* 跑步機

Track 9.10

Kelly: Hi, Brad. I haven't seen you here before!

Brad: Hi, Kelly. Oh, yeah? I come here regularly every other morning.

Kelly: Oh, right. I usually come in the evening, but I just joined a few weeks ago. I'm trying to *get into shape* for the summer.

Brad: Oh, good. Are you *following a routine*?

Kelly: Yes, I'm doing abs and thighs, and some work on the mats, then I do half an hour of jogging to *work up a good* sweat. What about you? You look pretty buff.

Brad: Oh, really? Thanks. Well, I'm just doing my normal workout. I'm trying to increase the *number of* reps I'm doing on this machine, as I want to strengthen my lower back. I've added some *more weights*, so it's kind of hard at the moment because I'm not used to it. I also need to *burn off* some of last night's beer, so I'm going to run a couple of miles on the treadmill.

Kelly: Wow, you sound *really into* it. It's really good for *working off* stress, isn't it, coming here?

Brad: Well, sometimes it's hard to maintain *motivation*, especially if you're really busy, but it's important to find a routine that works for you and *stick to it*.

Kelly: Yeah, don't *give in*, right.

Brad: You got it. Also, don't forget to *warm up* properly; otherwise you'll hurt yourself, and *cool down* afterwards, too.

Kelly: That's good advice. Well, catch you later.

Brad: You too. Enjoy your workout.

Kelly: You too.

中 譯

Kelly：嗨，Brad，我以前沒在這裡看過你！

Brad ：嗨，Kelly。是嗎？我每隔一個早上都會固定來這裡。

Kelly： 難怪，我通常是晚上來，不過我是前幾個星期才加入的。我想在夏天來臨前把身體練好。

Brad： 喔，不錯。妳有固定做什麼運動嗎？

Kelly： 有，我會練腹肌和大腿，在墊子上做一些伸展運動，然後慢跑半小時，讓身體痛快地流一場汗。你呢？你看起來體格很棒。

Brad： 哦，真的嗎？謝謝。我只有做普通的運動而已。我試著增加在這台機器上鍛鍊的反覆次數，因為我想要強化我的下背部。我多加了一些重量，我還沒習慣，所以目前有點費力。我還要把昨晚喝的一些啤酒消耗掉，所以我打算在跑步機上跑個幾哩。

Kelly： 哇，聽起來你真是投入。來這裡紓解壓力是很棒的事，對吧？

Brad： 嗯，保持動力有時候還挺難的，尤其是很忙的時候。但重點在於，要找一項對自己有用的固定運動，然後持之以恆。

Kelly： 沒錯，不要一曝十寒。

Brad： 妳說得對。此外，不要忘了適度地熱身，否則會受傷，而且事後還要做緩和運動。

Kelly： 這個建議不錯。好了，待會兒見。

Brad： 妳也是。好好練喔！

Kelly： 你也是。

利用語庫中的用語練習造句，熟能生巧喔！

提升字彙量

最後一節中，我們要來學習如何增進字彙。

Task 9.24

請研讀以下這則關於高爾夫球的報導。把下頁的敘述和文章的段落配對。

Although Tom Lehman is a fine golfer, he will always be remembered for his boorish behavior during the United States' Ryder Cup victory in 1999. It was his wild celebrations on the seventeenth green while Jose Maria Olazabal still had a putt to save the match which caused the most offense to fans and players alike. His subsequent apology was brave and we hope he will be a wiser man when he leads the United States at the K Club in 2006. However, some people maintain that Lehman's fist-punching display of triumphalism five years ago showed he cared passionately about the game. This kind of attitude was missing in the U.S. players in Detroit seven weeks ago.

Phil Mickelson, for example, changed his clubs only a few days before the event and then decided to skip practice with the rest of the team. Another team member, Chris Riley, did not want to play in the foursomes because he was "tired." In contrast, the European players performed as a team, enjoying the team spirit and celebrating each others' success. The U.S. players, on the other hand, seemed more like a disparate group of sulking superstars who were interested only in the money. As one commentator said: "The Europeans all went home on one plane, but our team left in twelve jets."

| Word List |

boorish [ˋburɪʃ] *adj.* 沒禮貌的；粗野的
foursome [ˋforsəm] *n.* 四人對抗賽；雙打
sulk [sʌlk] *v.* 慍怒；生氣

triumphalism [traɪˋʌmfəˏlɪzm̩] *n.* 必勝主義
disparate [ˋdɪspərɪt] *adj.*（本質上）不同的

Contrast this attitude with Lehman's reaction to being named U.S. captain for 2006. "What a thrill and an honor it is," he said. "Being the Ryder Cup captain is certainly beyond my wildest dreams. The Ryder Cup, to me, is the ultimate golf experience." Hopefully his enthusiasm will affect his team, because the 2004 event was simply too disappointing to be called sporting entertainment.

Paragraph _____ Tom Lehman's reaction to being named captain
Paragraph _____ Tom Lehman's mistake and how he dealt with it
Paragraph _____ The performance of the U.S. and European teams contrasted

● 答　案

段落 ___3___ Tom Lehman 對於被任命為隊長的反應
段落 ___1___ Tom Lehman 所犯的錯以及他的因應之道
段落 ___2___ 美國隊和歐洲隊的成績比較

　　各位可以參考下列的譯文

● 中　譯

　　雖然湯姆・李曼的高爾夫球打得不錯，可是隨著美國隊在 1999 年贏得萊德盃，他魯莽的舉動也將永遠被世人記住。當荷西・馬利歐・歐拉查寶還有一個推桿可以挽回比賽時，他卻在第 17 洞的果嶺上誇張地慶祝，而這對球迷與球員都造成了極大的侮辱。他在事後勇於認錯，我們也希望他在 2006 年率領美國隊到老 K 俱樂部時，頭腦能更清楚。不過，有些人則認為，李曼在五年前以揮拳來慶祝勝利的舉動代表他十分在乎這場比賽。在七週前的底特律，美國球員就缺乏這樣的態度。

　　例如菲爾・米克森在離比賽只剩幾天的時候更換球桿，然後又決定不跟其他隊員一起練習。另一位隊員克里斯・萊里則不想打四人賽，因為他「很累」。相較之下，歐洲球員就很有團隊風範。他們很注重團隊精神，並且會在有人打出好球時互相激勵。另一方面，美國球員似乎比較像是一盤散沙，那些鬧情緒的超級巨星只對錢感興趣。有一位球評說：「歐洲球員都是搭同一班飛機返家，我們則是分搭 12 架噴射機離開。」

　　李曼對於奉命擔任 2006 年美國隊隊長的反應和這種態度成了對比。他說：「這讓我倍覺興奮與光榮。我根本不敢妄想能擔任萊德盃的隊長。對我來說，萊德盃是至高無上的高爾夫球體驗。」希望他的熱情能帶動他的球隊，因為 2004 年的比賽簡直悽慘到完全抹殺了運動的娛樂性。

Task 9.25

找出報導中的 16 個 word partnerships。

答案

- fine golfer
- boorish behavior
- wild celebrations
- seventeenth green
- cause offense
- fist-punching display
- cared passionately
- U.S. players

- team member
- skip practice
- European players
- team spirit
- disparate group
- sulking superstars
- ultimate golf experience
- sporting entertainment

　　各位也可能有其他的答案。假如你不確定 word partnerships 的定義，不妨回頭看看本書「前言」中的說明。

　　各位現在應該已學會使用這些 word partnerships 來談論運動了。對於其他感興趣的運動，各位也可以如法炮製，以同樣的方式來增加自己的語彙。

　　結束之前，請回到本章的「學習目標」看看你達成了多少！

結　語

道別與總結

好了，本書到了結尾。希望各位有持之以恆地學習，收穫也比預期的多。各位學到了 short-turn 和 long-turn 的談話、要如何開啓一個 turn，以及要如何回應；各位學到了如何在餐廳裡點菜和取悅客戶，以及如何在宴會上閒聊和擴展人脈；各位也學到了許多話題的相關用語。一路學來也補充了許多文化方面的常識。

本章要來學的是如何道別，並做個總結。

道別

Task 結語 1

請聽 Track 結語 1，根據對話回答下列問題。

1. 對話 1 的兩個說話者在做什麼？
2. 對話 2 的兩個說話者在做什麼？
3. 兩段對話的不同之處為何？
4. 兩段談話的共同之處為何？

答 案

1. 他們在吃午餐。
2. 他們在吃晚餐。
3. 對話 1 比較不正式；對話 2 比較正式。
4. 兩段談話的進行模式相同，如下：
　　A 示意他想要告辭。
　　B 客氣地請他留下。這只是表示客氣的禮節。
　　A 感謝 B 的招待。
　　B 回應 A 的感謝。
　　A 道別。
　　B 也跟著道別。

我們可以把這個模式整理成下列三個步驟。

1. 示意結束（Signaling）。
   A 示意要告辭。
   B 客氣地請他留下。

2. 感謝（Thanking）
   A 感謝 B 的招待，並表示後會有期。
   B 回應 A 的感謝。

3. 離開（Leaving）
   A 道別。
   B 也跟著道別。

把這兩段對話多聽幾次，熟悉一下這種道別的模式。

Task 結語 2

將下列的用語分門別類，填入其後的表格。

說話者 A
1. Bye-bye!
2. Bye.
3. Goodbye.
4. Gosh, is that the time?
5. Gosh, look at the time.
6. Got to go.
7. I hope to see you again next year.
8. I really must be going.
9. I'd best be on my way.
10. I'd better be off.
11. I've enjoyed working with you.
12. It was a wonderful evening.
13. It's been good meeting you.
14. It's been nice to meet you.

說話者 B
1. Don't be a stranger.
2. Give my best wishes to _____.
3. Give my regards to _____.
4. Give _____ my best wishes.
5. Have a good journey.
6. Have a safe trip.
7. Have another one before you go.
8. It's been a pleasure having you.
9. It's been good meeting you.
10. Keep in touch.
11. Let's do it again soon.
12. My pleasure.
13. No, thank you!
14. Not at all.

15. It's high time I left.
16. It's time to go.
17. See you again soon.
18. See you later.
19. See you soon.
20. See you.
21. Talk to you soon.
22. Thank you for a lovely evening.
23. Thanks for lunch.
24. Thanks for the coffee.
25. Well, I have to be making a move soon.
26. You've been very helpful.

15. Oh, that's a pity. Can't you stay a bit longer?
16. So soon? Are you sure?
17. Stay for one more drink.
18. Take care.
19. The pleasure was mine.
20. We should do it again sometime.
21. Yes, I suppose I'd better be off, too.
22. You're very welcome.

說話者 A	說話者 B
Signaling	
Thanking	
Leaving	

答　案

┃ 請以下頁語庫核對答案。

社交必備語庫 結語 1　 CD 2-32

說話者 A	說話者 B
示意離開 Signaling	
• Well, I have to be making a move soon.	• So soon? Are you sure?
• I really must be going.	• Oh, that's a pity. Can't you stay a bit longer?
• I'd best be on my way.	• Stay for one more drink.
• Gosh, look at the time.	• Have another one before you go.
• Gosh, is that the time?	• Yes, I suppose I'd better be off, too.
• I'd better be off.	
• It's time to go.	
• It's high time I left.	
• Got to go.	
感謝 Thanking	
• Thank you for a lovely evening.	• No, thank you!
• It was a wonderful evening.	• The pleasure was mine.
• Thanks for lunch.	• It's been a pleasure having you.
• Thanks for the coffee.	• It's been good meeting you.
• It's been good meeting you.	• My pleasure.
• I've enjoyed working with you.	• Not at all.
• You've been very helpful.	• You're very welcome.
• I hope to see you again next year.	• We should do it again sometime.
• It's been nice to meet you.	• Let's do it again soon.
離開 Leaving	
• See you soon.	• Have a safe trip.
• See you again soon.	• Have a good journey.
• See you later.	• Give my regards to ____.
• Talk to you soon.	• Give my best wishes to ____.
• Bye.	• Give ____ my best wishes.
• Bye-bye!	• Take care.
• Goodbye.	• Keep in touch.
• See you.	• Don't be a stranger.

★ 語庫小叮嚀

Signaling

◆ 其中許多關於 B 請 A 留下的用語，只是表示客氣的禮節。

◆ 注意，It's high time I ... 後面所接的動詞一定是簡單過去式。

Thanking

◆ A 和 B 的用語大部分可以互相替換。

Leaving

◆ 注意，See you soon/later. 並非指這兩個人真的會很快地再見到對方，它只是用來道再見的非正式說法。

◆ A 和 B 的用語大部分可以互相替換。

Task 結語 3　　　　　　　　　　　　　　　　◉))) CD 2-32

請聽 Track 結語 2，練習語庫中用語的發音。

Task 結語 4　　　　　　　　　　　　　　　　◉))) CD 2-31

再聽一次 Track 結語 1，在語庫中勾選出你所聽到的用語。

● 答　案

▌ 請以下列的對話內容，核對答案。

◉))) Track 結語 1

Conversation 1

John: OK. Got to go.

Tracy: Yes, I suppose I'd better be off, too.

John: Thanks for lunch.

Tracy: Not at all. Let's do it again soon.

John: OK. See you later.

Tracy: See you.

Conversation 2

Mary: Gosh, is that the time?

Steve: Yes, it's late, isn't it?

Mary: Look, I'd better be off. I've got an early flight tomorrow.

Steve: Oh, no! Stay for one more drink.

Mary: Thanks, but I really must be going. Thank you for a lovely evening.

Steve: Oh, you're very welcome. It's been a pleasure having you.

Mary: Right. See you soon.

Steve: Yes, keep in touch. Give my regards to Tom.

Mary: I will. Bye.

Steve: Bye.

中 譯

對話 1

John： 好了，該走了！

Tracy： 嗯，我也該走了。

John： 謝謝妳招待的午餐。

Tracy： 不客氣，有空再一起吃午餐。

John： 沒問題，再見！

Tracy： 再見！

對話 2

Mary ： 天啊！那是現在的時間嗎！

Steve ： 是啊，已經很晚了，不是嗎？

Mary ： 嗯，我得走了，我明天一早還有班機得趕！

Steve ： 哦，不，再留下來多喝一杯吧！

Mary ： 謝謝，但我真的得走了。謝謝你給了我這個美好的夜晚。

Steve ： 不客氣，很高興很妳聚聚！

Mary ： 是呀，再見！

Steve ： 好，保持聯絡，替我向 Tom 問好。

Mary ： 我會的，再見。

Steve ： 再見。

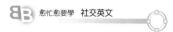
接著來做下一個練習。

Task 結語 5　　　　　　　　　　　　　◉))) CD 2-33

請聽 Track 結語 3，聽完 A 的部分，練習以 B 的身分作回應。如果無法完全聽懂，就參考下列的文字寫下答案。

A: Well, I have to be making a move soon.

B: ＿＿＿＿＿＿＿＿＿＿＿＿＿＿＿＿

A: Yes, I have an early flight tomorrow. I've enjoyed working with you.

B: ＿＿＿＿＿＿＿＿＿＿＿＿＿＿＿＿

A: Yes, I hope to see you again next year.

B: ＿＿＿＿＿＿＿＿＿＿＿＿＿＿＿＿

A: Indeed I will. Goodbye.

B: ＿＿＿＿＿＿＿＿＿＿＿＿＿＿＿＿

◉ 答　案　　　　　　　　　　　　　◉))) CD 2-34

各位可以聽 Track 結語 4 核對答案，若無法完全聽懂，可參考下列的對話內容。

◉))) **Track 10.4**

A: Well, I have to be making a move soon.

B: So soon? Are you sure?

A: Yes, I have an early flight tomorrow. I've enjoyed working with you.

B: It's been a pleasure having you.

A: Yes, I hope to see you again next year.

B: Give my best wishes to Marco.

A: Indeed I will. Goodbye.

B: Take care.

◉ 中　譯

A：好了，我該離開了。

B：這麼快，你確定嗎？

A：是啊，我明天一早的班機。我很高興和你一起工作。

B：有你的加入是件很棒的事。

A：嗯，我希望明年可以再見到你。

B：替我向 Marco 問候。

A：我一定會的，再見。

B：保重。

　　各位可以花一點時間寫一段對話，練習一下這些用語。可以參考我先前提到的模式。

總結

　　接著我要來做個總結，讓各位想想，讀完本書你的英文進步了多少。

　　各位也許還記得，在前言中請各位做了一項練習，就是從一段簡短的談話中找出 chunks 、 set-phrases 和 word partnerships 。現在不妨再把這項練習做一次，看看各位進步了多少。

Task 10.6

請找出下列對話中的 chunks 、 set-phrases 和 word partnerships ，填入其後的表格。請見範例。

A: Have you seen the new James Bond movie?

B: Oh, yes. You?

A: Yes. What did you think of it?

B: I thought it was better than the others — I really liked it. What did you think of it?

A: Yes, I liked it too. It was exciting, but not over the top, do you know what I mean?

B: Mmm. That's what I thought too. I really liked the car chase, and the opening credit sequence was very exciting. And I always enjoy watching Pierce Brosnan.

A: Oh, yes. He's brilliant. Did you like the title song?

B: Not as much as last time, actually. What's the name of the American actor who was in the supporting role?

A: Uhm, Edward Norton, or something like that. Did you like him?

B: Yes. He was excellent. They worked well together, don't you think?

A: I don't know, I think the woman was better. She provided a good love interest. Lucky James Bond!

B: Yes!

Set-phrases	Chunks	Word Partnerships
Have you seen ...	*... be better than ...*	*James Bond movie*

答案

請以下表核對答案。不妨把拿這次的答案和上次的答案作比較。如此，各位可看出讀完本書後你進步了多少。

Set-phrases	Chunks	Word Partnerships
• Have you seen ...	• ... be better than ...	• James Bond movie
• What did you think of it?	• ... like sth. ...	• American actor
• Do you know what I mean?	• ... be exciting ...	• car chase
• That's what I thought, too.	• ... enjoy Ving ...	• opening credit sequence
• ... or something like that.	• ... the name of ...	• title song
• Don't you think?	• ... be excellent ...	• love interest
• I don't know.	• ... work well together ...	• supporting role
• I thought so too.	• ... over the top ...	
	• ... as much as ...	

既然各位對 Leximodel 已有充分的了解，現在只要用第三部分所教的方法來增加字彙，就可以強化所學的內容。

　　好了，本書到此結束！希望在下次的交際場合中，各位能好好發揮；在和老外聊天時，本書的內容能讓各位變得更自在、更有自信。

　　祝交際愉快！

附錄一：社交必備語庫

 社交必備語庫 2.1　開啓話題的問題　　　　p. 68

一陣子未見某人時可以問的問題
Questions You can Ask When You Haven't Seen Someone for a While

- What have you been doing since I saw you last?
- Have you been busy?
- What did you do on the weekend?
- Did you do anything special this weekend?
- How was your holiday/weekend/trip/vacation?
- How are you?
- Are you well?
- How's it going?
- How's business?
- What happened?
- What have you been doing this week?
- Where have you been?

關於某人未來計畫的問題 Questions about Someone's Future Plans

- What are you doing this weekend?
- Are you doing anything nice this weekend?
- Where are you going for your next holiday?
- Any plans for ...?
- Are you going out later?
- Do you always want to work in ...?
- What are you thinking of doing next?
- Are you going to ...?

關於某人擁有的某樣東西的問題 Questions about Something Someone Owns

- Where did you get your ...?
- Was your ... expensive?
- What kind of computer do you use?
- What kind of car do you drive?
- What year is your car?
- What color is your ...?
- Where can I get a ... like yours?

關於某人的過去經驗或生涯的問題
Questions about Someone's Past Experiences or Career

- What did you major in?
- Where did you go to university?
- Have you been to ...?
- Where did you work before?
- Where did you live before coming here?
- Have you ever ...?

關於某人的看法的問題 Questions about Someone's Views

- What do you think of the current economic/political situation?
- What do you think of the long term (economic/political/business) prospects?
- What do you think of ...?
- What are your views on ...?
- Have you seen this?
- Did you read that report on ... in ...?

關於工作的問題 Questions about Work

- How is your company coping with the economic situation?
- How do you do this in your company?
- How does your company deal with ...?
- Do you get on with your boss?
- What are you working on at the moment?
- How did ... go?
- Did ... go well?

關於某人目前的生活型態的問題 Questions about Someone's Current Lifestyle

- How long have you been here?
- Where do you live?
- Do you live far from the office?
- How do you get to work?
- What are you reading at the moment?
- How long does it take you to get home/get to the office/get to work?
- Do you have your family with you?
- Do your children like it here?
- Where are you sending them to school?
- How many children do you have?
- Do you miss home?
- What does your wife/husband do?
- Does she like it here?

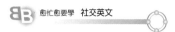
第一次遇到某人時可以問的問題
Questions You can Ask Someone You Are Meeting for the First Time

- How do you do?
- Where do you come from?
- Where are you from?
- What do you do?
- Where do you work?
- Who do you work for?
- What department do you work in?
- What does your company do?
- How long have you worked there?
- What's your job title?
- How big is your company?
- Where is it based?
- How do you find it here?
- Are you married?
- How long have you been married?
- Do you have any children?
- Can you speak Chinese?
- Where did you learn Chinese/English?

關於某人的興趣及嗜好的問題
Questions about Someone's Interests and Hobbies

- What's your handicap?
- How long have you been playing?
- Where do you play?
- Are you a (new) member?
- How long have you been a member?
- Do you do any (other) sports?
- How do you do that?
- Have you seen ...?
- What kind of music/food/books/movies do you like?
- What do you do in your free time?
- Have you ever played ...?
- Have you ever been ...?

社交必備語庫 2.2　延伸話題的問題　　　　　　　　　p. 75

用來鼓勵某人多說一點的問題 Questions to Encourage Someone to Talk More

- Why do you say that?
- What do you mean by that?
- Why is that?
- Why?
- What does that mean?
- What makes you say that?

社交必備語庫 3.1　Short-turn 的回應　　　　　　　　p. 91

表達意見 Expressing Your Opinion	表示同意 Expressing Agreement
• In my opinion, clause ...	• Oh yes.
• I personally think + n. clause ...	• Absolutely!
• To my mind, clause ...	• Definitely!
• I think + n. clause ...	• Indeed!
• I reckon + n. clause ...	• Oh, sure.
• My view is that + clause ...	• Right!
• I'm convinced that + clause ...	• I agree.
• I'd say that + clause ...	• I agree completely.
• I suspect that + clause ...	• I agree with you.
• Many people think that + clause ... but actually ...	• Exactly!
• In my experience, clause ...	• Well, that's exactly what I always say.
	• Yes, I know exactly what you mean.
	• Yes.
表示不同意 Expressing Disagreement	**表現出興趣 Showing Interest**
• Yes, but + n. clause ...	• Right.
• But the problem is that + clause ...	• OK.
• Possibly but + n. clause ...	• And then?
• What bothers me is that + clause ...	• Really?
• What bothers me is the n.p. ...	• Mmm.
• Yes, but don't forget that + clause ...	• Oh, my God, you're kidding me!
• Yes, but don't forget the n.p. ...	• No kidding!

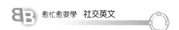
• That's probably true, but + n. clause ...	• Oh, that's good.
• But on the other hand, clause ...	• How wonderful.
• Yes, but look at it this way: ...	• How terrible for you.
• Very true, but + n. clause ...	• How awful!
• Hmm, I'll have to think about that.	• Wow!
• Oh, rubbish!	• Yuck!
• Come on, you can't be serious!	• Go on.
• I don't see it quite like that.	

社交必備語庫 3.2　　讓談話更為生動的形容詞　　　　　p. 103

Nice	Funny	Unpleasant	Strange	Boring	Interesting
• great	• entertaining	• nasty	• weird	• stupid	• fascinating
• fabulous	• hilarious	• terrible	• odd	• dull	• exciting
• marvelous	• ridiculous	• disgusting	• bizarre	• tedious	• appealing
• wonderful	• silly	• lousy	• crazy	• dreary	• noteworthy
• amazing	• wild	• awful	• peculiar	• wearisome	
• attractive	• humorous	• ghastly	• eccentric		
• brilliant	• comical				
• luxurious	• witty				
• beautiful					

社交必備語庫 4.1　　Long-turn 的發話　　　　　p. 124

開啓 Starting
• A funny thing happened to me ...
• Do you remember ...?
• Do you want to hear a joke?
• Have you heard the one about ...?
• Have you heard what happened to ...?
• I had a funny experience ...
• I had a great ...
• I had a terrible ...
• I heard this really funny joke the other day.
• I've got a good joke.

- It's about this ...
- Have you seen...?
- Have you read ...

鋪陳 Structuring

- Well, apparently, ...
- First of all, ...
- Then, ...
- Next, ...
- After that ...
- Finally, ...
- At the end, ...
- So then, ...
- What's more ...

重回 Returning

- So, ...
- Well, ...
- So as I was saying, ...
- Where was I? Oh yes, ...
- Yes, ...
- Well, anyway, ...

社交必備語庫 4.2　Long-turn 的回應　p. 133

回應 Responding	鼓勵 Encouraging	評論 Commenting
• Wow!	• So what happened next?	• He sure was (un)lucky.
• Yes.	• So what happened?	• He was really (un)lucky.
• Mmm.	• What happened?	• That's terrible.
• Really.	• So then what happened?	• That's amazing.
• Really?	• And then?	• That's incredible.
• OK.	• You're kidding!	• That's embarrassing
• Right.	• You're joking!	when that happens.
• Oh, no.	• My God!	• That's weird.
	• What do you mean?	• That's gross!
	• Oh, yes?	• That's a tricky situation.
	• Yeah, go on.	
	• So what did you do?	

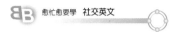
社交必備語庫 5.1　邀請　　　　　p. 147

邀請 Inviting
- Hungry?
- Are you hungry?
- Have you eaten?
- Shall we go get something to eat?
- Would you like to have dinner/lunch/breakfast?
- Would you like dinner/lunch/breakfast/a snack?
- Would you like something to eat?
- We'd like to invite you to dinner.
- We'd like to invite you to have dinner with us.
- We'd be very happy if you'd have dinner with us.

接受 Accepting
- Sure, why not?
- That'd be great, thanks.
- That would be lovely. Thank you.
- That's very kind of you. Thank you.

拒絕 Rejecting
- Another time perhaps? I've got to dash.
- Could we do it another time?
- That'd be great, thanks, but unfortunately + clause ...
- That would be lovely, but unfortunately + clause ...

社交必備語庫 5.2　討論菜單　　　　　p. 157

詢問菜單上的事項—客人 Asking about Something on the Menu — the Guest
- What's the ...?
- Can you tell me about the ...?
- What does ... mean?
- Is it spicy?
- Is it oily?
- Is it meat?
- Is it low-fat?
- Is it salty?
- Does it have ... in it? I'm allergic to ...

- What are you having?
- What can you recommend?
- What's good here?
- Why don't you just order for both of us?
- What does it come with?

推薦菜單上的事項－主人 Recommending Something on the Menu － the Host

- The ... is very good here.
- You should try the ...
- Try some ...
- Have you tried ...?
- It sounds horrible, but it's actually really good.
- You might want to try the ... It's a local delicacy.
- You could try ...
- How about ...?
- Would you like the ...?
- Would you like some ...?
- Would you like me to order for you?
- It's a little ...
- It might be too ... for you.

社交必備語庫 5.3　和服務生的應對　p. 163

點菜 Ordering Something on the Menu

- I'll have the ...
- Can I have the ...
- Not too spicy/salty/sweet, please.
- That's it.
- I'd like the ...
- For my starter I'll have the ...
- For my starter I'd like the ...
- Then I'll have the ...

開始、結束、抱怨和詢問 Starting, Ending, Complaining and Asking

- Excuse me?
- Can we have the menu, please?
- Can I have the check, please?
- Can I have the wine list, please?

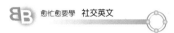
- Can you tell me what the specials are, please?
- Can you tell me what the soup of the day is, please?
- Can you tell me what the ... is, please?
- I'm sorry, but there's something wrong with my food.
- I'm sorry, but this is not what I ordered.
- I'm sorry, but we're still waiting for the ...
- I'm sorry, can you explain this item on the bill, please?
- I'm sorry, but I don't think this is what we ordered.

社交必備語庫 6.1　介紹 p. 179

自我介紹 Introducing Yourself

- Hello. _____
- Hello. I'm _____.
- Hello, my name's _____.
- I'm _____, by the way.
- Pleased to meet you.
- Pleased to meet you, too.
- It's a pleasure.
- It's a pleasure to meet you.
- It's a pleasure to meet you, too.
- How do you do?
- Nice to meet you.
- Nice to meet you, too.

介紹他人 Introducing Someone Else

- _____, I'd like to introduce you to _____.
- _____, let me introduce you to _____.
- _____, I want you to meet _____.
- _____, have you met _____?
- _____, do you know _____?
- _____, this is _____.
- _____, _____.
- Have you met _____?
- Have you two met?
- Do you know _____?
- Do you two know each other?

提供基本資訊 Giving Basic Information

- (S)he's in ...
- (S)he works in ...
- (S)he works for ...
- (S)he's based in ...
- (S)he works out of ...
- (S)he has his/her own ...
- (S)he runs his/her own ...
- I'm in ...
- I work in ...
- I work for ...
- I'm based in ...
- I work out of ...
- I have my own ...
- I run my own ...

社交必備語庫 6.2　　閒聊　　　　　　　　p. 193

轉述 PASSING IT ON

- According to sb. , ...
- According to the grapevine, ...
- Aren't they supposed to be Ving
- Aren't you supposed to be Ving
- From what I hear, clause ...
- From what I heard, clause ...
- Haven't you heard?
- I hear that + clause ...
- I hear you're thinking of Ving
- I heard it from the grapevine that + clause ...
- I heard that + clause ...
- I read somewhere that + clause ...
- I thought everyone knew.
- I thought it was common knowledge.
- I understand + n. clause ...
- I'm not one to gossip, but ...
- It appears that + clause ...

- It seems that + clause ...
- It sounds as if + n. clause ...
- Rumor has it that + clause ...
- Someone told me + clause ...
- They say + n. clause ...

保密 Keeping It Secret

- Don't tell anyone, but + clause ...
- I don't want this to get out.
- I won't mention any names, but ...
- If word gets out that + clause ...
- It's all a big secret.
- Just between ourselves, ...
- Just between us, ...
- Off the record, ...
- This is just between ourselves, of course.
- This is just between you and me, of course.
- This is not to go any further, of course.
- This is not to go outside the room.
- Well, apparently, ...
- You didn't hear this from me.

社交必備語庫 6.3　　轉換或中止話題　　p. 199

轉換話題 Changing the Topic

- Can I just change the subject before I forget?
- Oh, by the way, ...
- Oh, before I forget, ...
- Oh, I meant to tell you earlier.
- Oh, incidentally, ...
- Oh, that reminds me.
- Oh, while we're on the subject, ...
- Oh, you reminded me of something.
- That reminds me of n.p. ...
- On the subject of n.p. ...
- Talking of n.p. ...

中止談話 Breaking off the Conversation

- Could you excuse me a moment?
- Good talking to you.
- I have to be off.
- I have to make a phone call.
- I must just go and say hello to someone.
- I need another drink.
- I need to get some fresh air.
- I want a cigarette.
- I'll be back in a sec.
- I'll be right back.
- I'll catch you later.
- I'm just going to the bar/the buffet.
- If you'll excuse me a moment.
- It's been nice talking to you.
- It's getting late.
- There's someone I want to/need to talk to.
- Would you excuse me a moment?

社交必備語庫 6.4　關於酒的用語　p. 208

詢問是否需要飲料 Offering to Get a Drink	要求飲料 Asking for a Drink
• Drink?	• I'd like a nice stiff drink.
• Can I get you a drink of something?	• I need a drink.
• Would you like a drink of something?	• Can you get me a/another drink?
• Would you like a drink?	
• Can I get you a drink?	
• Would you like something to drink?	
• Would anyone like another drink?	

社交必備語庫 7.1 電影的種類 p. 222

- straight-to-video movie/straight-to-DVD movie/B movie
- cable movie
- sequel
- prequel
- documentary
- animated movie/cartoon
- biopic
- blue movie
- western
- horror movie
- ghost movie
- thriller
- spy movie
- costume drama
- romantic comedy
- musical
- gangster movie
- war movie
- road movie
- kung fu movie
- epic
- art movie

社交必備語庫 7.2 談論對電影的好惡 p. 226

正面 Positive	負面 Negative
• I'm crazy about n.p. ...	• I can't stand n.p. ...
• I love n.p. ...	• I can't bear n.p. ...
• I really like n.p. ...	• I really don't like n.p. ...
• ... n.p. is really good.	• I don't really like n.p. ...
• I quite like n.p. ...	• I'm not so keen on n.p. ...
• I'm rather keen on n.p. ...	
• ... n.p. is OK.	

社交必備語庫 7.3 電影人物 p. 229

- art director
- assistant director
- camera man
- cast
- casting director
- composer
- executive producer
- female lead
- male lead
- screenwriter
- sound director
- stand in/double

- director
- distributor
- editor
- star
- stuntman
- supporting role

社交必備語庫 7.4 　談論電影　　　　　　　p. 231

- adapt a screenplay
- be ahead of schedule
- be behind schedule
- be on schedule
- be over budget
- be within budget
- box-office receipts
- general release
- movie camera
- off-screen romance
- on-screen violence
- play a character
- play a part
- play a part
- shoot some footage
- sound effects
- take a shot
- write a screenplay

社交必備語庫 7.5 　談論電影： be 開頭的 chunks　　　　p. 232

•	be in	有演	Julia Roberts is in it.
•	be out	推出	It's not out yet.
•	be on at	在……上映	I think it's on at Warner Village.
•	be by	由……執導	It's by Steven Spielberg.
•	be about	描述	It's about a fish.
•	be from	產自	It's from Hong Kong.
•	be made in	拍攝於	It was made in London.

社交必備語庫 7.6 　談論《教父》的 Word Partnerships　　p. 241

- most highly regarded
- motion picture
- the ultimate "guy" movie
- cinematic favorite
- widespread appeal
- wonderfully realistic production quality

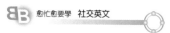

- three-film collaboration
- better written
- tightly edited
- emotional resonance
- full impact
- independent pieces
- stand alone
- quotable lines
- American tragedy

社交必備語庫 8.1　書的種類　　　　　　　　p. 247

- a play
- authorized biography
- autobiography
- classic novel
- criticism
- detective story
- ghost story
- history
- horror story
- modern classic
- novella
- philosophy
- poetry anthology
- pulp fiction
- self development manual/self help book
- short story
- thriller
- travel book
- unauthorized biography

社交必備語庫 8.2　談論書籍　　　　　　　　p. 250

書的內容 The Book As Story	書的物件 The Book As Object
• characterization • dialogue • setting • period • description • message • plot	• cover • jacket • blurb • review • binding

社交必備語庫 8.3　　評論書籍的好惡　　p. 251

正面 Positive	負面 Negative
• fully drawn characters	• flat descriptions
• gripping plot	• implausible events
• important message	• predictable plot
• plausible events	• trivial message
• vivid descriptions	• two-dimensional characters
• witty dialogue	• wooden dialogue

社交必備語庫 8.4　　談論書籍的 chunks　　p. 251

• bring sth. out	• BETA is bringing out its new book in the fall.
• sth. comes out	• His new book is coming out in the fall.
• get across sth.	• He didn't know how to get across all of the emotions he was feeling.
• get sth. across	• Her new book really gets her message across.
• sth. comes across	• Her message really comes across in her new book.

社交必備語庫 8.5　　音樂的種類　　p. 260

• album	• lead singer
• alto	• live recording
• backing vocals	• opera
• singer	• opera diva
• baritone	• pop group
• bass	• quartet
• brass instruments	• quintet
• chamber music	• record company
• choral music	• record label
• composer	• rock star
• concert	• sonata

- concerto
- conductor
- duo
- gospel choir
- hit single
- jingle
- keyboard instrument

- song writer
- soprano
- string instrument
- symphony
- tenor
- trior
- wind instrument

社交必備語庫 8.6　談論音樂帶來的感受　　　　　　　p. 265

快樂的 Happy	悲傷的 Sad
• cheerful	• nostalgic
• triumphant	• full of longing
• ecstatic	• introspective
• lighthearted	• heartbroken
• playful	• gloomy
振奮的 Energetic	放鬆的 Relaxing
• funky	• calming
• thrilling	• soothing
• exhilarating	• lulling
• wild	• consoling
• uplifting	• peaceful

社交必備語庫 8.7　無法精確描述感受時的「模糊」用語　p. 265

「模糊」的用語 Being Vague

* sort of ...
* ... kind of ...
* ... or anything
* ... like ...
* ... or something ...
* It's hard to describe, but ...
* It's difficult to say, but ...
* It's not easy to put into words, but ...
* I can't really describe it, but ...
* I'm not sure how to put it, but ...
* ... do you know what I mean?

社交必備語庫 8.8　談論《達文西密碼》的用語　p. 272

* good book
* fun book
* very well written
* fast-pacing
* quick-editing
* engrossing tale
* hard to put down
* resist the temptation to
* read ahead
* religious views
* great fictional mystery
* historical research
* making claims to
* historical precision
* descriptive errors
* historical inaccuracies
* complete hoax

社交必備語庫 9.1　　談論運動　　　　　　　　　p. 276

• It makes me feel really + adj. • Afterwards I feel so + adj. • While I'm doing it I feel so + adj.	• It does me good. • I really get a kick out of it. • It helps (me) to V

社交必備語庫 9.2　　從事某項運動的說法　　　　　p. 277

play	**do**	**go**
• soccer • football • basketball • volleyball • golf • tennis • ping-pong • rugby • backgammon • mahjong • chess	• a workout • exercise • athletics • aerobics • yoga • tai chi • martial arts • 25 laps	• climbing • jogging • swimming • running • hiking • sailing • diving • skiing

社交必備語庫 9.3　　足球、高爾夫球和網球的相關名稱　　p. 280

soccer/football	
	• pitch/field • team • game • goal • match • referee • player • stadium

golf	• course • player • caddy • cart • club • iron • ball • game

tennis	• court • ball • match • player • racket • umpire • net • doubles partner

社交必備語庫 9.4　　談論高爾夫球　　　　　　　　　p. 282

• on the range	• early holes
• on the course	• finishing holes
• play a shot	• practice tee
• feel your tempo	• smooth backswing
• selecting a club	• shoot in the 70s
• line of putt	• on the green

社交必備語庫 9.5　　談論網球　　　　　　　　　　p. 285

• tied thirty-thirty	• lost her serve
• match point	• change sides
• game, set, and match	• rain stopped play
• be up in the first set	• a formidable backhand
• go through to the semi-finals	• be seeded fourth

- clipped the net
- superb volley

- ace

社交必備語庫 9.6　　談論足球　　　　　　　　p. 288

- a penalty kick
- penalty area
- injury time
- foul sb.
- an equalizer

- full time
- decided on penalties
- end in a draw
- leads one-nil/leads one-nothing
- yellow card

社交必備語庫 9.7　　談論健身　　　　　　　　p. 292

• work out	I always work out in the morning because the gym is quieter at that time.
• burn off	I want to burn off some of those calories I ate last night.
• work off	I have a lot of stress from my job, so the gym is a good place to work it off.
• warm up	She forgot to warm up before her exercise class and she injured her back.
• cool down	I didn't cool down after my run, and, because I was all sweaty, I caught a cold.
• give up	Even when I feel exhausted after twenty minutes of jogging, I never give up. I always try to make thirty.
• stick to it	My routine is quite hard but I want to stick to it so I look good for my vacation.
• be into	I'm really into my gym instructor. He's so cool!

社交必備語庫 9.8　　更多談論健身的用語　　　　p. 293

- work up a good sweat
- add on more weights
- get into shape
- follow a routine
- number of reps
- maintain motivation

社交必備語庫 結語 1 ｜ 道別 p. 305

說話者 A	說話者 B
示意離開 Signaling	
• Well, I have to be making a move soon. • I really must be going. • I'd best be on my way. • Gosh, look at the time. • Gosh, is that the time? • I'd better be off. • It's time to go. • It's high time I left. • Got to go.	• So soon? Are you sure? • Oh, that's a pity. Can't you stay a bit longer? • Stay for one more drink. • Have another one before you go. • Yes, I suppose I'd better be off, too.
感謝 Thanking	
• Thank you for a lovely evening. • It was a wonderful evening. • Thanks for lunch. • Thanks for the coffee. • It's been good meeting you. • I've enjoyed working with you. • You've been very helpful. • I hope to see you again next year. • It's been nice to meet you.	• No, thank you! • The pleasure was mine. • It's been a pleasure having you. • It's been good meeting you. • My pleasure. • Not at all. • You're very welcome. • We should do it again sometime. • Let's do it again soon.
離開 Leaving	
• See you soon. • See you again soon. • See you later. • Talk to you soon. • Bye. • Bye-bye! • Goodbye. • See you.	• Have a safe trip. • Have a good journey. • Give my regards to ____. • Give my best wishes to ____. • Give ____ my best wishes. • Take care. • Keep in touch. • Don't be a stranger.

附錄二： CD 目錄

CD 軌數	章節軌數	內容
1-01		版權聲明
1-02	Track 前言 1	1 段對話
1-03	Track 前言 2	錯誤的句子
1-04	Track 1.1	3 段對話
1-05	Track 1.2	2 段對話
1-06	Track 1.3	1 段對話
1-07	Track 1.4	2 段對話
1-08	Track 1.5	2 段對話
1-09	Track 2.1	1 段對話
1-10	Track 2.2	1 段對話
1-11	Track 2.3	語庫 2.1
1-12	Track 2.4	語庫 2.2
1-13	Track 2.5	4 段話頭
1-14	Track 3.1	1 段對話
1-15	Track 3.2	1 段對話
1-16	Track 3.3	語庫 3.1
1-17	Track 3.4	問句
1-18	Track 3.5	問句與回應
1-19	Track 3.6	語庫 3.2
1-20	Track 3.7	問句
1-21	Track 3.8	問句
1-22	Track 3.9	問句與回應
1-23	Track 4.1	1 段對話
1-24	Track 4.2	1 段對話
1-25	Track 4.3	1 段對話
1-26	Track 4.4	1 段對話
1-27	Track 4.5	1 段對話

1-28	Track 4.6	語庫 4.1
1-29	Track 4.7	語庫 4.2
1-30	Track 4.8	2 段對話
1-31	Track 4.9	2 段對話
1-32	Track 5.1	2 段對話
1-33	Track 5.2	語庫 5.1
1-34	Track 5.3	4 個問句
1-35	Track 5.4	4 個問句與回應
1-36	Track 5.5	2 段對話
1-37	Track 5.6	語庫 5.2
1-38	Track 5.7	2 段對話
1-39	Track 5.8	語庫 5.3
1-40	Track 6.1	2 段對話
1-41	Track 6.2	2 段對話
1-42	Track 6.3	語庫 6.1
1-43	Track 6.4	2 段對話
1-44	Track 6.5	2 段對話
1-45	Track 6.6	語庫 6.2
1-46	Track 6.7	語庫 6.3
1-47	Track 6.8	1 段對話
1-48	Track 6.9	語庫 6.4
2-01	Track 7.1	對話
2-02	Track 7.2	語庫 7.1
2-03	Track 7.3	語庫 7.2
2-04	Track 7.4	語庫 7.3
2-05	Track 7.5	語庫 7.4
2-06	Track 7.6	語庫 7.5
2-07	Track 7.7	語庫 7.6
2-08	Track 8.1	對話
2-09	Track 8.2	語庫 8.1
2-10	Track 8.3	語庫 8.2

2-11	Track 8.4	語庫 8.3
2-12	Track 8.5	語庫 8.4
2-13	Track 8.6	對話
2-14	Track 8.7	語庫 8.5
2-15	Track 8.8	語庫 8.6
2-16	Track 8.9	語庫 8.7
2-17	Track 8.10	語庫 8.8
2-18	Track 8.11	語庫 8.9
2-19	Track 9.1	語庫 9.1
2-20	Track 9.2	語庫 9.2
2-21	Track 9.3	語庫 9.3
2-22	Track 9.4	對話
2-23	Track 9.5	語庫 9.4
2-24	Track 9.6	對話
2-25	Track 9.7	語庫 9.5
2-26	Track 9.8	對話
2-27	Track 9.9	語庫 9.6
2-28	Track 9.10	對話
2-29	Track 9.11	語庫 9.7
2-30	Track 9.12	語庫 9.8
2-31	Track 結語 1	2段對話
2-32	Track 結語 2	語庫　結語 1
2-33	Track 結語 3	問句
2-34	Track 結語 4	對話

附錄三：學習目標記錄表

利用這張表來設立你的學習目標和記錄你的學習狀況，以找出改進之道。

第一欄：寫下你接下來一週預定學習或使用的字串。

第二欄：寫下你在當週實際使用該字串的次數。

第三欄：寫下你使用該字串時遇到的困難或該注意的事項。

預計使用的字串	使用次數	附註

國家圖書館出版品預行編目資料

愈忙愈要學社交英文 / Quentin Brand作；戴至中譯.
－－初版. －－臺北市；貝塔，2005〔民94〕
　　面： 　　公分

　ISBN 957-729-487-1（平裝附光碟片）

　1. 英國語言－會話

805.188 　　　　　　　　　　　　　　93023988

愈忙愈要學社交英文
Biz English for Busy People — Socializing

作　　者 / Quentin Brand
總 編 輯 / 梁欣榮
譯　　者 / 戴至中
執行編輯 / 陳家仁

出　　版 / 貝塔語言出版有限公司
地　　址 / 100台北市館前路12號11樓
電　　話 / (02)2314-2525
傳　　真 / (02)2312-3535
郵　　撥 / 19493777貝塔出版有限公司
客服專線 / (02)2314-3535
客服信箱 / btservice@betamedia.com.tw

總 經 銷 / 時報文化出版企業股份有限公司
地　　址 / 桃園縣龜山鄉萬壽路二段 351 號
電　　話 / (02) 2306-6842

出版日期 / 2006年1月初版二刷
定　　價 / 380元
ISBN：957-729-487-1

Biz English for Busy People - Socializing
Copyright 2005 by Quentin Brand
Published by Beta Multimedia Publishing

喚醒你的英文語感！

對折後釘好，直接寄回即可！

| 廣　告　回　信 |
| 北區郵政管理局登記證 |
| 北 台 字 第 1 4 2 5 6 號 |
| 免　貼　郵　票 |

100 台北市中正區館前路12號11樓

貝塔語言出版 收
Beta Multimedia Publishing

寄件者住址 □□□

貝塔語言出版 Beta Multimedia Publishing

讀者服務專線（02）2314-3535　　讀者服務傳真（02）2312-3535
客戶服務信箱　btservice@betamedia.com.tw

www.betamedia.com.tw

謝謝您購買本書！！

貝塔語言擁有最優良之英文學習書籍，為提供您最佳的英語學習資訊，您可填妥此表後寄回（免貼郵票）將可不定期收到本公司最新發行書訊及活動訊息！

姓名：_____　性別：□男 □女　生日：____年____月____日

電話：(公)_____(宅)_____(手機)_____

電子信箱：_____

學歷：□高中職含以下 □專科 □大學 □研究所含以上

職業：□金融 □服務 □傳播 □製造 □資訊 □軍公教 □出版
　　　□自由 □教育 □學生 □其他

職級：□企業負責人 □高階主管 □中階主管 □職員 □專業人士

1. 您購買的書籍是？_____

2. 您從何處得知本產品？(可複選)

　　□書店 □網路 □書展 □校園活動 □廣告信函 □他人推薦 □新聞報導 □其他

3. 您覺得本產品價格：

　　□偏高 □合理 □偏低

4. 請問目前您每週花了多少時間學英語？

　　□ 不到十分鐘 □ 十分鐘以上，但不到半小時 □ 半小時以上，但不到一小時

　　□ 一小時以上，但不到兩小時 □ 兩個小時以上 □ 不一定

5. 通常在選擇語言學習書時，哪些因素是您會考慮的？

　　□ 封面 □ 內容、實用性 □ 品牌 □ 媒體、朋友推薦 □ 價格 □ 其他_____

6. 市面上您最需要的語言書種類為？

　　□ 聽力 □ 閱讀 □ 文法 □ 口說 □ 寫作 □ 其他_____

7. 通常您會透過何種方式選購語言學習書籍？

　　□ 書店門市 □ 網路書店 □ 郵購 □ 直接找出版社 □ 學校或公司團購

　　□ 其他_____

8. 給我們的建議：_____

_____

喚醒你的英文語感！

Get a Feel for English !

喚醒你的英文語感！

Get a Feel for English !